The Nancy Drew Mysteries

More 2 books in 1 in Armada

Enid Blyton
The Ring O'Bells Mystery / The Rubadub Mystery
The Secret Castle / The Secret Mountain
Mystery and Adventure Stories

Hardy Boys by Franklin W. Dixon
The Mystery of the Axtec Warrior /
The Arctic Patrol Mystery
The Haunted Fort / The Mystery of the Whale Tattoo

Hardy Boys Casefiles by Franklin W. Dixon
Dead On Target / Evil, Incorporated
Cult of Crime / The Lazarus Plot

Nancy Drew by Carolyn Keene
The Secret of Shadow Ranch /
The Mystery of the 99 Steps

Nancy Drew Casefiles by Carolyn Keene
Secrets Can Kill / Deadly Intent
Murder on Ice / Smile and Say Murder

Jinny by Patricia Leitch
For Love of a Horse / A Devil to Ride

Carolyn Keene

Nancy Drew

Mystery at the Ski Jump

The Spider Sapphire Mystery

Armada
An Imprint of HarperCollinsPublishers

Mystery at the Ski Jmp and
The Spider Sapphire Mystery
were first published in the USA in 1952 and 1968
respectively by Grosset and Dunlap, Inc.
First published in Great Britain in 1971
by William Collins Sons & Co. Ltd.

First published together in this edition
in 1993 by Armada
Armada is an imprint of
HarperCollins Children's Books,
part of HarperCollins Publishers Ltd
77-85 Fulham Palace Road
Hammersmith, London W6 8JB

1 3 5 7 9 10 8 6 4 2

Printed and bound in Great Britain by
HarperCollins Book Manufacturing, Glasgow

CONTENTS

MYSTERY AT THE SKI JUMP

·1·

The Strange Woman

"Brr-r, it's cold!"

Nancy Drew shivered and pulled the collar of her coat higher against the driving snow. Determinedly, she ducked her head and pushed along the darkening street, a new pair of skis slung over one shoulder.

Suddenly, out of nowhere, a long black car skidded across the pavement directly in front of the red-haired, eighteen-year-old girl.

"Oh!" Nancy cried out, leaping back just in time to escape being hit. A second later the car crashed into the porch of a nearby house.

As Nancy dashed forward to see if the driver were hurt, the door of the house flew open and the excited owner, Mrs Martin, rushed out.

"What happened?" she called. Then, seeing the car, Mrs Martin ran down the snowy steps. "Is someone hurt?"

Nancy had already opened the door on the driver's side. A slender woman in a fur coat was slumped across the steering wheel.

"Help me bring her into the house," Mrs Martin directed. Nancy laid down her skis. Together they carried the unconscious stranger inside and put her on a sofa in the living-room.

9

"I believe she's only stunned," Nancy announced, pressing her fingers to the victim's wrist. "Her pulse is regular and the colour's coming back to her cheeks."

"Just the same, I think we should call Dr Britt," Mrs Martin said nervously. "Will you do it, Nancy? The phone's in the hall. I'll get a blanket from upstairs to put over this woman."

Nancy went to call the doctor. The line was busy and it was a few minutes before she could get a connection.

"Dr Britt is out," the nurse reported, "but I'll give him your message."

"Thank you."

Mrs Martin came down the stairs with a blanket and Nancy told her Dr Britt would be there as soon as possible.

"Doctor! Who wants a doctor?" an annoyed voice called from the living-room. "I certainly don't need one. Say, how did I get here?"

Nancy and Mrs Martin were amazed to see the woman driver sitting up on the sofa. She was removing a make-up kit from the pocket of her coat. She calmly began to powder her face and dab on some exotic perfume as Mrs Martin explained what had happened.

"It was the storm," was all the unexpected visitor said.

Quickly Nancy appraised the woman. She was about thirty-five, strikingly handsome with blue-black hair, pale skin, and high cheekbones. An expensive-looking mink coat was draped nonchalantly over her slim shoulders.

"Why, Mrs Channing," Mrs Martin said suddenly. "I didn't recognize you. I'm glad you feel better. Nancy, this is Mrs Channing from the Forest Fur Company.

"Mrs Channing, I'd like you to meet Nancy Drew. She lives here in River Heights with her father, a famous lawyer. And Nancy herself is one of the best young detectives I ever—"

"Lawyer—detective!" Mrs Channing cried out. There was such a sharp expression in her dark blue eyes when she looked at Nancy that the girl felt slightly embarrassed.

"At least Dad is a fine lawyer," Nancy said, smiling. "Sometimes he asks me to help him on his cases. Your work must be interesting, too, Mrs Channing. I've never heard of the Forest Fur Company. Where is it?"

"Oh, we have many branches all over the country." Mrs Channing started to rise from the sofa but fell back weakly.

"I think you really should see a doctor," Nancy suggested kindly. "You're still shaky from the accident."

"I'll be all right!" Mrs Channing answered emphatically. "Perhaps if I could have a cup of tea—"

Nancy turned to Mrs Martin. "I think I'd better run along," she said.

"Oh, it's so cold outside, do stay and have some tea with us. It won't take a minute."

"Thank you, but I really can't," Nancy replied. "I'm leaving with Dad on a trip in the morning and have a lot of packing to do."

Nancy was looking forward to helping her father on a case in Montreal and enjoying some skiing. He had promised to tell her about his work at dinner that night.

A few minutes later she was shaking the snow from her coat and boots on the back porch of the Drew home. Opening the kitchen door, she called, "Hi, Hannah! I'm back."

"Well, I'm certainly relieved," replied a motherly voice from the hall. "What a storm! Did you buy the skis?"

"Yes, I did. They're real beauties. I can't wait to use them in Montreal."

Nancy recalled with pleasure her skiing weekend there the previous winter. What a wonderful feeling to stand on top of the mountain, in the cold crisp sunny morning, with the white world below her! Then off— down the fast trail to the bottom, concentrating on every turn and twist as the challenging trail demanded. Nancy had become so proficient that she had won the novice ladies' slalom race, successfully turning through all the slalom gates, in the fastest time.

Nancy smiled to herself as she thought of the "slalom gates", which were really just flags on tall poles stuck in the snow. Funny-looking "gates"!

The Drews' middle-aged housekeeper walked into the kitchen and smiled affectionately at Nancy. Hannah Gruen had been with the family ever since Mrs Drew had died when Nancy was a small child.

"I was delayed by an accident." Nancy explained what had happened. "I'm afraid Mrs Martin's porch will need a lot of repairing."

The conversation was interrupted by a telephone call from Nancy's friend, Ned Nickerson, inviting her to a fraternity dance at Emerson College the next month. She accepted gaily, then went upstairs to start packing. Five minutes later Hannah bustled into the bedroom.

"Look what I have to show you!" the housekeeper exclaimed.

Nancy's eyes gleamed. "A mink stole! It's beautiful!"

"It was such a bargain, I couldn't resist it," Hannah explained excitedly. "I've always wanted a fur stole but never felt I could afford it."

Nancy took the fur piece and laid it around her own shoulders. "It's gorgeous," she said. "Where did you buy it?"

"From a simply charming woman," Hannah replied. "She represents the Forest Fur Company. You see, she had already sold a stole to my friend Esther Mills. And Esther suggested—"

Nancy was not listening. At mention of the Forest Fur Company, her thoughts went racing back to the mysterious Mrs Channing.

"Nancy, do you think I was foolish?" the housekeeper asked anxiously as the girl frowned.

"I'm not sure," Nancy answered absently. "It does look like a good fur piece. But it's an odd way to sell expensive furs."

"I hope everything's all right," said Hannah, a worried look replacing her former eagerness. "I also invested some money in Forest Fur Company stock. The woman, a Mrs Channing, sold me ten shares. I paid her fifty dollars for it. But I'm sure it's okay. I have the certificate in my bureau drawer."

"Where is this woman staying?" Nancy asked.

"Why, I don't know. She didn't tell me."

At that moment Nancy heard the front door close and the sound of her father's footsteps in the hall. She put her arm about Hannah's shoulders and gave her a comforting squeeze.

"Don't worry. I'll run down and talk this over with Dad," she assured the housekeeper. "Perhaps he knows the Forest Fur Company."

"Hello, dear." Tall, handsome Carson Drew met his daughter at the bottom step and kissed her. "Do I detect a worried look in those pretty blue eyes?"

"Well, something's on my mind," Nancy admitted. She told her father about Mrs Channing and the Forest Fur Company.

"I've never heard of the firm," the lawyer remarked when she finished. "But I certainly don't like the way they do business. No reliable company would peddle expensive furs and stock from door to door at bargain prices. Please ask Hannah to let me see her certificate.

After reading it, he admitted it looked all right, but added that he thought the company should be investigated.

"Mrs Channing must still be at Mrs Martin's," Nancy said excitedly. "Suppose I go over there and talk to her."

"Fine." Carson Drew nodded. "I'll join you. We can't let our Hannah be taken in by swindlers."

The Martin home was only two blocks away. As the Drews reached it, Nancy noticed that Mrs Channing's car was gone. She dashed up the broken porch steps and rang the bell hurriedly. The door swung open.

"Mrs Martin," Nancy asked, "has Mrs Channing left already?"

"Yes." Mrs Martin's eyes blazed. "To put it bluntly, Nancy, Mrs Channing ran out on me. When I brought that tea she asked for, she was gone. And her car too! And not one word did she say about paying for the damage she did to my porch!"

"What's her address?" Nancy asked quickly.

Mrs Martin looked startled. "I don't know!"

·2·

A Serious Loss

MRS MARTIN invited Nancy and her father into the house and offered them chairs before the crackling blaze in the fireplace.

"I suppose I'll never find Mrs R. I. Channing," she spluttered. "But that Forest Fur Company will pay for repairing my porch! Don't you think they should, Mr Drew?"

"That depends on whether or not Mrs Channing was using a car of theirs, or at least was doing business for them at the time of the accident. Suppose you tell us everything you know about this woman."

Before Mrs Martin could start, they heard the sound of heavy feet on the porch stamping off snow. This was followed by the sound of the door bell. The caller was Dr Britt, tired and cold after his long drive through the storm. When he learned that the accident victim had left in such a rude way, the physician was indignant.

"I don't blame you for being angry, Mrs Martin," he agreed, stepping into the living-room. "Anyone as ungrateful as Mrs Channing doesn't deserve sympathy. Good evening, Mr Drew. Hello, Nancy."

Mrs Martin indicated a fourth chair facing the fire. "You sit here and rest, Doctor," she urged. "I was just going to tell what I know about Mrs Channing.

"She came here two days ago and sold me a mink boa and some stock in a fur company. She promised that the stock would make me a great deal of money. But now I don't trust her. You know what I think? That she ran away from here because of you, Nancy."

"What!"

"Before I went to get the tea," Mrs Martin explained, "I told her how many cases you had solved yourself—not just for your father. Now that I think of it, I believe Mrs Channing got scared and left. We'll never find her."

"Mrs Channing also sold a mink stole and some stock to our housekeeper, Hannah Gruen," Nancy volunteered. "That's why I came back here."

Dr Britt looked thoughtful. *"Channing—Channing!"* he murmured. "I thought that name sounded familiar. Now I remember. My nurse, Ida Compton, showed me a fur piece and a certificate for stock she had purchased from a woman named Channing."

"This is very interesting," Mr Drew spoke up. "Nancy, why don't you see Miss Compton and find out if she can give you some additional information about Mrs Channing?"

"I certainly will, Dad. But by the time we get back from Montreal—"

"I suggest that you stay here a couple of days and see what you can find out," the lawyer said. "You can follow me later."

He rose, adding that Hannah Gruen probably was becoming uneasy over their absence. She would want to know what they had learned about Mrs Channing.

"And the delicious dinner I smelt will be spoiled," Nancy said, smiling.

"Let me drive you," the doctor offered. "Fortunately

the storm is dying down. It should be fair by morning."

When the Drews arrived home, Mrs Gruen met them with questioning eyes. They told her the truth but begged her not to worry about the fur company stock.

"It may be a good investment," the lawyer said cheerfully, although he doubted it. "And now, how about some food? This is the best eating place in the country, Hannah."

The housekeeper beamed. "Tonight it's pot roast and big browned potatoes exactly as you like them."

"Dessert?"

"Your favourite. Apple tart with lots of cinnamon." Mrs Gruen turned to Nancy. "Bess Marvin phoned. She's coming over after dinner. And George—I never can get used to a girl with a boy's name—will be here too."

"Great!" said Nancy. "The three of us will hold a farewell party for you, Dad."

Bess and her cousin George Fayne arrived at eight o'clock. Clad in boots and ski pants, they were in the highest spirits in spite of the cold. George, a trim-looking girl with short, black hair and an athletic swing to her shoulders, was the first through the door.

"Isn't this storm something? she exclaimed. "Old Man Winter is certainly doing his best to blow our town off the map." She panted. "One more big puff and I'd probably have landed on top of a church steeple."

Bess giggled. "That would be something—you flapping about like a weather vane!"

"Bet I could point in all directions at once," George retorted.

"Well, I'd rather stay inside," said Bess, blonde and pretty. "Maybe we can make some fudge," she added hopefully. Bess loved sweets and worried little about her weight.

"I'm afraid there won't be time for fudge," said Nancy. "The fact is, I have some work for both of you."

"Nancy! You don't mean you're on the trail of another mystery?" George asked eagerly.

"Could be," Nancy answered, her eyes twinkling. Quickly she briefed her friends about Mrs R. I. Channing and her questionable method of selling stock and furs.

"I've just been examining the stock certificate she gave Hannah," the young detective went on. "It gives the headquarters of the Forest Fur Company as Dunstan Lake, Vermont. But, girls, I've looked in the atlas and there's no such place as Dunstan Lake, Vermont."

"Too small, maybe," George suggested.

"Dad has a directory published by the Post Office Department," Nancy went on. "It's not in there, either."

"Then it must be a phoney outfit!" Bess declared.

"Perhaps," Nancy agreed. "Anyway, I must find that Mrs Channing as soon as possible."

"We'll help you search," George said eagerly. "Just give the orders!"

"Okay." Nancy grinned. "Suppose you two call all the garages in town and see if anyone brought in a long black car with damaged front fenders. Meanwhile, I'll use the private phone in Dad's study and call the local inns and motels to see if a Mrs Channing has registered."

When the girls met again twenty minutes later, all of them reported complete failure. Because of the weather, Bess and George were sure Mrs Channing could not have driven far. She probably had stayed with a friend.

"Unless she registered at a hotel under another name." Nancy mused.

Mr Drew joined them in a farewell snack, then kissed Nancy good night. He told her he would be gone before the three girls were awake, then asked:

"What's your next move?"

"To call on Ida Compton."

The next morning was crisp and sunny. Giant snow-ploughs, working all night, had effectively cleared the roads. At ten o'clock the three girls were seated in Nancy's sleek convertible, on their way to consult the nurse. Nancy pulled up at Dr Britt's office.

After hearing the story, Miss Compton was eager to co-operate. She explained that a few days previously, a tall, muscular man of about forty and his wife had called to see the doctor. They had given their names as Mr and Mrs R. I. Channing.

While they waited to see the doctor, the nurse had expressed her admiration for the mink stole Mrs Channing wore. To her surprise, the woman had removed the fur and offered to sell it cheap. She had also suggested Miss Compton buy a block of Forest Fur Company stock.

"Mrs Channing doesn't miss a trick, does she?" George remarked. "Always on the lookout for clients!"

"Mrs Channing seemed pleasant and honest." The nurse sighed. "Are you sure she isn't?"

"Well, I haven't proved anything yet," Nancy admitted. "But Mrs Channing's methods are very strange, and I couldn't locate Dunstan Lake."

Miss Compton said she never left the office when strangers were in it. But at Mr Channing's request she had gone to make a cup of tea because his wife felt faint.

"I'm afraid the tea business was just an excuse," Nancy said. "Those two wanted you out of here for some special reason. But why?"

The young detective's glance passed swiftly about the room and came to rest on a steel cabinet. "Of course!" she exclaimed. "The Channings wanted to look in the file. They hoped to get names and addresses of persons they might sell to."

"I guess that's true, Nancy," the nurse admitted. "Because as soon as Mrs Channing drank the tea and I handed her a cheque for the stole and the stock, she said they couldn't wait to see the doctor and hurried away."

"Miss Compton, will you do me a favour?" Nancy asked. "Call a few of the doctor's patients on the telephone right now. Ask if a Mrs Channing—or at least a dark-haired woman—has called on them, offering to sell them stock or furs."

She had no sooner made her request than the nurse began to dial a number. Within a few minutes Nancy learned that several patients had made purchases from a smooth-talking woman named Mrs Channing. Nancy spoke to each one but picked up no further information.

"I think we had better be on our way," she said finally. "I don't want to take any more of your time, Miss Compton. But if you will continue to check the people in those files, we can stop in later for the list. Somewhere there's bound to be a person who can give us a real clue."

"Where do we go from here?" George asked as the three friends got into the convertible.

"I don't know," said Nancy. "It's too near lunch-time to make any calls and—girls!"

Nancy's voice was excited as she bent over the steering wheel and stared down the street. "There! Just crossing the intersection in that car," she gasped. "I believe it's Mrs Channing!"

As soon as the light changed, Nancy turned left to follow the black car. She trailed it down the side street for a block, then on to a highway that led to open country. All at once the girls heard the warning wail of a siren. A police car drew up alongside the convertible. The driver waved Nancy to the kerb.

"Where do you think you're going in such a hurry?" the officer demanded.

"Oh!" Nancy flushed. "I'm sorry if I was going too fast. You see, I was trying to catch another car."

The policeman ignored her apology. "Let's see your driver's licence."

"Certainly, Officer."

Nancy reached for the wallet in her inner coat pocket. She snapped open a flap and suddenly her face was the picture of dismay.

Her driver's licence and all her other identification papers were gone!

·3·

Missing Earrings

"Now, young lady, I suppose you're going to tell me you lost your driver's licence?"

The policeman's tone was sceptical as he looked at Nancy. The man was a stranger to her, which was unusual, since Nancy knew most of the local police and all were her friends.

"Oh dear! This is certainly a disaster!" wailed Bess. "Now we can't catch that awful Mrs Channing."

George spoke up. "Officer, this is Nancy Drew," she said. "We're after a thief. Please let us go."

The policeman stared. "You're what? Listen, miss, if that's the case, there are two reasons for my taking you to headquarters. Suppose you tell the chief your story." He directed Nancy to follow him.

Chief of Police McGinnis was surprised to see Nancy. He listened while she explained her predicament of being without a licence.

"I just can't figure out what happened to it," she continued. "I know I had it in my purse yesterday."

"I'm aware you have a driver's licence, Nancy," the chief assured her. "That's why I'm going to be lenient in your case. You've helped the police department on so many occasions that it's almost as if you were a member of the force."

At this remark the traffic policeman's jaw dropped.

"Oh, thank you, Chief McGinnis," Nancy said gratefully. "I'll make application for a duplicate licence at once."

"Good." The officer nodded. "But remember, young lady, keep your car in the garage until that new licence arrives."

"Chief, I have a driver's licence," Bess interrupted. "See—it's right here in my handbag. I can drive Nancy's car for her."

"You girls!" Chief McGinnis laughed. "You don't miss a trick, do you? Yes, Miss Marvin, I suppose you can act as chaffeur. And now what's this about a thief? Are you up to something we police don't know about?"

Nancy's eyes were teasing as she answered, "I'll let you know the instant I find out."

As the girls left, George exclaimed, "Whew, that was close! I thought you were going to have to tell him about Mrs Channing and I knew you didn't want to yet."

"No, not until I have some proof she's dishonest." There was a thoughtful frown on Nancy's brow. "I wish I could figure out what happened to my licence."

"You don't suppose someone stole it, do you?" Bess asked as she slid in behind the steering wheel.

"I can't decide," Nancy admitted. "In the first place, that licence isn't worth a thing to anybody but me. So why would it attract a thief? And why would he want my identification papers?"

"Maybe the thief was looking for money and took the other things by mistake," George suggested. "Did you have much money in your purse?"

"No, just an emergency five dollars," said Nancy. "I

have another purse that I carry silver and bills in. That wasn't tampered with."

"Well, we can put our heads together at lunch," said Bess. "You're both invited to my house. And, girls, I promise chicken pie and angel cake."

The food was delicious, but what interested Nancy even more was a message for her from Bess's father. Hearing of the case, Mr Marvin had telephoned his broker in New York and learned that no such organisation as the Forest Fur Company was listed among legitimate stock companies.

"Poor Hannah!" thought Nancy, deciding to redouble her efforts to find Mrs Channing.

That afternoon Nancy, Bess, and George stopped at Dr Britt's office and picked up the list Miss Compton had prepared. It contained the names of several patients who had bought furs or stock from the mysterious Mrs Channing.

"I think Mrs Clifton Packer would be a good one," decided Nancy. "She's a wealthy widow and bought several hundred shares of stock in the Forest Fur Company."

"Then, Mrs Packer, here we come," George said with a grin. "Step on it, chauffeur," she commanded, tapping her cousin Bess on the shoulder. "But for goodness sake—don't speed!"

The Packer house was a large stone building that looked more like a French château than an American residence. A maid, clad in a black uniform and a starched cap and apron, answered the doorbell. She ushered the three girls into the entrance hall.

Mrs Packer was a stout, talkative woman. She knew Nancy by reputation and was plainly curious as to the purpose of the young detective's call.

"Don't tell me I have a mystery here at Oak Manor, Nancy?" she began as soon as the three girls were seated in her luxurious living-room.

"Perhaps you have, Mrs Packer." Nancy smiled. She hastily sketched her reasons for suspecting Mrs Channing and her questionable sales activity.

"Why, I'm astounded—simply astounded!" gasped the plump widow. "Mrs Channing appeared so charming. Such a lady."

"I understand she sold you some furs," prompted Nancy.

"Oh, she did. She did indeed," babbled Mrs Packer. "And then, of course, there is that block of stock I bought. I paid her a thousand dollars for that."

Bess and George exchanged startled glances.

"Did Mrs Channing give you any information about this fur company?" Nancy asked. "Where it's located, for instance?"

"I don't think so," admitted Mrs Packer. "I just remember her saying they have mink ranches throughout the United States and Canada. That's why I thought the stock was all right. Good mink, you know, is very scarce. And very expensive."

"But suppose the stock you bought is worthless," said Nancy, and told what Mr Marvin had learned.

"Oh dear! I suppose I was foolish," Mrs Packer admitted. "But it was the lovely mink furs Mrs Channing showed me that convinced me. You see, I'm quite an authority on pelts.

"Come up to my bedroom, girls," the widow invited, leading the way. "I'll show you what I bought. All mink, you know, isn't equally fine. There are four different grades. The best fur comes from the northern

United States and Canada. It's the cold weather that makes it lustrous and thick."

Mrs Packer opened a wardrobe and removed a luxurious mink cape. "The minute Mrs Channing showed this to me I knew I had to have it," she rattled on. "Notice the rich dark-brown colour and how alive and silky the fur is!

"That shows the cape was made from young mink. In older animals, the fur is much coarser and the pelts are larger, too. A sure indication that you have a less valuable piece of merchandise."

George winked at Nancy. They were surely getting Mrs Channing's sales-talk secondhand!

Bess giggled. "Young mink, old mink—who cares?" she said. "I'd settle for any kind of a mink coat."

They went back to the living-room. Mrs Packer rang a bell and her maid, Hilda, a woman of thirty, appeared. She was asked to serve tea. After the maid had left, their hostess dimpled coyly.

"I just love tea parties, don't you?" Evidently she was not too concerned about her missing thousand dollars. "Hilda makes the most divine little cakes. I served them when I had the party for Mrs Channing."

"What!" George burst out, then added apologetically, "I'm sorry."

Mrs Packer explained that she had held a party for Mrs Channing to introduce certain friends who were always "looking for bargains in clothes". The friends had purchased both furs and stock. Nancy was about to ask their names when the woman abruptly changed the subject.

"Now that you're here, Nancy Drew, I want to consult you about the disappearance of my favourite earrings."

Nancy looked doubtful. "I don't know, Mrs Packer. I'm pretty busy just now. Perhaps you just misplaced the earrings."

"Of course I didn't," her hostess protested. "I always put everything back in my jewel case the minute I take it off. Besides, I was very careful of those earrings. They're part of a valuable set.

"See, I'm wearing the brooch that matches them. Nancy, how would it be if you take this with you, so you can trace the earrings for me?" the widow continued, removing the brooch and handing it to Nancy.

Despite the fact that the young detective had one mystery to solve and was to help her father on another, she found herself saying, just as Hilda walked in with the tea tray:

"I'll do what I can, Mrs Packer. When did you first miss your jewellery?"

As the woman pondered the question, Nancy saw Hilda stop short. The maid placed the tray on top of the piano and hastened back to the kitchen, as if she had forgotten something. Perhaps the napkins, Nancy thought, but she immediately noticed them protruding over the corner of the tray. Did Hilda's action have anything to do with the conversation?

"Do you remember when you missed your jewellery?" Nancy prompted Mrs Packer, who seemingly had not noticed the strange procedure.

"Oh, yes, now I remember," the woman said, her hands fluttering in agitation. "It was the day after that party."

George shot a glance towards Nancy, but let the young detective do the talking.

"Do you know of anybody at the party who might have wanted the earrings?" Nancy asked.

Hilda hastened back from the kitchen, picked up the tray, and approached her mistress. The maid was pale and nervous.

"No, unless it was—Why, Nancy, do you think it could have been Mrs Channing, the woman you said sold me the fake fur stock?"

At Mrs Packer's words an agonized wail burst from Hilda. She went chalk white.

"O-oh!" she cried.

Nancy looked up just in time to see the tray tilt precariously in the maid's hands. Hilda clutched at the dishes, but too late. The tray slipped from her grasp!

The lid of the teapot fell off and a cascade of hot water poured down upon the arm of Hilda's startled mistress. With it the cups and saucers clattered to the sofa.

Hilda, with a terrified scream, turned and ran from the room.

·4·

More Trouble

"Oh! I'm burned!" Mrs Packer cried out. She jumped up and shook her wet sleeve. "Such stupid clumsiness!" she sputtered, seizing a napkin and swabbing her arm.

"Girls," she went on, "did you notice how Hilda jumped when I spoke of my stolen earrings? It's plain the girl knows something. Why, she may have taken them herself!"

"She certainly acted strangely," George agreed.

"Yes—and while we've been talking, she's escaped!" Bess added excitedly.

"Hilda looks like an honest person," said Nancy, coming to the girl's defence. "I think she's only worried or scared. Mrs Packer, do you mind if I look for your maid?"

"Go right ahead," the widow replied. "But I think I should call the police."

"Wait a little, please," Nancy urged. "And tell me, are there any other servants in the house?"

"No," said Mrs Packer. "My butler and cook have the afternoon off. If Hilda hasn't run away already, she's probably in her room. That's on the third floor. The second door to the left."

Nancy found Hilda's bedroom door tightly closed. But she knew by the sound of hysterical sobbing that the maid was inside. She knocked softly.

"Hilda, let me in," she called. "Don't be afraid. I just want to help you."

"Go 'way," said a muffled voice. "Mrs Packer—she'll fire me! She thinks I'm a thief!"

"No. I want to talk to you, Hilda," pleaded Nancy. "I'm your friend. Won't you listen to me, please?"

The sympathy in Nancy's voice must have convinced the nervous young woman, for she opened the door. "I was packing my suitcase," she admitted, dabbing at her reddened eyes with a handkerchief. "Oh, Miss Drew, I've been such a fool!"

"We're all foolish now and then," Nancy said soothingly. She led the maid gently to the bed and sat down beside her. "Hilda, why don't you tell me about it?" she suggested.

Ten minutes later Nancy and a subdued and calmer Hilda rejoined the others in the living-room. Nancy's blue eyes twinkled as she addressed her hostess.

"Mrs Packer, Hilda hasn't committed any crime. Her only mistake was that she did exactly as you did!"

"What do you mean?"

"Simply this," explained Nancy. "Hilda heard Mrs Channing tell you about the stock in the Forest Fur Company and how it would make you a lot of money. When she saw you buy some of it, Hilda decided to do the same thing."

"*Ja*," said Hilda, bobbing her white-blonde head. "That's just what I did. I think what's good for a smart lady like Mrs Packer is good for me."

Mrs Packer's grim face softened. "Why, Hilda," she said, "in a way, that's a compliment."

"Of course it is," said Nancy. "Hilda feels doubly bad because the money she used was the twenty-five dollars she borrowed on her salary to send to her family in Europe."

"Never mind," her mistress said gently. "I'll see that you don't lose by this, Hilda. Suppose you get busy now and clear away those broken cups and saucers."

Nancy and her friends left, the valuable brooch pinned on the young detective's blouse. She promised to try to find the earrings as soon as possible.

"I'm glad poor Hilda didn't lose her money and her job," said Bess as the three girls drove to Nancy's house. "I think Mrs Packer was to blame, anyway."

"We didn't get much farther in tracking down Mrs Channing," George remarked.

"No," said Nancy. "But I believe we've advanced a bit. We'd nearly forgotten Mr Channing. I'm sure that he's part of our puzzle."

"And what a puzzle!" Bess sighed as they drove into the Drew garage. She and George walked home.

Togo, Nancy's alert little terrier, was waiting for her when Nancy stepped into the house. The little fellow scampered joyfully ahead of her as she climbed the stairs and went into her father's deserted study. Togo cocked his head. He was hoping his mistress was going to play a game with him.

"I love this room, Togo," Nancy confided to him. "It makes me feel so close to Dad. Let's pretend he's here, shall we?" She sat down in the big leather chair and held out her arms to the eager dog.

"You sit right here—on my lap—Togo. That's it. Now we'll hold our conference.

"First of all, I know what Dad would advise. He'd say: 'Use your head, daughter! You can't just chase after this Mrs Channing as if she were a butterfly. You must outsmart her!'

"Hm-m, that's right," Nancy mused. "Probably Mrs Channing has exhausted her prospects in River Heights. This means she has moved into new territory. But where? Got any suggestions, Togo? Speak up, boy!"

At the word "speak" the little terrier gave a sharp bark. "Oh, I see." Nancy grinned. "You advise that we try one town in every direction from here. If Mrs Channing has been seen in any of these places, we'll know whether she has headed north, south, east, or west. And a very good idea it is."

Nancy heaved a sigh of relief and set Togo on the floor. "Okay. Conference is over," she announced. "Now we'll go and see about dinner, partner."

Nancy spent the evening at the telephone. First, she followed up the rest of the names on Miss Compton's list. No information of value came of this.

Next, she called several out-of-town physicians who were friends of Dr Britt. To her satisfaction, she found that three had been visited by Mr and Mrs Channing. Later the physicians called her back to say certain patients of theirs had been approached by the couple but only one woman had bought furs and stock. Three others, more cautious, had turned down the proposition. One of those, a saleswoman herself, had considered notifying the Better Business Bureau, but had not done so.

Before retiring, Nancy wrote a letter to the Motor Vehicle Department advising them of her lost licence. She hoped it would not be too long before a replacement was sent.

When Bess and George arrived the next morning, Nancy greeted them with, "We're going to Masonville. . . . Why? Because it's north of here."

"Nancy, it's too early in the day for riddles," George complained.

Nancy smiled mysteriously, then said all of Mrs Channing's victims to the west, south, and east of River Heights had been called upon at least a month before.

"So our saleswoman won't go back there," Nancy theorized. "But apparently she hasn't tackled Masonville yet. If we can only find her at work there—"

"Let's go!" George said impatiently.

Halfway to Masonville, Bess suddenly gasped. "Our fuel gauge says *empty*. I hope we don't get stuck."

Luck favoured the girls. A quarter of a mile further on, they came to a petrol station. The proprietor was a gaunt, grey-haired man in frayed overalls. Nancy lowered a window of the convertible and asked him to fill the tank. Then she said:

"Has a woman in a mink coat and driving a long black car stopped here lately?"

The old fellow looked at her shrewdly and scratched one ear. "Was the lady purty and was that a fine mink coat?" he countered.

At his words Nancy's heart gave an exultant leap. "Oh, you've seen her, then! Do you mind telling us when it was?"

"No, I don't mind," said the man. "The lady come by here yesterday mornin' on her way to Masonville. My wife was with me. The minute she spotted that coat she ohed and ahed, the way womenfolks do."

"Did she sell your wife a fur piece?" Bess interrupted, unable to restrain her excitement.

The man shook his head. "Nope. She didn't sell us nothin', young lady. But she claimed to be from a big fur outfit. Even offered to get my wife a mink coat cheap

—that is, if we'd buy some stock in her company first."

"Did she show you this stock?" persisted Nancy.

"She did, but I'm an old Vermonter myself. I never heard o' that town, Dunstan Lake, listed on the certificate."

"Did you ask her about it?"

"Sure, miss. She said Dunstan Lake was only a village with too few people for a post office. Sounded fishy to me."

"How right you are!" George said grimly. "I'm glad you didn't buy anything from her."

As the girls drove off, Bess exclaimed enthusiastically, "We're on the right track!"

Masonville was only five miles from the petrol station. The three young detectives were excited as they drove into town, convinced that they were on Mrs Channing's trail at last.

"Let's not celebrate too soon," Nancy cautioned. "Mrs Channing may have finished her work here and driven further north. But we'll investigate."

"I'll park in front of this bank," said Bess.

"All right," Nancy agreed. "We can walk from here. But first let's decide what to do."

"Shouldn't we try the hotels, Nancy?" George suggested. "If Mrs Channing is registered at one of them, it might save us the trouble of going to any other place."

"Do you know the names of the hotels here?" Bess asked.

Nancy thought a moment. "There's the Mansion House, but I don't think Mrs Channing would like that. It's a commercial hotel."

"Isn't the Palace in Masonville?" George recalled. "Famous for lobster or something?"

"Yes, but it's no longer a hotel, Dad told me. It's an office building now."

"We're getting nowhere fast," George groaned. "Let's go ask a police—"

She broke off abruptly as Bess's eyes suddenly grew wide with fear and she whispered excitedly:

"Girls! Look at those two men across the street! They're staring at us as if we'd just escaped from jail!"

"You're being silly," George remarked, not taking her scared cousin seriously.

"I mean it," Bess insisted. "You see for yourself."

George turned to look and Nancy leaned forward to observe the men. One was a short, stout man in a grey overcoat, with soft grey hair. The other was slim and younger. He wore a blue raincoat with the collar turned up, and a cap pulled low on his forehead.

At a nod from him, the stout man walked determinedly across the street towards the convertible, with the younger man close behind.

As the girls watched, the two men slowly circled the car and examined the licence plate at its rear. Then a big hand pulled open the door beside Bess.

"Which of you is Nancy Drew?" he demanded in a deep voice.

"I am," Nancy admitted. "Why do you want to know?"

"You're wanted for shoplifting, Nancy Drew," said the stout man. "I place you under arrest!"

·5·

The Second Nancy

THE man in the grey overcoat motioned the girls to get out of the car. For several seconds they sat still, too astonished to speak. Then Nancy faced the men and said calmly, "Suppose you tell me who you are and why you're making this ridiculous charge."

The stout man opened his coat. A police badge gleamed on his inside pocket. His companion showed one also.

"We're plain-clothes men," he explained. "We were told to pick up a car with this licence number and a Nancy Drew who owns it."

"You can't arrest Nancy!" Bess asserted.

George spoke up indignantly. "Nancy's a detective herself. You'd better be careful what you say."

The stout man looked grim. "Well, somebody detected *her* when she entered a fur store here and stole two expensive mink stoles."

"I did no such thing," Nancy declared quickly.

"Oh, yes, you did," the slim man insisted. "After you showed your licence and charged a cheap fur piece on credit, you took two expensive furs that you didn't charge! What did you do with them?"

Nancy realized that the woman who had her driver's

licence was pretending to be Nancy Drew! If it were Mrs Channing, she probably had altered the age and personal data on the card.

"Let's go to headquarters, girls," Nancy said. "We'll clear this up in no time."

At headquarters a sergeant took down Nancy's name and address. "Any relation to the lawyer in River Heights?" he asked.

"He's my father," said Nancy.

"Good grief!" Sergeant Wilks said, shaking his head. "You never know where these juvenile delinquents will come from!"

Nancy turned scarlet and George sputtered with anger. Neither noticed that Bess was no longer with them.

Suddenly the door was flung open. A distinguished-looking man hurried in, followed by Bess.

"Judge Hart!" Nancy cried, rushing forward to greet her father's old friend. "You're just the person I need!"

"That's what Bess tells me."

"You—you know the judge?" Sergeant Wilks stammered.

"Very well," said Nancy.

Judge Hart turned to the sergeant. "Why are you holding this young woman?"

The officer repeated the charges.

"There's a mistake somewhere," the judge insisted.

"It's because my driver's licence was stolen two days ago, Judge," said Nancy. "I've been telling these officers someone evidently is using it, but they won't believe me."

"I see." Judge Hart frowned. "Let's call in that

fur-shop owner and settle this matter properly."

The man was summoned to headquarters. He looked at Nancy and shook his head. "No, this is a different person. The thief was older."

"Was the woman wearing a mink coat, and did she have blue eyes and blue-black hair?" Nancy asked.

"Why, yes," the man said. "That describes her."

"Well, Sergeant," said Judge Hart, "is Miss Drew free to go now?"

"Certainly. Miss Drew, can you tell us where we might find the woman you spoke of?"

"I wish I could," said Nancy. "I only know that sometimes she calls herself Mrs Channing. Besides being a shoplifter, she sells fake stock."

"We'll be on the lookout for her," Wilks promised.

The girls walked with Judge Hart to his nearby office. Nancy thanked him for his help and told of the stock swindle.

"I've spent many summers in Vermont," the judge remarked, "but I've never heard of Dunstan Lake. Let me make a phone call and find out where it is."

The judge placed a call to the Vermont capital. When he finished his conversation, he declared, "There is no such place as Dunstan Lake anywhere in the State of Vermont. You have a real mystery on your hands, young lady. Let me know if I can help you."

"I surely will," Nancy promised.

As the girls walked back to the car, Bess asked, "Nancy, how do you suppose Mrs Channing got her hands on your licence?"

"Well, Mrs Martin and I left her alone on the sofa after the accident. When Mrs Channing regained consciousness and saw that we were out of the room, she must have slipped the papers out of my purse. It was in my coat on a chair."

"Shoplifters *are* quick with their hands," Bess pointed out. "Just like pickpockets."

Nancy nodded and said, "Well, girls, let's head further north!"

"North!" chorused the cousins in surprise.

"I'm sure Mrs Channing left Masonville right after that theft," Nancy answered. "She wouldn't dare turn back, so I believe she continued north."

The girls rode rapidly, stopping frequently at small towns to inquire if anyone had seen a woman of Mrs Channing's description.

At the town of Winchester, George went into the Crestview Hotel and soon came rushing back. "We've found her!" she cried. "The desk clerk says a dark-haired woman in a mink coat registered here last night. But she isn't in now."

"She's probably out robbing somebody," Bess remarked.

"And listen to this!" George said, growing more excited every moment. "Nancy, she's still using your name!"

Nancy's eyes flashed angrily. "I've always been proud of my name and I resent having it connected with a thief! Come on, girls. We'll wait for her in the lobby."

The three waited for an hour. Finally Nancy walked up to the desk. "We're here to see a guest registered as Nancy Drew," she told the clerk. "Do you suppose she came in another entrance?"

"That's impossible," the man said. "There's only the back door used by our employees. I'll ring her room if you like."

There was no answer to the call. Nancy decided to take the clerk into her confidence. When the man heard the story, he offered to unlock the suspect's room and see if there were any evidence that she was the thief.

"Please do that," Nancy asked the clerk, who said his name was Mark Evans.

When they reached the room, Bess and George remained in the hall to watch for Mrs Channing. Nancy followed Mr Evans inside. The man glanced about, threw open the wardrobe door, and cried out, "Her luggage is gone! She left without paying her bill!"

Nancy could detect the scent of the woman's exotic perfume in the air. The young detective walked to a window, lifted it, and stared at the ground below. The snow was marked with scrambled footprints and several deep indentations.

"I can see how Mrs Channing got away," Nancy said. "She slipped up here by the servants' stairway and dropped her bags out the window. Then she went down the stairs again, picked up her luggage, and hurried off."

"She can't be allowed to get away with this!" Mr Evans spluttered.

"Perhaps she left a clue that will help us find her," Nancy suggested. She moved slowly about the room, searching the floor and furniture. Methodically she opened and shut bureau drawers. All were empty.

Suddenly Nancy stooped to pick up something from beneath the bed. It was a small black label used by stores to identify their merchandise. The name on the label was : *Masonville Fur Company*.

"Here is a clue !" Nancy thought elatedly.

"Here is a clue!" Nancy thought elatedly

At the moment Nancy made her discovery a voice said, "What's wrong, Mr Evans?" The speaker was a plump woman who peered curiously into the room.

"Good morning, Mrs Plimpton," the clerk answered. "We're looking for a guest who occupied this room."

"Miss Drew, you mean," said Mrs Plimpton. "We ate breakfast together and had a nice chat."

Nancy suspected another stock sale. "I came a long way to see this woman," she said. "I wonder if I might talk with you privately."

"Why, certainly," Mrs Plimpton agreed. "My room's just across the hall. Come over there."

While George and Bess went to wait in the hotel lobby, Nancy listened to the woman's story. Mrs Plimpton had admired the fur coat which Mrs Channing wore. The younger woman offered to sell her a mink stole at half price.

Later that morning Mrs Channing had come to Mrs Plimpton's room and persuaded her to buy the fur stole. "But I didn't have the five hundred dollars she urged me to invest in her stock," the woman told her.

"Lucky for you," Nancy said, and explained that the value of the stock was questionable. "Mrs Plimpton, in your conversations with her, did this woman say where she might be going from here?"

The older woman shook her head. "I understood that she was to stay at Crestview for some time."

"Mrs Channing must have caught a glimpse of me as we entered the hotel," Nancy thought. Aloud she said, "May I see the stole?"

"Certainly," Mrs Plimpton replied, and brought out a fur piece. There was no label on it.

"Mrs Channing must have removed it," Nancy said

to herself. "But perhaps there's some other way to identify it as stolen goods." She explained her suspicions to Mrs Plimpton and asked to use the telephone.

Nancy called the Masonville Fur Company and learned that every fur piece sold there had MFC stamped on one of the skins. At the time of purchase, the date was added.

Nancy borrowed scissors and quickly opened the lining of the stole. Near the neckline was the MFC mark. There was no date.

"I'll let the fur company know," Mrs Plimpton said tearfully.

"I hope to recover your money," Nancy said. "By the way, that thief is not Nancy Drew. Her name is Mrs Channing. If you should ever see her again, be sure to call the police."

When Nancy joined her friends in the lobby, Bess suggested that they go to lunch at a tearoom she had noticed a few blocks away. As the three walked towards it, Nancy told what she had learned from Mrs Plimpton.

"Has Mrs Channing been doing this all along? Stealing furs and then selling them as a come-on for her fake stock?" George asked.

"I'm not sure where she got her first supply," said Nancy. "But evidently business has been so good that she ran out of merchandise and had to resort to shoplifting."

"Well, what next?" Bess asked.

"Before we leave town," Nancy said, "I'd like to canvass all the exclusive shops and find out if they've missed any furs or—" Her voice trailed away. She had seen an elegantly dressed woman with shiny blue-black hair walking briskly along the opposite side of the street.

"I'll be back!" she said quickly, hurrying across the street to follow the woman. Mrs Channing was moving so rapidly that the girl had no chance to trail her subtly.

Nancy had nearly caught up to Mrs Channing when the woman paused to look in a gift-shop window. An instant later she turned, ran down the street, and slipped into a small fur shop.

"She saw my reflection in that shop window!" Nancy thought, and walked rapidly to the fur shop. She gazed cautiously through the window. Mrs Channing was not in sight.

Nancy stepped inside. A small, stout man moved briskly to meet her, followed by a smaller and equally stout woman. "Something my wife and I can do for you miss?" the man asked.

"I came in to inquire about a woman I saw enter this place a minute ago," Nancy replied. "A tall woman in a mink coat. She has bluish-black hair."

The storekeeper raised his eyebrows and shook his head, at the same time glancing quickly at his wife. "Perhaps you are mistaken?"

"I saw her come in here," Nancy insisted. "I must find her."

"Who are you, please?" the man demanded.

"My name is Nancy Drew, and—"

With a yelp of rage the little man leaped towards the girl, pinning her hands behind her back. The woman threw a dark cloth over Nancy's head. Despite her resistance, the couple over-powered the young sleuth and dragged her to a back room.

"Unlock the cupboard!" the man directed.

Nancy heard the click of a door latch. She was shoved among some fur coats. The door slammed shut and a key turned in the lock.

"You'll never try to rob this store again!" the proprietor cried mockingly.

·6·

Curious Dealings

THE cupboard in which Nancy was a prisoner was dark and stuffy. Fur garments crowded against her, nearly suffocating her. She pressed an ear to a crack in the door and listened to the murmur of excited voices in the shop.

"I say we call the police!" the woman shrilled. "Tell them we have captured this thief ourselves and no thanks to their protection!"

"But, Mama, suppose the lady in the fur coat was mistaken?" persisted the proprietor. "All we know is that she said a thief named Nancy Drew was coming to steal furs."

"And didn't Nancy Drew come in here?" insisted his wife. "That's good enough for me!"

Nancy heard the door of the shop open. "Pardon me," said a familiar voice. "Did a red-haired girl come in here?"

"George!" thought Nancy.

"Why do you ask?" the proprietor demanded.

"Because she's a friend of ours," Bess answered. "We saw her come into this shop."

After a moment of silence, the woman asked, "What's your friend's name?"

"Nancy Drew," George declared.

47

"You've come to help her rob us!" the woman shrieked. "Papa, lock them up too!"

Nancy doubled her fists and banged on the closed door with all her might. "Bess! George!" she shouted. "I'm locked in this cupboard!"

She heard a startled exclamation and the sound of running feet. In a moment the door swung open. "Nancy!" Bess gasped. "What happened?"

"Mrs Channing told these people I'm a thief!"

The proprietor frowned. "Mrs Channing?"

"The woman in the fur coat," Nancy told him. "She stole two mink pieces in Masonville yesterday. I believe she planned to rob you, but saw me coming and used this means to get rid of me."

"Nancy's a detective," Bess spoke up.

The mouths of the shop owners dropped open. "I meant no harm, miss," the man said quickly.

"Where did Mrs Channing go?" Nancy asked.

"Out the back door," The proprietor pointed. "I'm so very, very sorry—" he began.

"It's all right," Nancy said. "Come on, girls. Maybe we can pick up that woman's trail."

But Mrs Channing was not hiding in any of the alleys or shops in the vicinity. The three friends cruised up and down the streets of Winchester, and inquired at two other hotels and all the fur shops. No one had seen the woman.

Finally the girls decided to return home. When they stopped for petrol on the way back to River Heights, Nancy picked up a clue. She questioned the service-station attendant, who informed her that a long black car with dented fenders had stopped there for petrol a short time before.

"The driver was a dark-haired woman in a fur coat," the employee said. "I remember her because she seemed so nervous. Kept looking back over her shoulder all the time."

"Did she mention where she was going?" Nancy asked.

"No. But she said to fill her fuel tank—said she was starting on a trip. Maybe to Vermont, I thought. The car had a Vermont licence."

"Did you happen to notice anything she had in the car with her? Luggage or packages or anything?" George asked.

"Now, why are you girls so curious?" the man countered. "I'm pretty busy here."

Before Nancy could stop Bess, she revealed their suspicions of Mrs Channing. The attendant became cordial once more.

"You know, that woman did have two extra fur coats on the back seat," he said.

Nancy thanked the man for the information. While paying for the petrol, she asked, " Have you a telephone?"

"Yes, inside. Use it if you like."

Nancy phoned the local police, told what she had learned, and asked them to alert the Vermont authorities.

When Nancy finally reached home, Hannah greeted her with a broad smile and said, "I'm sorry you had such a long, tedious trip."

"Well, I picked up some good clues."

"What were you doing, anyway? Trailing that nice Mrs Channing?" Hannah asked.

"I wouldn't call her nice!" Nancy declared.

"Well, now, I think you're prejudiced," Hannah said. "That's fine stock she sold me!"

"What makes you think so?" Nancy asked.

"In the afternoon post I received some money from the Forest Fur Company—a nice, fat dividend," Hannah stated triumphantly.

Nancy stared at her in amazement. "That fake fur company actually paid you?" she asked.

"Yes, indeed!" said Hannah. "And Mrs Martin phoned to say that she received her payment, too."

"Why—why, it simply doesn't make sense," Nancy said, walking to the telephone. "I'm going to call Mrs Clifton Packer."

The wealthy widow greeted Nancy cordially, and admitted she had been mailed a sizeable dividend. But Mrs Packer did not sound pleased.

"I suppose the payment was not very large," Nancy remarked, thinking that the woman was no doubt accustomed to receiving sizeable dividends.

"It's not that," Mrs Packer replied. "Nancy, there's something queer about the way the money was sent. And one doesn't get dividends so soon after buying stock. I wish you'd investigate!"

Nancy's fingers tightened on the telephone receiver. "Something odd about the payment?"

"Yes," Mrs Packer went on. "As you might guess, I have stock in various companies. They all send their dividends by cheque. The cheques are signed by the treasurer of the company."

"And this payment was different?"

"It certainly was!" said the widow. "It was a money order posted from New York. No legitimate business would work that way."

Nancy thanked Mrs Packer for the information and hung up. "Well?" asked Hannah Gruen.

"Mrs Packer agrees that something is wrong," said Nancy. "Do you still have the letter that came with your dividend?"

"There wasn't any letter." The housekeeper frowned. "Just the money order in an envelope." Hannah said that she had cashed the money order and thrown the envelope away.

After a frantic search, Nancy located it in a wastebasket. She smoothed out the crumpled bit of paper to study the sender's name and address. There was no name, and the street number was blurred.

"Who sent the money orders?" she asked herself. "Not Mrs Channing—she was in River Heights at the time this was posted."

Nancy concluded that the woman must have a confederate in New York, someone to whom she sent lists of her victims and who then mailed the dividends. Could the person be Mrs Channing's husband? she wondered.

Nancy was eager to follow up the clue. "If Dad doesn't need me yet, I'll take the early plane for New York tomorrow," she decided.

After supper she telephoned her father and told him the news. "May I make a quick trip to New York before I join you?" she asked.

"If you think it's worth while, go ahead," the lawyer replied. "I've found some extra work up here that'll keep me busy a few days."

The next morning Nancy was optimistic as she boarded the aircraft. She always enjoyed trips to New York, which invariably meant a visit to Mr Drew's younger sister, a schoolteacher.

The slim, red-haired woman resembled Nancy in more than looks. Eloise Drew had assisted her niece in solving several mysteries.

Nancy took a taxi from the airport to Miss Drew's apartment. Her aunt greeted Nancy with a warm smile. "I was just hoping I could see you during my holiday next week!" she declared. "And here you are, and with that old twinkle in your eyes. You're involved in another mystery. Right?"

Nancy laughed. "Right! Will you help me?"

While she and her aunt prepared lunch, Nancy told of the case and the envelope clue.

"What do you plan to do next?" Aunt Eloise asked.

"Go to the address on the envelope. I think Mrs Channing's husband may be there. If he sent the money orders, I'll call the police."

"I'll go with you," Aunt Eloise announced.

After the two finished lunch, they started out. The address on the envelope proved to be that of a hotel in a run-down district.

At the desk in the lobby, a clerk glanced up as Nancy approached him. "Is a Mr R. I. Channing registered here?" she asked.

The clerk shook his head.

"Perhaps I was mistaken in the name," Nancy said quickly. "Have you a guest who works for the Forest Fur Company?"

The clerk grew impatient. "No, young lady. This is a residential hotel, and we don't handle business, so—"

"Did you mention the Forest Fur Company?" interrupted a voice behind Nancy.

The speaker was a red-haired woman in her early

forties. She was wearing a tight dress and too much make-up and jewellery. Nancy turned to her.

"I'm Miss Reynolds," the woman said. "I live here and I couldn't help overhearing you. I know the person you're looking for. I'm a stockholder in his company."

Nancy's heart leaped. She introduced herself and her aunt, and said, "Can you tell me where I can find the man you mentioned?"

"Why, he's Mr Sidney Boyd, and he lives in the suite next to mine!" the woman said loftily. "He is a true student of the theatre, Miss Drew. He said that my performance in *Wild Lilacs*—"

"I'm sure he was very complimentary, Miss Reynolds," Nancy interrupted. "But do you mind telling me how you happened to purchase stock in the Forest Fur Company?"

"Well, I had to coax Mr Boyd to sell it to me," the woman said coyly.

The clerk listened to the conversation. After Miss Reynolds nodded goodbye to the Drews and sauntered to the elevator, the man came over. "Hm!" he snorted. "Bunny Reynolds hasn't had a theatre engagement in years!"

"What about this Sidney Boyd?" Nancy prompted.

"Yes, tell us about him," Aunt Eloise put in.

"Ladies, I'm manager as well as clerk here. We don't want trouble on the premises."

"Then I imagine you want to avoid trouble with the law too," Eloise Drew said. "Suppose this Mr Boyd is involved in a stock swindle?"

"A swindle!" the manager gasped. "Well, I did suspect there was something phoney about that glib talker," he added defensively.

"What does he look like?" Nancy asked.

The man shrugged. "The usual ladies' man. Slender. Dark eyes. Kind of long, uncombed hair."

"He can't be Mr Channing," Nancy thought, "because he's a big broad-shouldered man." Aloud she said, "May I question some of your staff about Mr Boyd? It won't take long."

The man hesitated, then nodded. "Step into my office, ladies. I'll send the porters in first."

The men could tell nothing about Sidney Boyd except that he tipped generously. All the maids but one were unable to add anything. Katy, the fourth-floor maid, had such an uneasy manner of speaking that Nancy felt she might know something important about the suspect. She questioned the woman further.

"Mr Boyd gets up late," Katy said, growing more talkative. "Sometimes, while I'm waiting to clean up, he chats with me."

"What does he talk about?" Nancy asked.

"Oh, once he told me about when he was a little boy in Canada," said Katy. "He said his mother was French and his pa was a fur trapper—and he learned up there about furs. That's how I came to buy some of his fur stock."

"Forest Fur Company stock?" Nancy asked.

"Yes. I had a little money saved up," said Katy. "Maybe I shouldn't have spent it. But Mr Boyd wants to help me make more money. He says I'll get big dividends."

"Have you had any yet?" Nancy asked.

"No, but Mr Boyd promised some soon."

"The man's completely unscrupulous!" Eloise Drew cried out. "He swindles hard-working people like you!"

"Swindles?" Katy said. Tears began to stream down her face. "I've been robbed?"

"I think you'll get your money back," Nancy said soothingly. "Just try to tell me—"

Katy had already leaped to her feet. Sobbing, she flung open the door and rushed from the office.

Eloise Drew shook her head. "This is terrible. What do you propose to do next, Nancy?"

"See Sidney Boyd," the said grimly. "And turn him over to the police!"

As she and her aunt returned to the lobby, they heard the clang of the elevator door and the click of high heels.

"Wait! Please wait!" Bunny Reynolds called as she ran across the lobby towards the two. The woman's eyes were full of alarm. "Katy told me everything!" she wailed. "It's dreadful!"

"I'll try to help you—" Nancy began.

"And the earrings!" the actress interrupted. "What about the diamond earrings I bought from Sidney Boyd? I suppose they're worthless too!"

·7·

The TV Tip-off

THERE was no quieting Bunny Reynolds. The woman was so agitated that Nancy and her aunt went with her to her room on the fourth floor.

Miss Reynolds paced the floor dramatically. "To think how I trusted that villain!" she lamented, flourishing her handkerchief. "Oh, oh, oh! I shall punish that unworthy soul!" The woman sank into a chair. "Only yesterday I let him sell me those no-good earrings."

"Are you sure the earrings are worthless?" Nancy asked.

"The stock's worthless. The earrings must be."

"Do you know where he got the earrings?" Nancy persisted.

"He said he inherited them from his mother and never intended to see another woman wear them until he met me. He said that only a woman of fire and artistic temperament should have them."

'I'm no jewel expert," said Nancy, "but I'd like to examine the earrings."

"Of course." Miss Reynolds went to her wardrobe. From a shelf she took a rolled stocking, which she unwound to disclose a small velvet-covered box.

Nancy took the case and opened it. *The case was empty!*

Bunny Reynolds let out a shriek. "He stole them!" she cried. "That horrible man took my money and then stole the diamond earrings!"

"It looks that way," Nancy said. "The diamonds must be real after all."

The actress burst into tears again. "I can't afford to lose all that money," she sobbed.

"Neither can a lot of other people who have bought Forest Fur Company stock," Nancy said grimly. "Miss Reynolds, what did the earrings look like?"

"Beautiful! Beautiful!" The actress sighed. "Tiny platinum arrows, tipped with diamonds."

Nancy opened her handbag and took out Mrs Packer's diamond brooch. "Were they anything like this?" she asked.

"Why," Bunny Reynolds exclaimed, "this matches the earrings exactly! How did you get it?"

"I'm afraid I have more bad news for you," Nancy said. "The earrings probably are part of a set that was stolen a few days ago from Mrs Clifton Packer in River Heights."

"Sidney Boyd robbed her, too?"

"I believe an accomplice of his—Mrs R. I. Channing —stole the earrings. Did Sidney Boyd ever mention her to you?"

"No," the actress answered. "Well, I'm going to call the police this minute!" She smiled coyly. "I have a special friend on the force," she said. "Police Sergeant Rolf."

Nancy spoke softly to her aunt. "I'm going to do some more investigating and see if I can find Mr Boyd," she confided. "Will you stay here with Miss Reynolds?"

Eloise Drew nodded. Nancy crossed the room. As she

flung open the door to the corridor, she collided with a crouching figure. Katy had been listening to the conversation.

Nancy smiled at the embarrassed girl. "Naturally you want to know what's going on, Katy."

"Yes, ma'am, I do," the maid said nervously. "Will the police get that awful man, Miss Drew—now that he's run away?"

"Run away!" Nancy exclaimed. "You mean Sidney Boyd has left the hotel?"

"His bed wasn't slept in last night," the maid said. "And all his things are gone. I didn't go in there till a few minutes ago because he had a *Do Not Disturb* sign on his door."

"Does the manager know this?" Nancy asked.

"I just told him," Katy said. "Mr Boyd checked out late last night. The night clerk forgot to report it to the day man."

"I'll bet he left right after he stole the earrings from Bunny Reynolds!" Nancy thought.

At Nancy's request Katy took her to the swindler's room. While the young detective investigated, a booming voice from the hallway announced the arrival of Sergeant Rolf. Nancy hurried to speak to him.

After hearing the actress's story, the tall sergeant asked to see the brooch which matched the stolen earrings. Nancy gave him the brooch and told him that Sidney Boyd had fled.

"The villain!" Miss Reynolds said bitterly.

The officer listened to the details of the case, then said, "I'd like to take the brooch to the police laboratory and have some photographs made. We can give the pictures to our men and alert them to be on the lookout in case Boyd tries to sell those earrings again."

"You're a remarkable detective!" Miss Reynolds cooed. "You'll get my money back, won't you, Sergeant? Right away?"

The man looked embarrassed. "Now, Miss Reynolds, it may take time," he protested.

The actress rolled her green eyes at him. "Can't you get some action by tonight?"

Sergeant Rolf fidgeted. "Well—er—the fact is that a lot of the men will be off duty tonight, Miss Reynolds. It's the Policeman's Ball."

The actress grew tearful. "You'll be dancing and having a good time while I—"

The sergeant took a deep breath. "Look, I've got no special lady friend," he said. "Suppose you come along with me?"

Bunny Reynolds was all smiles. "Why, Sergeant! How delightful! I'd love to go!"

Nancy beckoned to her aunt. "I think this is our cue for an exit." She chuckled. "If the sergeant will write a receipt for this brooch, we'll be on our way."

"Yes, ma'am." The officer wrote the receipt and gave it to Nancy. Then he made a note of her aunt's address and promised to return the brooch within a day or two.

"You certainly accomplished a lot, Nancy," Eloise Drew said when they entered her apartment. "And now, please relax for the rest of your visit. I've planned a special dinner tonight."

Later Miss Drew set the table with gleaming silver and tall lighted candles.

"I was so intrigued by your fur mystery that I ordered things for a trapper's dinner," she said.

When it was time to sit down to eat, Nancy was delighted. "How delicious everything looks!" she said. "Venison, wild rice, and my favourite currant jelly! Why, Aunt Eloise, this is a real north country feast!"

As they ate, their conversation returned to the mystery. "What was it you said about Dunstan Lake?" Aunt Eloise asked. "Is that the location of the Forest Fur Company?"

"So it says on the stock certificates," her niece answered. "But not even the United States Post Office has ever heard of such a place."

"Maybe it's not a town at all," Aunt Eloise suggested. "You know, Nancy, I recall that name from somewhere, but I can't remember when or how. I hope you'll let me help in your mysteries even though my memory's failed me!" she added with a chuckle.

"I call on you whenever I can," Nancy reminded her. "You've always been a help to me. Remember when you took my dog Togo to your summer home in the Adirondacks—"

"Togo!" Aunt Eloise interrupted. "I remember now. Someone came to the cottage while we were there. I believe he was a trapper. He was looking for a mink ranch and a Dunstan Lake. But there's no lake by that name around there. I remember thinking it might be the name of the owner of the mink ranch."

"That's a wonderful clue!" Nancy exclaimed.

"Please don't follow it tonight," her aunt teased, "or we'll be late for the theatre."

The next day Nancy and her aunt waited for word from the police. By evening they had received none, and Nancy finally declared that she could remain in New York only until noon the next day.

"Then I'll have to take a plane home in case Dad needs my help in Montreal. If the brooch hasn't arrived by that time, will you phone me as soon as it comes and then send it to me by registered mail?"

Aunt Eloise agreed, and the two spent the evening watching television. The late movie was an old film depicting a skating carnival. It began with a picture of the skating queen and individual close-ups of her ladies in waiting.

Suddenly Nancy cried out, "Aunt Eloise, look! That tall, dark-haired attendant!"

"She's very attractive," Miss Drew commented. "In fact, she's more striking than the queen."

"I know her!" Nancy cried.

"Friend of yours?"

"No, no. Aunt Eloise, she's the woman I'm trying to find. That's Mrs R. I. Channing!"

·8·

Trapper's Story

NANCY and Aunt Eloise waited eagerly for the motion picture to conclude. At the end the cast was named. Mrs Channing was listed as Mitzi Adele.

"Her stage name," her aunt guessed.

Nancy nodded. "Yes, or her maiden name. The film is seven or eight years old."

"She may have given up professional skating when she married," Eloise Drew suggested.

"Still, this helps," Nancy said. "If Mrs Channing was a skater, perhaps I can find some people in the profession who know where she comes from and something about her."

After breakfast the next morning Nancy phoned the television studio and asked for information about the skater Mitzi Adele. The man on the other end of the line advised Nancy to write to the Bramson Film Company, which had made the motion picture.

"Did you find out anything?" Aunt Eloise asked as Nancy put down the phone.

"Only the name of the film company. I hope they have that woman's address!"

Eloise Drew prepared to leave for school. Nancy thanked her for the visit and kissed her goodbye. After her aunt had gone, Nancy sent a telegram to the film company, asking that the reply be sent to her at River Heights.

As she was packing, the doorbell rang. Police Sergeant Rolf was in the lobby and asked to see her.

"I'm here to return that diamond brooch, Miss Drew," the officer told her. "If Sidney Boyd tries to sell the matching earrings, we'll get him!" The sergeant thanked Nancy for her help and left.

The weather was clear that afternoon and Nancy's flight was smooth. She took a taxi home from the River Heights Airport, and slipped quietly into the Drew home. Hannah was in the kitchen. Tiptoeing up behind the housekeeper, Nancy called loudly, "I'm home!"

"Oh!" gasped Hannah. "Nancy, you startled me!"

"Aunt Eloise sent her love," said Nancy as she removed her hat and coat and started for the hall cupboard. When she returned, Mrs Gruen was taking a pie from the oven.

"If Bess saw that cherry pie—" Nancy began.

"Bess and George have a surprise for you," Hannah interrupted. "Bess left word for you to phone her. George is there. Then tell me about the trip."

"I'll tell you first," Nancy said, laughing.

Ten minutes later she telephoned Bess, who reported that through a merchant who sold hunting equipment, she and George had met another investor in the Forest Fur Company.

"The old man's a fur trapper from up north," Bess went on. "He lives with his niece."

"When can I speak with him?" Nancy asked.

Bess consulted George, who took up the extension phone. "We'll drive him over tomorrow morning,"

George said. "That is, if we can persuade him to ride in a car. John Horn is strictly a high boot and snowshoe man."

Nancy laughed. "I'll get out my buckskin leggings and my coonskin cap!"

"We'll come early," George promised.

Mail for Nancy had accumulated on the hall table. As soon as she finished the conversation, she began to read it. Her duplicate driver's licence had arrived. There was also a note from her father, who was eager to have her join him.

"Did you see this?" Hannah asked, pointing to a telegram half-hidden by an advertising circular.

The message was from the Bramson Film Company. It stated that they did not know Mitzi Adele's address. However, a representative of the firm would call on Nancy shortly in regard to the woman skater.

"I wonder why," Nancy remarked. "Now I can't go to Montreal until I find out what the representative has to say!"

In the morning loud voices announced the arrival of Bess, George and the fur trapper. Stocky and round-faced the man strode up to the porch with the easy gait of a man of half his seventy years.

John Horn was dressed like Daniel Boone, Nancy thought, and his long white beard reminded her of Santa Claus. At her invitation, the three entered the Drew living-room.

The woodsman declined to take a chair. He stood before the mantel, his legs wide apart and his hands deep in the pockets of his heavy jacket.

"Well, young woman, what do you want to ask me?" he demanded, his bright blue eyes boring into Nancy's.

"Is it true that you bought Forest Fur Company stock from a Mrs Channing?" she asked.

"Yep. I was an old fool," John Horn admitted candidly. "I leaped to the bait—stupid as a wall-eyed pike!"

"I wonder if she told you anything that would help us trace her," Nancy said. "Did she mention a Dunstan Lake, for instance?"

The old man pulled at his beard. "No-o. Never heard that name, miss. All we chinned about was mink. I've worked on a mink farm and I been trappin' the little rascals for years. That's how I came by Arabella, here."

From a pocket in his coat, he pulled out a small, squirrel-like creature with bright black eyes and a long tail.

"Why, it's a mink!" cried Bess.

"Sure, she is!" John Horn said proudly. "Four months old and with as prime a pelt as I ever seen. Notice that glossy dark-brown fur? See how thick and live-looking the hair is? Arabella's an aristocrat. Yes, sir-ree!"

"Is she tame?" George asked.

"She's tame because I raised her myself," explained John Horn. "A wild mink, though, will bite—and his teeth are plenty sharp."

"Where did you get her?" Nancy asked.

"Arabella was born on a mink ranch. The first time I saw her she was a pinky white and not much bigger than a lima bean. All baby minks are like that. Tiny and covered with silky hair."

John Horn gave his pet an affectionate stroke and replaced her in his pocket. "You want me to help you catch that crook, don't you, Miss Drew?" he said.

Nancy had no such thing in mind However, if the fur company was located in the Adirondacks, as Aunt Eloise believed, it would be handy to have an experienced woodsman around

"Mr Horn, I may need your help if I have to travel up north or into the mountains, she said.

"You can count on me!" said the old man.

"Excuse me, Nancy," said Hannah from the doorway. "I thought perhaps these folks would like some hot chocolate and cinnamon toast."

At the sight of the older woman, John Horn became ill at ease. "No, thank you, ma'am," he said hastily. "Fact is, I gotta be goin'."

"We'll drive you," Bess offered.

"No. No, I'd rather walk." The old trapper turned to Nancy. "I like you, girl. You—you talk sense," he stammered. "Here—take this!"

Nancy felt something warm and furry wriggle in her hands. Startled, she gasped and stepped backward, dropping the little mink to the floor.

Arabella instantly leaped away, straight towards the astounded Hannah. The housekeeper clutched at her skirts and hopped on to the nearest chair. "A rat!" she shrieked.

"It's a mink," Nancy said. She reached down and tried to catch the little animal.

"It'll bite!" Hannah warned. "Like a rat!"

Arabella was terrified by the strange surroundings and the squeals of Bess and Hannah. The tiny animal scuttled frantically here and there in search of a hiding place.

John Horn held up one hand. "Quiet, everybody!

You women stay put! And cut out that yammering! You'll skeer my poor pet to death!"

The trapper located Arabella crouched in a corner of the entrance hall. He spoke to his pet softly as he approached. Then, kneeling, took the mink into his arms.

Just then the doorbell rang. Nancy opened the door to a well-dressed, middle-aged man.

"How do you do?" he said. "Is this a bad hour to call? I've rung several times."

"I'm sorry," Nancy said. "We were chasing an escaped mink and we—"

"A mink?" The stranger stared at Nancy.

She blushed and pointed to the little animal nestled against John Horn's chest. "It's a tame mink," she said.

"I see," said the newcomer, still bewildered. "I'm Mr Nelson from the Bramson Film Company, and I'd like to speak with Miss Nancy Drew."

"I'm Nancy Drew. Please come in and sit down in the living-room. I'll be with you in a few minutes."

The man walked inside and Nancy turned to the trapper. "I'd love to keep Arabella," she said, "but I think she'd be happier with you. Besides, we have a dog here. That might make trouble."

Horn nodded, tucking the mink back into his pocket. "My offer to help catch that crook is still good."

Nancy smiled. "I'll call on you."

The cousins departed with Arabella and her master, who rode away in the back seat of Bess's car. Evidently he had changed his mind about walking!

Nancy entered the living-room and sat down.

"Miss Drew," said Mr Nelson, "I understand that

you want to find Mitzi Adele. Just how close a friend of hers are you?"

"Friend?" Nancy shook her head. "Not a friend."

After she had told what she knew of the woman, Mr Nelson's voice became more cordial. "I'm glad you told me this, Miss Drew," he said. "Frankly, we thought you might have been mixed up in Mitzi's dealings. A few years ago Mitzi stole several valuable costumes from the Bramson Film Company. We've been looking for her ever since."

"Do you know where she came from?" Nancy asked.

"Her home was in northern New York State. Somewhere near the Canadian border. That's all I know about her." After a little more conversation, the caller left.

Nancy went to the kitchen to tell Hannah what she had learned. "Now I must go to Montreal," she said. "In fact, I'll leave this evening if I can get a train reservation."

Nancy secured a sleeper on the late express and sent a telegram telling her father the hour she expected to arrive. Hannah helped her pack, and went with her in a taxi to the railway station.

Next morning Nancy looked out the window eagerly as the train pulled into the Montreal station. She hurried down the steps into her father's arms.

"Nancy! I'm so glad to see you!" he cried, taking her skis.

"I'm twice as glad to see you," she replied.

"How goes the great fur mystery?" Mr Drew asked as they followed a porter to the taxi stand.

"I'm stymied, Dad," Nancy admitted.

"Well, sometimes a change of work helps. Suppose

you give me a hand. A young man, Chuck Wilson, is my client here. I'm puzzled about him and I'd like your opinion. If you can, get Chuck to tell you about his case himself."

Nancy smiled. "When do I go to work?"

"You'll meet Chuck in an hour. I told him we'd be at the ski jump of the Hotel Canadien, where I'm staying."

"I'll have to go to the hotel first and put on ski clothes," Nancy said.

The hotel, a few miles out of the city, nestled at the foot of a majestic hill. Nancy was shown to her room, where she dressed in a trim blue ski outfit. Then she and her father went out to a nearby ski slope and ski jump. As they approached the foot of the jump, a man prepared to descend it.

The skier waited for his signal. An instant later he came skimming downward, fast as a bullet, only to rise into the air, soaring like a bird, with arms outstretched. He made a perfect landing.

"Good boy!" cried Mr Drew.

"That was beautiful!" Nancy exclaimed. "I wish I could jump the way he does."

"That's my client—perhaps he'll give you some instruction," said Mr Drew. "Chuck—Chuck Wilson— come over here!"

The slender youth waved. He stomped across to them, his blonde hair gleaming in the sunlight.

After Nancy's father had completed introductions, Chuck asked, "Do you ski, Nancy?"

"Yes. But not very well."

"Perhaps I can give you some pointers," Chuck suggested eagerly. "Would you like to come and ski with me?"

"A good idea," Mr Drew agreed. "I'll leave my daughter with you and get back to work. Take good care of her!"

"I sure will!" the young man answered in a tone that made Nancy blush. They waved goodbye to Mr Drew. Then Chuck Wilson seized Nancy's hand and pulled her towards the base of the jump. "I must see this next jump, he said.

The skier made a graceful take-off. Then something went wrong. The man's legs spread-eagled on landing and one ski caught in the icy snow, throwing him for a nasty spill.

The watching crowd gasped, then was silent. A spectator, a short distance away from Nancy and Chuck, rushed towards the man. "You idiot!" he yelled. "What will happen to Mitzi if you kill yourself?"

Hearing the name Mitzi, Nancy elbowed her way quickly through the crowd. She was too late. By the time she reached the spot, the unfortunate jumper and his friend had disappeared.

"Why did you run off?" Chuck asked as he reached Nancy's side.

Nancy apologized. "I'm looking for someone. Can we go to the ski lodge? Perhaps he's there."

"Okay," Chuck said, leading the way.

The lodge was crowded with skiers but the men were not inside. Nancy asked Chuck if he knew the skier's name.

"No. But say, would his initials help?"

"Oh yes! Where did you see them?"

"On his skis—if they were his. Big letters."

Nancy's heart skipped a beat. "What were they?"

"R.I.C."

Nancy's spine tingled as if someone had put snow down her back. Could this be Mitzi Channing's husband? And the other man—was he, perhaps, Sidney Boyd?

·9·

A Disastrous Jump

CHUCK WILSON chatted cheerfully as he and Nancy went up in the chair lift to the station where they were to begin their ski lesson. But Nancy's thoughts were far away. She kept wondering about R. I. Channing and whether her hunch was correct. Was Mitzi Channing's husband really in Montreal? Was he the mystery jumper?

"Maybe I should have tried harder to find him," she chided herself.

The ski instructor noticed her faraway look. When they reached their destination, he said:

"Time for class? Suppose you take off from here. I want to watch you do parallel turns down the practice slope."

Nancy gave a quick shove with her sticks and glided away.

"Not bad. Not bad at all!" Chuck called as she completed her trial run. "You have self-confidence and a fine sense of balance. Have you ever done any wedeln?"

"Yes," Nancy admitted. "But not very well."

"We can try some steeper slopes tomorrow," her companion said, smiling. "You shouldn't have any trouble. Now take another run. Remember always to lean away from the hill. Keep your skis together all the time. You need more of what the French call—abandon."

"Abandon?"

"You know—relax." Chuck smiled. "Bend your knees, keep your weight forward. You have a natural rhythm. Use it when you wedeln. It is just half turning in rhythm all the way down the hill."

When the lesson was over, Nancy turned to her instructor. "Thanks for everything," she said. "Tomorrow I'd like to try some jumping. But now I mustn't take up any more of your time."

"My time is yours," Chuck said. "I have no more lessons scheduled for today."

Nancy was pleased. Perhaps she could get Chuck to forget skiing and talk about himself.

"I'd like to take you out to dinner tonight," he said, "and perhaps go dancing."

Nancy hesitated. The young man read her mind. "If your father would care to come—"

"Suppose I ask him," Nancy replied. She liked Chuck Wilson.

"Then it's settled," Chuck said. "I'll drive you back to the hotel now and be on hand again at six-thirty. Or is that too early?"

"Six-thirty will be fine," Nancy agreed.

Mr Drew was pleased when Nancy told him that Chuck Wilson had invited them to dinner, but he said that he would not go along.

"I'd rather have you encourage him to talk without me there," he said. "Sometimes a young man will talk more freely to a girl than to his lawyer. I feel Chuck has been holding something back. See if you can find out what it is."

Promptly at six-thirty Chuck walked into the hotel lobby and greeted the Drews. He expressed regret that Mr Drew was not joining them.

"Your daughter could become a very fine skier, Mr Drew," Chuck observed. "All she needs is practice."

"I've no doubt of it." The lawyer smiled proudly. "But I guess Nancy will always be better on ice skates than she is on skis. She was fortunate in having a very fine teacher. I sometimes thought he might encourage her to become a professional!"

"Why, Dad, you're just prejudiced," Nancy protested.

"If you like skating," Chuck spoke up, "how about going to see an exhibition that's being held here tomorrow night? I'm going to skate. If you could use two tickets—?"

Mr. Drew shook his head. "I'm afraid Nancy and I won't be here, my boy. Thank you, though. And now, I must leave you two."

Nancy wondered if her father's decision to depart from Montreal had anything to do with Chuck. Mr Drew had said nothing about their time of departure. In any case, she had better get started on her work!

It was not long before Nancy and Chuck were seated in an attractive restaurant. "Chuck," she said, "have you skated professionally very long?"

"Several years."

"Did you ever hear of a Mitzi Adele?"

"No, I never did. Is she a skater?"

Before Nancy could reply, the orchestra started a catchy dance number. Chuck grinned, rose, and escorted her on to the floor.

Nancy had never danced with a better partner. She

"Chuck thinks he's skating," Nancy said to herself

was thoroughly enjoying it when suddenly Chuck seemed to forget he was on a dance floor. The musicians had switched to a waltz and Chuck became a skater.

He gave Nancy a lead for a tremendous step backward, then lifted her from the floor as if to execute a skating lift.

"Chuck thinks he's skating," Nancy said to herself. But with a laugh he gracefully put her down again, continuing to dance. "What next?" she wondered.

Chuck swung round beside her and they glided arm in arm in skating style around the dance floor. He gave her a twirl, then the music ended. Chuck clapped loudly.

"Nancy, you're wonderful," he said.

Back at the table, she remarked that he must have been dancing all his life. Chuck looked at her searchingly for a moment, then said:

"My parents were dancers. Would you like to hear about them?"

"Oh yes."

"They were quite famous, but they were killed in a train crash when I was twelve years old. It stunned me and for a long time I wished I had died too. I had to go to live with an ill-tempered uncle. He hated dancing, and would never let me even listen to music."

"How dreadful!" Nancy murmured.

"That wasn't the worst of it," Chuck went on. He explained that only recently he had found out that his grandfather had left him an inheritance, but apparently it had been stolen from him by his uncle.

"Uncle Chad had a small ranch in the north country," Chuck went on. "He gave me a miserable time in my boyhood. My only friend was a kindly old trapper. He took me on long trips into the woods and taught me forest lore. It was from him that I learned to ski and snowshoe and to hunt and fish, too. I guess Uncle Chad became suspicious that the old man knew about the money my grandfather had left me and might cause trouble. So he scared him away.

"Later on, as soon as I was old enough, I ran off to Montreal," Chuck continued. "And now I've asked your father to be my lawyer. I want him to bring suit to recover my inheritance."

"Dad can help you if anybody can," Nancy said confidently.

"Yes, I know that. But it's such a hopeless case. I have no legal proof of my uncle's dishonesty, Nancy. My one witness has disappeared."

"You mean the old trapper?" Nancy asked.

"Yes." Chuck nodded. "And there never was a finer man than John Horn."

John Horn! The name of the old trapper! Could there be another such man besides the one in River Heights?

Nancy decided to say nothing to Chuck of the possibility that she knew the one person who could help him. After all, there was no need to arouse false hopes until she had made a definite check.

Four hours later, after an exciting evening of conversation and dancing, Chuck left Nancy at her hotel, with a promise to meet her at the ski lift the following morning. She hurried to her father's room to tell him her discoveries. The lawyer was not in, so Nancy decided to make a long-distance call to her home in River Heights. Hannah Gruen answered the telephone but there was little chance for conversation.

"I can't hear a thing you say, Nancy," the house-keeper protested. "There are two jaybirds chattering at my elbow. I'm so distracted I can hardly think."

"Oh, you mean Bess and George?" Nancy laughed. "Put them on the line please."

"Nancy, I'm so happy it's you!" cried Bess an instant later. "George and I came over here to spend the night because we thought Hannah might be lonely."

"Besides, we had a feeling you might call," George put in on the extension phone.

"Tell us what you've been doing. Tell us everything!" Bess urged eagerly.

"Well, I had a skiing lesson this afternoon. My instructor was a client of Dad's named Chuck Wilson."

"And what did you do this evening?" Bess persisted.

"Chuck and I had dinner together, and danced, and talked."

"And I suppose this Chuck Wilson is young and very good-looking?" Bess asked. Nancy could detect dis-approval in her tone.

"He is." Nancy chuckled. "But I don't see—"

"I'm thinking of Ned Nickerson," Bess reproached her. "Don't you break Ned's heart, Nancy Drew!"

"Nonsense," Nancy countered. "Now listen care-fully, Bess. I have a job for you and George. I want you to see that old trapper, John Horn. Ask him if he ever knew a boy named Chuck Wilson."

"We'll do it first thing tomorrow," Bess promised.

Nancy was up early the next morning. At breakfast she told her father Chuck's complete story, ending with the item about the old trapper.

"That's a stroke of luck for us." The lawyer nodded.

"If your man proves to be our missing witness, Chuck Wilson may really have a case. You've done a fine job, my dear. Are you seeing Chuck today?"

"I'm meeting him at the ski lift at ten."

"Well, have a good time. I'll join you at lunch. By the way, we have reservations on the five o'clock train."

"I'll be ready."

Chuck Wilson was waiting for Nancy at the ski lift. "You're going to enjoy jumping," he predicted. "It's a great thrill and it might come in handy someday if you're schussing a mountain and you suddenly come upon a sizeable hummock.

"Now there's a slope with a big mogul in the middle. Moguls," he explained, "are big lumps of snow formed by many skiers turning in a certain path on a steep slope. The more the steep area is used for turning, the bigger the lumps or moguls become. Suppose we climb up there and have a go at it."

"Just tell me what to do," Nancy urged.

"The first thing to remember is that when you hit a bump it will lift you into the air," Chuck cautioned. "Your job is to crouch down before you hit your obstacle. You spring upward and sort of synchronize your spring with the natural lift the bump gives you. Is that clear, Nancy?"

"I think so."

"Good! Then here are a few other rules," Chuck continued as they reached the crest of the little hill. "Try to pull your knees up under your chest as you jump, Nancy. And push down hard on your heels so that the points of your skis won't dig into the ground and trip you. Hold the upper part of your body erect and balance with your arms outstretched."

"That's a lot to remember," Nancy replied. "I'd feel better if there weren't so many people milling about the hill. When I come down, I want a clear track."

"Oh, you'll be okay," Chuck assured her. "All you need is practice. Well, Nancy, this is it. Don't use your sticks. I'll hold them. Get set— GO!"

In an instant Nancy was off. Flying gracefully as a bird down the long, smooth slope, she watched the snow-covered bump ahead of her loom larger— LARGER. And then, suddenly, her heart skipped a beat, and she gave a gasp of dismay.

"A snow bunny!" Nancy exclaimed.

The inexperienced skier ahead floundered directly into her path, stumbled, and fell just over the edge of the mogul. Nancy had to choose between jumping over his prostrate body or crashing into him.

She must jump!

Nancy crouched and sprang upward, jumping as far as she possibly could. She came down in a heap.

Chuck Wilson cried out as she spilled, and sped down the slope to his pupil's rescue.

"Nancy! Nancy!"

The girl lay motionless!

·10·

A Surprise Announcement

"NANCY! Are you hurt?"

She opened her eyes slowly and looked up into Chuck Wilson's worried face. He was kneeling beside her and chafing her wrists.

"W-what happened?" she asked in a faint voice.

"You spilled," Chuck explained. "You made a clean jump over that skier and then you pitched on your face. But it wasn't your fault."

"Not my fault? You mean that man—"

"He got in your way, all right," Chuck answered. "But it was a loose binding on one of your skis that caused your fall." The instructor showed it to her.

Nancy sat up. "I want to try again," she said.

"Do you think you should?" Chuck asked.

"Of course I should!" Chuck helped Nancy rise to her feet. "See?" She smiled. "No bones broken. Nothing injured except my dignity!"

For the next hour, Chuck helped Nancy with her jumps. "You're learning fast!" he declared. "I wish you didn't have to return to the States so soon. Can't you persuade your father to stay, at least until after the ice show tonight?"

"Maybe I can," Nancy said. "I have an idea!"

"Please try!" Chuck beamed. "Here are some tickets

to the ice show. I'll expect to see you and your father there tonight."

"I can't promise," Nancy reminded him. "But thanks! So long for now, Chuck. I'd better go back to the hotel and meet Dad."

Nancy and her father had a late lunch in the hotel dining-room. The lawyer looked amused when his daughter told him she wanted to stay longer in Montreal. "For the winter sports or for young Wilson?" he teased.

Nancy made a face, then grew earnest. "I'm thinking mainly of the Channings," she said. "They may be selling more of that fake stock right in this area!" She told about the expert ski jumper and her suspicion that he was R. I. Channing.

"Mrs Channing may be here too," the lawyer mused. "Yes, I think we ought to stay until you can investigate. Will you still have time for that skating exhibition tonight?"

"Of course!" Nancy said. "That's part of my plan. Have you forgotten that Mrs Channing is a professional skater—or used to be one?"

Mr Drew smiled. "You think this woman may attend the show, or even take part in it?"

"Exactly. And if she does show up. I think I have enough evidence to have her arrested. Even if she's not there, I may be able to get some information about her from the skaters."

The head waiter suddenly appeared. "Pardon me, but are you Miss Nancy Drew?" he inquired. When she nodded, the waiter said, "There's a long-distance call for you in the lobby."

Nancy excused herself and hurried to the telephone.

The caller was George Fayne, who told her excitedly, "Bess and I just spoke with John Horn. He remembers Chuck Wilson!"

"George, that's marvellous!"

"And he says that if he can do anything to help Chuck, he's willing to go to Canada!"

"That's just what I'd hoped for!" said Nancy. "I'll be home soon and tell you all the news."

"Another mystery?" George asked.

Nancy laughed. "This one is Dad's. I'm just helping!"

She returned to the table and told her father of John Horn's offer.

"Now, that's progress!" the lawyer declared. "I'll tell Chuck as soon as possible. Meanwhile, Nancy, why don't you do some sightseeing in Montreal this afternoon?"

"A fine idea!" Nancy agreed. "I can combine sightseeing with a visit to fur shops and hotels."

Nancy walked around the picturesque city all afternoon, but did not find a clue to the Channings at the fur shops she visited. By the time she returned to the hotel it was early evening, and heavy snow had begun to fall.

"It's a good thing the ice show wasn't planned for outdoors," Mr Drew remarked as he and Nancy waited for a taxi.

When they were seated in the big arena, Nancy studied her programme and saw that Chuck would skate first. Neither Mitzi Adele nor Mitzi Channing was listed. "Perhaps she's among the spectators," Nancy thought. She borrowed binoculars from the man seated next to her and carefully scrutinized the audience.

Nancy concluded that Mrs Channing was not present. "I'm afraid my guess was wrong, Dad," she sighed.

"Mrs Channing might be using another name, or be wearing a disguise," Mr Drew suggested.

"If she does appear," Nancy mused, "I'd like to know how to reach the police in a hurry."

"Just go to one of those little black boxes along the wall," her father said. "They connect with a police booth in the balcony."

"Dad, how did you figure that out?" Nancy asked admiringly.

"I didn't," the lawyer said with a chuckle. "I called the police station this afternoon and asked what kind of protection they'd have here."

Suddenly the loudspeaker blared, "*Attention!* We have a late entry in the Pair Skating. Miss Nancy Drew and her partner from the United States."

Nancy's father turned to her in astonishment. "Why didn't you tell me you were going to skate?"

"Because I'm not," Nancy declared. "Mrs Channing must be using my name again!"

Nancy left her seat, her face flushed with anger. She followed signs that pointed the way to the skaters' dressing rooms. But as she neared the area, a uniformed attendant blocked her path. "Sorry, ma'am, nobody's permitted back there except skaters."

"But I'm Nancy Drew!" she protested, showing the man her driver's licence.

The attendant glanced at it, then stepped aside as he declared, "I thought Miss Drew came in before. Well, you dressing room is straight ahead. Your name is on the door."

Nancy found the corridor crowded with skaters in

colourful costumes. Mrs Channing was not among them. Suddenly an eager voice exclaimed, "Nancy! Are you looking for me?"

Nancy turned to see Chuck, who wore a black and red pirate's suit. "No, Chuck. It would take some time to explain why I'm here."

"So you entered the exhibition!" Chuck said. "I wish you'd told me!"

"It's a mistake," Nancy said, moving on hurriedly. "I'll explain later, Chuck."

She edged past the dressing rooms until she came to one with her name on it. She knocked on the door. There was no response. Nancy took a deep breath and opened the door.

The dressing room was empty!

Nancy was crestfallen. She had missed Mrs Channing again! A quick survey of the room convinced her that the woman had been there recently. The scent of her heavy perfume was thick in the air.

Had Mrs Channing been frightened away? Who had warned her? Had she seen Nancy come into the arena?

Nancy left the dressing room and made her way back through the crowded corridor. She questioned the skaters she met, but none recalled having seen the woman she described.

Chuck Wilson greeted her again. "I have a solo part in the first number," he told her. "I'd like you to see it. You'll still have time to get into your costume."

"Chuck, I'm not going to skate—really!" Nancy said. "I'm not the girl who signed up for the Pair Skating!"

"What?"

"Tell me, did you speak about me to anyone here

after that announcement on the loudspeaker?"

Chuck grinned. "Maybe I did mention to some of the performers that I know you," he admitted. "I said you were with your father in the arena."

"When you said that, were you standing anywhere near the dressing room with my name on it?"

"Well, I guess I was," Chuck replied. "Now, won't you tell me what all the mystery is about?"

"Not yet—not in this crowd," she said. "Too much has been overheard already!"

"*Is Miss Drew here?—Miss Nancy Drew?*"

A short, plump man with a waxed moustache came down the corridor, looking about him as he asked the question.

"That's Mr Dubois, the manager of the show," Chuck told Nancy.

"I can give you information about Nancy Drew," the young detective told the man.

Mr Dubois motioned to Nancy and Chuck to follow him to an unoccupied dressing room. "Tell me where this young woman is," he urged. "She must perform in thirty minutes."

"I'm sure she has left," Nancy said. "The woman who entered the exhibition isn't Nancy Drew at all. That's my name. This other woman is Mitzi Channing, and she's wanted by the police."

The manager threw up his hands. "The police! Are you saying that I've been sponsoring a criminal?"

"I know you've done nothing wrong," Nancy said quickly. "But surely you want to help catch a thief. Please tell me what you know about this skater. What does she look like?"

The description Mr Dubois gave identified the

woman as Mitzi Channing. She and a man named
Smith had come that afternoon to try out for the show.
Mr Dubois described the man, but Nancy did not
recognize him.

"They were excellent skaters," the manager said,
"and I gave them permission to enter the Pair Skating.
The woman wouldn't allow her partner's name to be
announced."

Nancy thanked Mr Dubois. Just then a bell sounded.
The manager and Chuck hurried off, and Nancy went
to a telephone to tell the police of her suspicions.

In the auditorium, Mr Drew was becoming increas-
ingly anxious about Nancy. Once he considered going
to search for her. "No," he told himself, "she works fast
when she has a lead, and I trust her to act intelligently."

The lawyer assumed that the late entry in the Pair
Skating would be scratched. He was surprised when
the announcer declared that the next skater would be
Miss Nancy Drew and that her partner would be
Charles Wilson.

Mr Drew watched his client, wearing close-fitting
black slacks and an open-necked white satin shirt, glide
gracefully on to the ice. Then the young man was
joined by a red-haired girl in a white satin ballet
costume.

The lawyer gasped. "*Nancy!*"

The two skaters danced in unison, then spun off to
skate individually. While Nancy executed some simple
steps, her partner jumped and whirled in intricate
patterns.

Nancy had conceived the plan while Chuck was
skating his first number. When he had returned to the
dressing room, Nancy had asked him, "Do you think I

danced well enough with you last night to try it on skates?"

"Why, sure! You're cool."

"I can't tell you the whole story now," Nancy had said, "but I'd like to take the place of that woman who called herself Nancy Drew."

The young sleuth thought, "Some of Mrs Channing's friends might be in the arena, unaware that the woman has left. When I come on instead, one of them may be so startled that he'll reveal himself. I'll ask the police to hold anyone who tries to leave the building during or immediately after the number."

Turning to Chuck, she had said, "Will you skate with me if Mr Dubois will let me and if I can borrow a costume and skates?"

"You bet I will!"

"I'm no expert," Nancy warned. "So don't try anything tricky. I'll leave the fancy steps to you, and while you're in the spotlight, I'll have a chance to do some detective work."

"To do what? Well, all right!"

Mr Dubois had agreed to the plan and a girl Nancy's size had offered to lend the young sleuth skates and a costume.

Nancy's heart had pounded with fright when the loudspeaker had announced their number. But with Chuck's confident voice encouraging her, she soon lost her nervousness.

At the end of the number, the young man grasped Nancy's wrists, swept her from her feet and spun round and round with her until the music blared the last note. Nancy was dizzy as applause rang in her ears.

As her vision cleared, she noticed that a tall, heavy-set man had risen from his seat and was moving quickly towards an exit. Was he R. I. Channing?

Nancy turned to her partner. "Come on, Chuck," she urged. "Let's get off the ice quickly. I think the mystery is about to be solved!"

·11·

The Password

"WELL, here he is, Miss Drew!"

A big policeman thrust his prisoner through the open door of Nancy's dressing room.

"We've been watching for this fellow ever since you warned us that he might try to make a getaway," the officer went on. "He denies everything."

"Of course I deny it," the prisoner snarled, twisting away from his captor's grasp and glaring at Nancy. "My name is Jacques Fremont. I'm a respectable citizen of Canada, and I've never heard of R. I. Channing!"

The man was bluffing, Nancy felt sure. The tall, muscular body, the touch of grey at his temples—both tallied with the description of Mitzi's husband that Dr Britt's nurse had given.

"I suppose you have never heard of Mitzi Adele, either?" Nancy asked.

For an instant the man looked startled. Then his eyes met Nancy's in a glare of hate. "No, I've never heard of her either," he sneered. "See here, Officer, this is outrageous. I have an identification. Here's my driver's licence. It'll show that I'm Jacques Fremont."

The policeman looked at the licence in the man's wallet, then nodded. "Everything seems to be in order," he admitted. "I'm afraid that if you have no more proof than this, Miss Drew, we'll have to let the man go."

Nancy was taken aback. She was sure of her accusation. But there was nothing she could do but thank the officer for his trouble and watch as the man who called himself Jacques Fremont slammed angrily out the door.

"If only I weren't in costume and could follow him!" Nancy sighed, then looked up in relief to see her father standing on the threshold.

"Congratulations, daughter!" Mr Drew called. "I was never so surprised as when—"

Nancy did not let him finish. "Dad! Quick! That tall man you just passed—the one in the brown overcoat. Follow him!" she implored.

"But, Nancy—"

"I'm sure he's R. I. Channing. I asked the police to stop him," Nancy went on rapidly, "but Channing insisted his name is Jacques Fremont and they let him go. Oh, Dad, trail him, please!"

"All right, Nancy," the lawyer agreed, dashing off.

Nancy had just put on her street clothes when Chuck Wilson knocked on her door. "I thought perhaps you'd like to go out somewhere for a late supper, Nancy," he suggested. "After all that exercise, I'm hungry as a bear."

"I'd like to," Nancy replied. "But I must go to the hotel and see Dad as soon as he gets back. I'll tell you what. Suppose you drive me there and we'll have a bite in the coffee bar."

Once they were in the car, Chuck Wilson glanced curiously at Nancy. "I suppose I shouldn't ask why you were expecting the police?" he began. "You've shown me there are a number of things you don't care to divulge."

"I can tell you now," Nancy replied. "I'm trying to catch a woman who stole my driver's licence and goes around using my name. This evening I tried to have the police arrest her husband. But the man was too clever and they had to release him. Dad went to trail him, though."

"And you can't wait to get the report." Chuck grinned. "I don't blame you. To be honest, I was afraid your secrecy might have had something to do with my case. When the policeman went to your dressing room—"

"Oh, I'm sorry, Chuck. Didn't Dad get in touch with you this afternoon?"

"No. I wasn't at home. Can you tell me what he wanted?"

"I suppose I can. It's good news. Your old friend John Horn has been found," Nancy announced.

"What! Oh boy! That's great!" Chuck shouted, and yanked the steering wheel hard. In his excitement he had let the car head for a snow drift, and barely got out of the way.

When they reached the hotel, Nancy left word at the desk for Mr Drew to meet her and Chuck in the coffee bar. Half an hour later he came in and dropped wearily into a chair beside them.

"Mr Drew," Chuck spoke up, "Nancy says you've located John Horn."

The lawyer smiled. "Nancy did," he answered. "Actually, my daughter has done more on your case than I have," he confessed. "But as soon as we get back to River Heights, I'll see this man Horn and have a talk with him about your uncle."

"And what did you learn on my case, Dad?" Nancy asked. "Did you find Mr Channing?"

"I did and I didn't, if that makes any sense," her father replied. "Chuck, will you order me a hamburger and coffee while I start the story? That rascal Channing moves fast, Nancy. I spotted him soon after I left you, and almost caught up with him."

Nancy's face fell. "But you missed him?"

"Yes," her father admitted. "The man hopped into a taxi. But I did manage to get the car's licence number and later located the driver. He told me that Channing —or Fremont as he calls himself—went to the New Lasser Hotel."

"Oh, Dad, that's wonderful!" Nancy cried triumphantly. "All we need do is watch the hotel and wait for all the thieves to show up there."

"It isn't that simple," her father replied. "I talked to the manager of the New Lasser. He's a fraternity brother of mine and very friendly. He said that a Jacques Fremont, a Miss Nancy Drew, and Miss Drew's brother occupied a suite of several rooms on the second floor. Unfortunately for us, Miss Drew's brother checked out for the trio an hour before I arrived."

"Oh dear!" Nancy groaned. "Now we must start hunting for them all over again. Did you get any clues about where they went, Dad?"

Mr Drew took a bite of his hamburger sandwich, chewed it slowly, and swallowed before answering. Nancy knew from the twinkle in his eyes, though, that he had something important to reveal. Finally he spoke.

"It seems that Mitzi was expecting an important long-distance call at ten tomorrow morning. When she found she must leave town in such a hurry, Mitzi wrote out a message and entrusted it to the clerk. The message read:

" '*Foxes after stock. Transferring to camp.*' "

"What does that mean?" Chuck asked, puzzled.

The lawyer and his daughter shrugged, but Mr Drew prophesied that Nancy would soon learn the answer. Then he changed the subject.

"The performance you two put on this evening was most commendable," he said. "Nancy, I knew you were good on skates, but I didn't know you were that good."

Nancy smiled at Chuck. "I didn't know it, either!" she said.

The gay little party broke up soon afterwards. Mr Drew confessed to being very sleepy, but Nancy remained wide awake for hours. She kept thinking of the message Mitzi Channing had left with the hotel clerk, wondering about its true meaning.

At breakfast she joined her father in the coffee bar with a brisk air that indicated she had come to a decision. With laughter in her eyes, she said:

"Good morning, Dad, you old fox!"

"Fox?" Mr Drew raised his eyebrows in surprise.

"I was thinking of Mitzi," his daughter explained. "I believe when she wrote that message '*Foxes after stock*,' she meant us, Dad. You and I are the wily foxes."

"That might be," the lawyer admitted.

Nancy confided a daring plan she had conceived before going to sleep.

"Well, good luck," he said when she finished. "But be careful!"

Shortly before ten o'clock Nancy entered the lobby of the New Lasser Hotel, and strolled over to the telephone switchboard operator.

"My name is Drew. Miss Nancy Drew," she explained, displaying her duplicate driver's licence. "I'm expecting a long-distance call at ten o'clock—"

"But I was told Miss Drew had checked out," protested the operator. "In fact, the clerk gave me a message to deliver when the call comes in."

"I know," said Nancy. "I intended to leave town but decided to stay. I'll just sit here and you can let me know when the call comes through. That is, if it's not too much trouble."

"No trouble at all," said the operator. "Wait, Miss Drew. I think your party's on the line now. Take the end booth, please."

Nancy's heart was pounding as she hurried towards the telephone. So much depended on whether the person on the other end of the line was convinced that she was Mitzi Channing. Cautiously she lifted the receiver and said:

"Hello!"

"Hello," snapped back a man's brisk voice. And then it added a second word—"Lake."

For an instant there was silence. Nancy thought frantically. "Lake?" That must be a password between the swindlers, she told herself. Suddenly a possible answer snapped into her mind. She set her jaw and tried to make her voice sound coarse.

"Dunstan," she replied.

· 12 ·

Slippery Sidney

THE word "Dunstan" seemed to satisfy the man at the other end of the wire. He identified himself as Sidney.

"Listen, Mitzi!" he said. "I've got a deal cooking here for a thousand dollars' worth of stock. Old Mrs Bellhouse will buy it, but I've got to work fast."

"Swell," Nancy murmured in a low voice.

"Sure, it's swell," Sidney agreed. "But the trouble is, I'm nearly out of certificates. You'll have to get more printed and rush 'em to me!"

"You mean to River Heights?"

"Speak a little louder!" Sidney ordered.

"I said, where do you want the stock sent?"

"Why, to the Winchester Post Office, of course. General Delivery," the man snapped. "As soon as I make this sale, I'll beat it to Dunstan."

The receiver clicked as the man abruptly ended the conversation. Nancy hurried back to the Hotel Canadien, where she found her father waiting in the lobby.

"I'm glad you're here," he said. "I've been called home on urgent business. I've already notified Chuck that we'll be leaving on the next plane."

Nancy had no chance to tell about the man on the telephone until she and her father were seated in the plane.

"I'm sure I was talking to Sidney Boyd," she declared. "The one who sold stock and earrings to that actress in New York. And then stole the earrings from her!"

"Obviously you're right," the lawyer agreed. "But in order to trap this man, you'll have to supply him with new stock certificates."

"I know. Dad, would it be possible to make copies from Hannah's certificate?"

Mr Drew looked thoughtful. "I know a printer who would do a rush job for us. However, I must warn you that it's illegal to print fake stock even for a worthy purpose. I'll contact the authorities and get permission."

As soon as the plane landed at River Heights, Mr Drew went to his office. Meanwhile, Nancy searched several telephone directories for a listing of Mrs Bellhouse. There was none, so she went to the public library and thumbed through the city directories. Apparently no one by the name of Sidney Boyd's intended victim lived in Winchester or in any of the nearby towns.

At dinner Mr Drew reported that he had received permission to have Hannah's stock certificate copied. The printer would have the papers ready by noon the next day, and Mr Drew would rush them to Montreal where a colleague would remail them to Winchester.

"That's great," Nancy said. "But something worries me, Dad. I can't find Mrs Bellhouse's address anywhere."

"Never mind!" the lawyer reassured her. "As soon as those stocks are mailed, we'll notify the Winchester police. They can watch the General Delivery window at the post office and shadow Sidney Boyd after he picks up the package."

Nancy shook her head. "Mr Boyd may call for the package under another name. Perhaps Mitzi always sends the stocks that way."

"Well, ours will be addressed to Sidney Boyd, since that's the only name we know. Of course, the fellow may send someone else to the post office to get the parcel, and he may collect the money from Mrs Bellhouse before he goes to the post office. We'll have to remember that we're taking a gamble."

Nancy nodded. "But the odds would be with us if we could find Mrs Bellhouse and catch that man in the act of selling her his fake stock."

Hannah Gruen spoke up. "If this Mrs Bellhouse is elderly, she probably sees a doctor from time to time. Why not ask Dr Britt about medical people in the area who might know her?"

"A wonderful idea!" Nancy exclaimed, hurrying to the telephone. At her request, Dr Britt agreed to do this.

The next morning Bess and George arrived at the Drew home, eager to trade news with Nancy. George reported that John Horn had gone ice fishing, but would speak with the Drews as soon as he returned.

"He says Chuck Wilson's a right handsome fellow," she added.

Bess sighed. "Nancy has all the luck!"

"Well, wish that my luck holds out," Nancy said, smiling, "at least until Dr Britt contacts me." At that moment the telephone rang.

The caller was Miss Compton, Dr Britt's office nurse. She told Nancy, "Dr Green recently placed a woman named Mrs Bellhouse in the Restview Nursing Home, at the edge of Winchester. Visiting hours are between two and three-thirty."

Nancy thanked the woman and hung up. After telling the cousins what she had learned, she said, "Let's have a talk with Mrs Bellhouse."

The girls started off immediately. Just before two o'clock they reached the rambling white nursing home. A uniformed nurse greeted them and Nancy explained their mission.

"Can you come back tomorrow?" the woman asked. "Mrs Bellhouse has been ill and she's sleeping now. She shouldn't have callers today."

As the girls returned to the car, Nancy proposed that they stay near the nursing home to see if Sidney Boyd showed up. They waited an hour but the suspect did not appear.

The next day Nancy learned from the detective on duty at the Winchester Post Office that Sidney Boyd had not been there. "It's probably too soon," she thought.

At two o'clock Nancy and her friends were again at the nursing home. The nurse they had spoken to the previous afternoon led the girls to a sunny front room on the second floor.

Mrs Bellhouse was a fragile old lady with silver hair and faded blue eyes. She smiled as Nancy approached her bed. "Who are you?" she asked.

"I'm Nancy Drew, Mrs Bellhouse, and these are my friends, George Fayne and Bess Marvin."

"So young," murmured the old lady. "Did my relative Sidney Boyd send you? Sidney's the husband of my dear cousin Elsie."

"Are you expecting him today?" Nancy asked.

"This very afternoon!" Mrs Bellhouse said. She motioned for Nancy to bend nearer. "I have something for Sidney, but I don't want that starchy old nurse to know," she said with a chuckle. "See?"

The old lady pulled out a drawer of her night table. Under some tissues lay a pile of currency.

"It's a thousand dollars!" the woman confided.

Nancy pretended surprise. "That's a most generous gift," she remarked.

"No such thing," Mrs Bellhouse answered. "Sidney's selling me stock in a wonderful fur company. The dividends will end my financial worries."

George had posted herself near a front window. When a car parked and a man got out, George gave Nancy a signal and the three girls said a hasty goodbye to Mrs Bellhouse.

In the hall Nancy said quickly, "George, you go downstairs and call the police. Bess and I will hide in the room that connects with the one Mrs Bellhouse is in. It's empty."

The girls retreated just as a man with a pencil-thin moustache strode upstairs and into the woman's room.

"Cousin Clara!" he exclaimed.

Nancy and Bess, watching through a crack in the connecting room, saw Sidney Boyd clasp Mrs Bellhouse's hand. "You look well today. Charming! I wish I were free to spend the afternoon with you. However, I've brought you the stock certificate."

"Sidney, I've been thinking of dear Elsie," Mrs Bellhouse quavered. "She never let me know when she married you."

"I'm sure she did. You've probably forgotten," he said quickly. "Now, before that crabby old nurse comes back—do you have the money?"

"It's right here," said Mrs Bellhouse.

"Fine, Cousin Clara. Here's the stock." He handed her an envelope. "And I'll take the money. Wasn't that easy?"

Nancy and Bess watched indignantly. Then they heard footsteps behind them. It was George, who tiptoed forward and whispered, "Police on the way!"

As Boyd started to leave his victim, he cocked his head and listened. An automobile had just stopped in front of the house. The man looked out a window, then ran from the room.

Nancy followed him as he bolted down the back stairway. "Come on, girls!" she urged.

The steps were narrow and unlighted. Halfway down, they turned sharply. Here Bess tripped and fell against Nancy, who was just ahead of her.

"Oh," Nancy murmured, grasping for the rail and managing to regain her balance.

George quickly helped Bess to her feet but the delay had given Sidney Boyd a head start. When the girls reached the rear porch of the nursing home, their quarry was nowhere in sight.

"I'm so sorry," Bess said tearfully.

"Never mind," George said, "but you sure were clumsy," she chided.

"Let's separate and look for him," Nancy suggested. George dashed around the east side of the house, while Bess raced towards the rear of the grounds.

Nancy made a beeline for the grove of birches at the west side of the nursing home. She spotted Sidney Boyd crouched behind a clump of saplings.

The man saw her coming. He jumped up and sprinted towards the road. Nancy, still running, cried out loudly, "Help! Help!"

Hearing Nancy's cry, George flagged down the two approaching policemen. "Hurry!" she urged, jumping into their police car. "The thief is down the road, and my friend is chasing him!"

Boyd now crossed the road and started into a field. The officers left their car and sprinted after the swindler. Within seconds the man was a prisoner.

"What's the meaning of this outrage?" he spluttered.

"You'll know fast enough," one of the policemen told him as they walked towards the road where Nancy and George were waiting. "Suppose you listen to this young lady."

"Who's she?" Boyd snapped.

"I'm Nancy Drew," the young sleuth spoke up.

"I've never heard of you," the man said, sneering.

The policemen, the prisoner, Nancy, and George rode back to the nursing home. Bess was waiting at the entrance.

"Nancy, I've been talking with the nurse," she said. "We'd better not tell Mrs Bellhouse about this—the police can give her her money back somehow. If she knew the stock is worthless she might have another attack."

"What do you mean—worthless?" Boyd demanded.

"You know there's no Forest Fur Company," George said, "and Dunstan Lake, Vermont, isn't on the map."

Boyd smiled slyly. "If there's anything phoney about the Forest Fur Company, that's not my fault. I'm merely a broker, and I find this news quite shocking."

"There's a warrant out for your arrest," said one of the policemen. "Let's go!"

The other officer turned to Nancy and said, "I'd like you to follow us."

At the Winchester police station, the captain praised Nancy for her fine detective work. "Miss Drew," he said, taking a piece of paper from his desk, "I think you'll be interested in this. The arresting officers recovered it from Boyd's pocket, along with the thousand dollars he took from the woman in the rest home. It's part of the reason that fellow's behind bars now."

The letter, postmarked New York, read:

Dear Sid,
Tell the boss to come across with some pay or there won't be any more stock printed.

Ben

"That's clear evidence," Nancy said. Returning the paper, she added, "I haven't heard of Ben."

The captain smiled. "We know now that the fur stock is printed in New York and that Boyd is definitely one of the gang. I'll have the New York police trace Ben."

"I'll appreciate it if you'll let me know what comes of this," Nancy said, and wished the captain goodbye. She returned to her car, where Bess and George were waiting.

"At last!" George exclaimed. "You were in there so long we thought we might have to bail you out!"

As Nancy drove towards River Heights, she told her friends what had happened.

"It seems to me this case is pretty well cracked," said George. "Don't you think you need a holiday, Nancy?"

Nancy's eyes twinkled. "Good idea," she said. "How would you like to go to Aunt Eloise's lodge in the Adirondacks? She has a holiday coming up. Maybe she'd come with us—"

"Why, we'd freeze up there!" Bess exclaimed.

"It's between terms at Emerson," Nancy pointed out, ignoring the protest. "We could invite the boys."

The girls began making enthusiastic plans. Suddenly Bess exclaimed, "I'll bet there's something behind this idea of yours. Does it have to do with the fur mystery?"

"Could be," Nancy admitted. "Remember, Aunt Eloise first heard of Dunstan Lake when she was at her summer home. It's possible the gang has headquarters in that vicinity."

"And you want to add detectives Ned Nickerson, Dave Evans, and Burt Eddleton to your investigation squad." George declared.

"Exactly," Nancy admitted. "Suppose you come to my house while I phone Aunt Eloise. I hope we can start day after tomorrow."

Bess looked worried. "What if the boys can't go? It wouldn't be safe up there without some men. The Adirondacks are full of bears."

"Who sleep all winter!" George hooted.

Nancy laughed. "There probably won't be anything more dangerous than a few minks."

"But the stock swindlers—" Bess began.

"No need to worry yet," Nancy advised. "First, I must ask Aunt Eloise if she can go."

·13·

The House Party

NANCY telephoned at once to her aunt. Eloise Drew readily agreed to act as hostess for a house party. "I never dreamed that my clue about Dunstan Lake would bring such an interesting holiday!" she said.

"My hunch may be wrong," Nancy warned. "But we'll have fun, anyway."

"Suppose you pick me up at the station in York Village near camp," her aunt suggested. "I'll arrive there at three-thirty."

Bess and George hung over Nancy's shoulder as she said goodbye, and then made a call to Emerson College. The three boys were enthusiastic about a trip to the Adirondacks. Burt said they could take his family's station wagon.

"Wonderful," said Nancy. "But we'd better have two cars, so I'll take mine, too."

The boys said they could stay only a few days, however, since they had only a short holiday between terms.

This news made Bess pout. When the long-distance conversation was over, she complained, "That's not much time to solve a mystery and have some fun, too!"

Everybody was excited about the excursion to the Adirondacks except Hannah Gruen. The housekeeper worried about possible accidents on the icy roads and a blizzard that might keep them snowbound. "And then you don't know the ways of the woods in the wintertime."

"Hannah," Nancy said, "would you feel happier if someone like John Horn was around to guide us?"

"I certainly would," Hannah answered. "And I'm sure your father would too."

That evening Nancy and Mr Drew went over to call on John Horn, who had just returned from his ice-fishing trip.

To Nancy's delight, the trapper verified Chuck Wilson's story about his ill-tempered uncle. He told of several incidents which had made him suspicious that the elder Wilson was helping himself to certain funds and not making an accounting of them to the Probate Court.

"But I never could prove it," the trapper said.

"You've been very helpful," the lawyer told him. "And I may call on you to be a witness."

Before the Drews left, Nancy made her request about the trip. The elderly man's eyes glistened.

"You couldn't 'a' asked me anything I'd ruther do," he beamed. "But I won't ride in any of them motor contraptions. No sir-ree. The train for me. And I'll mush in from the station at York. I was brought up on snowshoes."

"Your going relieves my mind," Mr Drew said, and added with a laugh, "Keep my daughter from making any ski jumps after those thieves, will you?"

John Horn chuckled. "Don't you worry. I'll pick up their tracks in the snow and call the police while your daughter's off gallivantin' with the young folks."

Two mornings later the young people began their trip. With skis, sticks, snowshoes, and suitcases in their cars, the girls dressed in colourful ski clothes and the boys in anoraks and fur caps, their group resembled a polar expedition.

"Too bad that old trapper wouldn't let us give him a lift," said Ned as he joined Nancy in the convertible.

"Oh, John Horn's like that. A mind of his own and very independent." Nancy laughed. "When I asked him to help find those swindlers, the old fellow became really excited. Patted his hunting rifle and announced that he intended to snare the varmints!"

For the next three hours everything went well for the travellers. The station wagon followed close behind the convertible. Then, as they reached the foothills of the Adirondacks and began to climb, the roads became icy and the drivers were obliged to decrease their speed to a bare crawl.

Nancy frowned. "I'm worried about Aunt Eloise," she confessed to Ned. "Her train reaches York Village at three-thirty and she's expecting us to pick her up."

"York? That's where we buy the supplies for camp, isn't it?" Ned asked.

"Yes, I'd hoped to get there in time for us to shop before Aunt Eloise arrives."

At that moment a series of loud hoots behind them caused Nancy to slow down and look round. "Oh dear! Burt's car has skidded into a ditch!" She groaned. "We'll have to pull it out."

It took half an hour and considerable huffing and puffing on everybody's part to haul the station wagon back on to the road. When it was once more on its way, Burt realized that the steering gear needed attention.

"Burt's car has skidded into a ditch!" Nancy cried out

He signalled to Nancy and drove forward to tell her they must stop at the first town and have it adjusted.

Nancy nodded. "Suppose Ned and I go ahead and leave the food order at the general store. You pick it up. We'll drive Aunt Eloise to camp and start a fire."

Soon the convertible was again on its way. At the store Nancy ordered ham, eggs, bacon, sausages, meat, huge roasting potatoes, bread, fresh fruit, and other necessities.

"Friends of mine will call for the order in a station wagon," Nancy explained to the proprietor.

"Come on. We'd better hurry," Ned warned. "I can hear the train pulling in."

He and Nancy dashed to the station, half expecting to see John Horn alight as well as Eloise Drew. But the trapper was not aboard.

"Hello, Ned!" Miss Drew greeted him, after she embraced her niece. "And where are the rest of my guests?" she inquired.

"They were delayed," said Nancy. "A little trouble with Burt's station wagon. We're to go on ahead."

"I'm glad we're starting at once," Miss Drew observed. "In an hour it will be dark. And that narrow, snowy road leading to my place can be very hazardous."

Nancy and Ned helped Aunt Eloise into the convertible and they began the long climb to the lodge. The road was indeed deep in snow and Ned had to drive very slowly. All were relieved to see the house.

"Look at that snow!" Aunt Eloise exclaimed. "Why, it's halfway up the door."

"Are there any shovels in the garage?" Ned asked as he climbed out of the car.

"I think so," Miss Drew answered.

Ned struggled round the corner of the house to the garage. He came back swinging a shovel and started clearing a path. Soon the station wagon arrived.

"Reinforcements are here," Dave and Burt announced.

In a few minutes they were carrying in the suitcases. The girls and Aunt Eloise followed, shivering in the huge, icy living-room.

"We can soon have some heat," Aunt Eloise said, taking swift charge of the situation. "Boys, there's plenty of wood in the shed outside. Suppose you start a roaring fire in the grate."

"Girls," said Nancy, "let's bring in those groceries from the station wagon."

"Groceries?" Bess gaped.

Nancy's heart sank. "Bess! George!" she gasped. "Didn't you remember to stop for the food? Didn't Burt tell you?"

The blank consternation on her friends' faces was answer enough.

Tired and hungry, the campers had to face it. *There was no food in the house!*

·14·

The Fur Thief

"CHEER UP!" Aunt Eloise encouraged her guests. "The situation isn't too black. I left a few cans in the pantry here. If you don't object to beans—"

"Beans! Oh, welcome word!" cried Bess, rolling her eyes ecstatically. "I'm ravenous enough to eat tacks."

"Then you'll have to earn your supper," George said firmly. "Get a mop. This place must be cleaned before we eat."

In the midst of their tidying the lodge a knock came on the door. John Horn walked in. The old fellow looked ruddy and fit after his trek on snowshoes. He explained that he had come up the day before and was camping out in the hills Indian style. When they told him of their predicament about food, he looked amused.

"Shucks, nobody here need go hungry." He chuckled. "I shot some rabbits on the way. I'll bring 'em in and give you folks a real treat!"

After consuming the nourishing beans and John Horn's delicious rabbit, cooked on a spit in the fireplace, everyone felt satisfied and content. Then, gathering around him, Aunt Eloise and her guests listened for two hours to the old trapper's yarns. Later, when Nancy asked him if he had found out anything about Dunstan Lake, he shook his head.

"Nope. Nobody I met ever heard of the man, Nancy.

Nor of that Forest Fur Company, either. But they say there's three mink ranches around here owned by outside folks."

Suddenly Eloise Drew snapped her fingers. "I just recalled that I heard the name Dunstan Lake twice. The second time was last summer at the Longview Inn five miles from here. I was leaving the dining-room when I overheard a woman mention the name."

"Maybe it's another clue," Nancy spoke up. "I think I'll go over there right after breakfast tomorrow and speak to the manager. I'd like to hike over. Could I make it on snowshoes, Mr Horn?"

"Oh, sure—that is, if you got good muscles, and you look as if you do. Well, folks," the trapper said, rising, "I'll be on my way."

He would not accept a bunk with the boys and went off whistling in the darkness. The house party guests rolled wearily into bed and slept soundly.

Next morning the prospect of a second meal of beans for breakfast had little appeal for the campers. At Nancy's suggestion the young people tramped down to the frozen lake, resolved to try some ice fishing.

The boys hacked a hole in the ice fifty feet from shore and carefully lowered several lines with baited hooks. But although they waited patiently, there was not a bite.

"I guess we'll eat beans—and like it," George groaned.

"Hal-loo there! What you doin'? Lookin' for a walrus?" called a voice from the shore.

They turned to see John Horn standing there with a heavy pack on his back. The old trapper explained that he had risen before daylight and gone down to York Village.

"I brought your grub." He grinned. "Wanta eat?"

"Do we!" cried Burt, dropping the line he was holding. "I'll swap an uncaught fish for a stack of hotdogs any day!"

The others echoed his sentiments as they rushed to join the trapper and relieve him of the food.

Directly after breakfast Nancy and Ned fastened snowshoes to their hiking boots and set out for Longview Inn. The snow was crisp and just hard enough for firm going. Shortly before noon they arrived at the entrance to the big resort hotel.

"What a grand spot for winter sports!" Nancy exclaimed. She gazed admiringly at the high ski jump and the numerous ski trails and toboggan slides.

"Sure is." Ned nodded. "I wish we had time to try 'em. But I suppose you want to find out about Dunstan Lake. Well, where do we begin our investigations?"

"Pardon me. But would you two be interested in purchasing tickets to our charity contest? a strange voice inquired.

The couple looked round to face a smiling elderly woman. She went on to explain that the tickets were for a skiing party the next afternoon, to be followed by a trapper's dinner at the inn.

Ned was just about to say that they could not make it, when Nancy surprised him by telling the woman they would take seven tickets! Ned dug into his pocket for the money.

But as they entered the hotel, he asked, "Nancy, why did you do that?"

"Sorry, Ned, I'll pay for the tickets."

"That's all right, Nancy, but maybe the others won't want to go."

"I was thinking of Mitzi Channing," Nancy said. "If she's in the neighbourhood, she might show up."

"You're right. Well, let's call on the manager."

Mr Pike had been with the inn for five years, but he had never heard of a Dunstan Lake, nor anyone named Channing. He promised, however, to make inquiries among the guests and to let Nancy know.

When they left the hotel, Ned said eagerly, "Let's go over and look at that Olympic ski jump."

The jump was truly spectacular and near the base of it was a skating pond. At the edge of the ice stood two mammoth figures which had been carved out of snow.

"Aren't they wonderful!" Nancy cried out.

As she and Ned stood staring at the snow giants, Nancy felt a hand on her arm.

"Nancy Drew—this *is* a surprise!" said a familiar voice.

"Why, Chuck Wilson!" Nancy gasped. "What are you doing here?"

Working as a ski instructor." Chuck grinned. "The regular pro has a broken leg. And now tell me what you're doing here."

Nancy introduced the two young men, then told Chuck about the house party at her aunt's camp.

"Oh, Chuck, I have a grand surprise for you!" she added. "Guess what! John Horn's here!"

"Here!" The skier looked incredulous. "At your camp? I'll be right over!"

Ned looked none too pleased at this suggestion. "John's not staying with us," he said.

Ned lost his glum look, however, when Chuck insisted upon lending the couple skis, boots and sticks, and suggested that they take a few runs. For the next half hour Ned and Nancy enjoyed themselves on the ski slopes.

"Nancy, your skiing has certainly improved," Ned said, smiling.

"The credit for that goes to Chuck."

Below them, Chuck Wilson waved his hand. "Hey, why don't you try jumping off that mogul?" he called.

"I'm game," Nancy cried, pushing off, after leaving her sticks against a tree. "Come on, Ned!"

Nancy went first, taking off beautifully from the top of the huge bump. Ned followed but his was by far the higher and the longer jump.

"Well, at least I didn't spill." Nancy laughed as they pulled up alongside the ski instructor. "And now I think we'd better start back to camp."

"Nancy, I'll see you again soon, won't I?" Chuck pleaded.

"We're all coming over here tomorrow," she promised. Then, with a teasing glance at Ned, she added, "But there's no reason why we can't see more of each other today. Ned and I haven't had lunch, so why don't you join us in the dining-room?"

"Thanks, I will. But let's go downstairs to the snack corner."

Nancy and Ned returned the borrowed equipment, and Chuck checked his skis and sticks at the long rack outside the beam-ceilinged room, which was crowded with skiing enthusiasts.

Their appetites whetted by a morning in the crisp mountain air, the trio ate heartily. When they finished, Ned and Nancy insisted they must leave, instead of joining the group which lingered by the fireplace discussing slalom and downhill racing.

Outside, as they were fastening on their snowshoes for the long hike back to camp, Nancy turned to Chuck. "By the way, do you know of any mink ranches around here?"

"There's one up on that ridge where the run for the ski jump starts. The ranch is owned by Charlie Wells."

"Let's go home that way," Nancy suggested to Ned. "We may pick up some information about the Forest Fur Company and Dunstan Lake."

They rode up on the lift and trekked off along the ridge. Half a mile further on, they neared the ranch buildings. A man came running towards them.

"Did you meet anyone or see anyone leaving here?" he asked excitedly.

"No," Ned replied. "Is something the matter?"

"I'll say there's something the matter," the man growled. "Some of my finest mink pelts have been stolen!"

Racing a Storm

STOLEN!

An idea clicked in Nancy's mind. Could the person who had taken the pelts from Wells's ranch be one of the Forest Fur Company gang? Quickly she introduced Ned and herself.

"Did you lose many minks?" Nancy asked.

"About two thousand dollars' worth," the man replied. "Half my take for the year."

"You own the mink ranch?" Ned inquired.

"Yes. I'm Charlie Wells."

"When were the pelts stolen?"

"I'm not sure. Just a few minutes ago I noticed the door of the storage house was half open."

"Did you see any new tracks in the snow?" Nancy asked.

"No, but we had a hard blow here early this morning. The snow could have filled up the tracks."

"Perhaps the furs were taken last night," Nancy commented. "A thief wouldn't dare prowl around in the daylight. May we see where you kept the pelts, Mr Wells?"

"Certainly." He led them to a small building attached to the back of the house.

As they approached the door, Ned remarked, "I

notice only one set of footprints here, and they must be yours, Mr Wells."

Nancy stooped down. With her glove she lightly brushed away some of the powder snow. Another man's prints were visible in the crust underneath the recently blown powder. "I wish we could follow these tracks," Nancy said.

"You're not going to try brushing away all this snow!" Ned exclaimed.

Nancy smiled. "If I thought it would lead us to the thief, I'd try it."

"I'm afraid my pelts are in another state by this time," Mr Wells said mournfully.

"Maybe we can help you get them back," Nancy suggested. "Have you ever heard of the Forest Fur Company? Or Mr and Mrs R. I. Channing? Or Dunstan Lake?"

At each question Mr Wells shook his head.

"Have you notified the police about the theft?" Nancy asked.

"No."

"I'll do it for you," she offered.

The rancher led them into his small house, which was furnished with rustic pieces. A large deer head hung over the living-room fireplace.

Nancy telephoned the State Police. She reported the theft at the Wells Ranch and then told about the stock swindle and the arrest of Boyd.

"I believe a man named Channing may know something about this theft," she said.

The officer was grateful for the information and said, "We'll follow up your lead right away!"

When Nancy returned from the telephone, she found

Mr Wells pointing to the deer head and telling Ned how he had shot the animal in the nearby woods.

Ned was impressed. "I'd like to shoot one and hang the head in our fraternity house!"

The ranch owner winked at Nancy. "It's all yours, son, if Miss Drew nabs the fur thief."

"I'll do my best," the young detective promised. "Mr Wells, this is my first chance to see a mink ranch. May Ned and I look around a bit?"

"I'll go with you," the rancher replied. As they stepped outside, he glanced at the low, dark clouds rolling in from the north. "More snow on the way," he predicted.

"Then we mustn't stay long," Ned said.

Mr Wells led them to one of several small, shed-like buildings set back some distance from the house. The shed was about six feet wide and had separate pens on either side of a central aisle. Some fifty glossy little animals occupied the pens.

"They're beautiful," Nancy remarked. "But they must require a lot of care."

Mr Wells shook his head. "All they need is the right kind of food and a clean, cool place where there isn't too much sunlight."

"Sounds like a good business," Ned said.

"It is, for an outdoor man," the rancher replied. "If you want to establish a mink farm, you should start with the finest, healthiest animals you can buy. Then get settled in a cold climate—makes the fur grow thick. In this country you find most of the mink ranches in Maine, Vermont, New Hampshire, Massachusetts, and northern New York."

"What do minks eat?" Nancy asked.

"A mink likes lean meat and fish best," Mr Wells said enthusiastically. "But he'll eat table scraps, vegetables—even field mice. Wild minks are fierce little fighters and very cunning."

"Very interesting," said Ned. "Now we'd better leave. We want to get home ahead of the storm."

As they left the building, Nancy suddenly spied a small, dark object half hidden under the snow. "The thief may have dropped this!" she thought excitedly.

The rancher, walking ahead of the couple, did not see Nancy run over to the spot, stoop down, and reach for the object. Suddenly Ned cried, "Don't touch that!"

He gave Nancy a shove which sent her reeling away from the object.

"Ned, what—"

"It's a trap, Nancy!"

Mr Wells turned and hurried back to them. "That's a fox trap!" he warned. "I keep them all around the grounds to catch foxes who try to raid the mink pens."

"Thanks, Ned," Nancy said. "I'm glad you recognized it."

The young people said goodbye to Mr Wells and started off. "Hurry!" Ned urged. "I don't like the look of that sky."

"Let's go along behind the mink sheds," Nancy suggested. "The thieves may have left clues."

"Okay."

Behind the sheds a thick row of evergreens marked the Wells property line. Nancy and Ned followed it, scanning the ground hopefully.

Once Ned happened to look up. Near him, hanging from a shoulder-high branch, was a strand of white yarn. "Here's something!" he exclaimed.

Nancy plodded over. "Well, Mr Detective, what's your theory?"

"Anyone trying to keep out of sight against the snow would wear white," Ned said. "Maybe our man snagged his shoulder or sleeve on these trees as he approached the mink pens."

"How right you are," said Nancy. "Let's see if we can find more of that yarn."

The two followed the line of evergreens into dense woods. From time to time, wisps of white wool on tree branches marked a clear trail.

But soon the woods gave way to open ground, dotted with knee-high clumps of berry bushes. A brisk wind hit Nancy and Ned with full force as they emerged into the open. The cold stung their faces.

"We'd better make for camp in a hurry," Nancy said. "We'll retrace our steps."

They turned, then stopped. The wind had blown snow over their tracks.

"Seems to me we came from over that way," Nancy said, trying to sound cheerful.

Ned nodded. "Let's go! And make it fast!"

Neither spoke as they tramped along. The daylight grew dimmer. For two hours they trudged ahead through the snow.

Finally Nancy called, "Ned! We should have reached camp long ago."

"I know that," the youth said grimly. "I don't want to worry you, Nancy, but I'm afraid we're lost!"

·16·

An SOS

FOR several seconds neither Nancy nor Ned spoke. Each was trying to figure out how to get back to the lodge before the storm.

Ned sheltered his eyes with one hand and peered through the rapidly falling dusk. All he could distinguish at first were rolling stretches of snow-covered landscape. The lost couple might have been in the arctic wastelands. Then Ned spied a lean-to and they hiked to it.

"Wood!" he exclaimed, seeing a pile of logs in one corner. "I'm going to build a fire. That may attract someone's attention."

"And we can eat," said Nancy. "I have two chocolate bars in my pocket."

The crackling fire and the chocolate revived their spirits, though no one came to guide them out of the snowy wilderness. Finally, when the fire died down, they set off again. Their way lay downhill, which at this moment seemed the easiest to take.

"I have a pocket torch," said Nancy. "I'll blink an SOS. Three short, three long, then three short. Right?"

"Right," Ned agreed.

Nancy clicked the signal several times as they crunched along. Again they had just about given up hope of help, and were floundering in a snowbank, when Ned said:

"Listen! I thought I heard a shout."

Nancy glanced quickly over her shoulder. "You're right!" she cried. "There *is* a man over there. John Horn!"

The trapper came plunging towards them through a drift. "I saw your distress signal, folks!" he yelled. "You lost? Why, Nancy! Ned!"

When Ned explained that they were indeed lost, the old man looked hurt. "You shoulda asked me to guide you," he reproached them. "But anyway, I can show you a short cut through the woods. You can make it home before it snows."

"You're certainly a lifesaver," Nancy said gratefully. "As a reward, I'll tell you some good news. Chuck Wilson is staying at the inn. We saw him this afternoon."

"You don't say!" Horn exclaimed, his leathery face spreading into a delighted grin. "Well, I'll sure have to tramp over there in a hurry and visit the boy."

He started off, with Nancy following and Ned bringing up the rear. Presently Nancy noticed that the trapper had about a dozen beautiful mink pelts strapped to his knapsack. She admired them, then asked where they had come from.

"Oh, I picked 'em up," John Horn answered vaguely. "They're the best mink there is!"

Nancy frowned worriedly as she tramped silently behind the trapper. Twenty minutes later they came to a well-defined trail, marked with the stompings of many feet.

"Just follow this," said their guide, "and you'll come

to your camp. So long, I'll drop over tomorrow."

As the couple watched their rescuer's sturdy figure vanish into the night, Ned said, "Nancy, you look upset. Surely you're not afraid we'll get lost again?"

"No, it's not that," she replied. "I was wondering about those valuable pelts John Horn was carrying, and the ones that were stolen from Mr Wells."

"Good grief! You don't think that old man's a thief, do you?" Ned demanded.

"I hate to think that," Nancy admitted. "He could have set a lot of traps, I suppose, and had some luck."

Ned shrugged, then said if Horn had stolen the pelts, more than likely he would have hidden them.

Nancy agreed, saying, "I guess I'm so tired and hungry that my suspicions are getting the better of me."

The trail led almost directly to the back of the lodge. "We were going in circles," Ned remarked ruefully, "before John Horn found us." As they climbed the porch steps, snow began to fall.

They were welcomed by a frantic group. Aunt Eloise had been chiding herself for letting the couple go off without a guide, and actually wept with joy to see her niece and Ned.

Again they all enjoyed supper before a blazing fire, while Nancy and Ned recounted their adventures. The prospect of attending the big ski party at the hotel aroused the young people's enthusiasm. They agreed to follow Aunt Eloise's advice and retire early in preparation for the big day.

Nancy was so weary that she tumbled into bed like a rag doll. It seemed as if her head had barely touched the pillow when she heard her aunt's voice.

"Nancy! Wake up!" Miss Drew urged. "It's a lovely,

sunny day. And there's a telegram for you, dear. A boy just brought it from the village."

"Read it to me, please," mumbled sleepy Nancy.

"Very well." Her aunt hurriedly slit the envelope and scanned the teletyped lines. Then she read the message aloud: " 'Nancy, phone me from Longview Inn. Love, Father.' "

"Aunt Eloise, I don't understand," Nancy said, now fully awake and sitting up in bed. "Why should Dad send me a telegram like that?"

"Perhaps he has learned something that will help solve this fur mystery," her aunt suggested.

"Perhaps. But why should Dad ask me to phone from the hotel instead of the village? And why would he sign the message 'Father' instead of 'Dad' as he always does? Aunt Eloise, it looks as if that telegram might be a fake."

"Oh dear!" said Aunt Eloise. "Those thieves have probably found out you're here. Well, that settles it. No more trips except in a group. And I'm going to phone your father myself from the village."

When Nancy entered the living-room a short time later, she found George and the three boys busily waxing their skis. "We've decided to go to the party on skis," Ned explained. "The snow's just right, and we'll work up a better appetite for that trapper's dinner." He grinned.

"Dinner?" Nancy asked. "How about breakfast?"

"We've eaten, sleepyhead," George replied.

Nancy prepared bacon, eggs, and toast for herself. She had just finished eating when Bess came running in, her cheeks flushed with excitement.

"Listen, everybody!" she cried out. "Someone's been

snooping around this house! I saw a lot of strange tracks."

The others rushed outside. In the new-fallen snow there were indeed a series of footprints encircling the house. A man had been both peering and eavesdropping!

The young people trailed the tracks away from the lodge and on down to the edge of a small grove. Here they disappeared as mysteriously as they had begun.

Where had the eavesdropper gone and who was he?

Back at the lodge, an ugly possibility came to Aunt Eloise's mind. The gang of fur thieves and stock swindlers had learned of Boyd's arrest and wanted to get revenge on Nancy! Also, they would stop at nothing to keep her from tracking them down.

Miss Drew felt the responsibility for her niece's safety weighing heavily on her. Nancy must be protected. It might be only a matter of time before the mysterious eavesdropper would return, not to observe, but to strike!

· 17 ·

The Hidden Cabin

DISAPPOINTED not to have found any trace of the eaves-dropper, the boys and girls returned to Eloise Drew's lodge and made plans to go to Longview Inn.

"I'm driving to the village with Aunt Eloise," announced Bess. "We'll meet you at the hotel for lunch."

The teacher recommended that the others start out at once. "It will take you until noon to reach the inn," she reminded them.

Just as the hikers were about to set off, John Horn strode up with a telegram.

"Did you get one of these this morning, Nancy?" he asked. "Woman at the telegraph office in the village sent a boy out with one, but he didn't come back there and they wondered if he delivered it."

"Yes, he did," said Nancy. The telegram proved to be a duplicate of the one she had received.

Nancy told John Horn about the mysterious eaves-dropper. "Would you look at the spot where the tracks end and see what you think? His tracks simply vanish."

The trapper followed Nancy to the place. He chuckled. "The fellow used the old Injun method of covering his tracks," he declared. "Walked backward and brushed the prints away with a broom he'd made of an evergreen bough. He wouldn't keep that up for long, though. Maybe we'll pick up the tracks some distance on. I'll go with you."

Nancy went back for her skis, then the group set off for the inn, watching carefully for footprints.

"Hey, gang!" Dave called suddenly. "Look at the circle of ski tracks just ahead."

"How odd!" said Ned. "It looks as if two or three people met here and—"

"And had a conference," Nancy finished. "I'll bet that evesdropper has skis! The tracks seem to lead away in three directions—so why don't we separate and see where they go?"

Burt grinned. "Give us our orders, ma'am!"

"Okay. Dave, will you follow the tracks that lead towards the hotel? Tell Aunt Eloise and Bess that the rest of us may be delayed. George and Burt, will you swing right towards the Wells Ranch?" She pointed.

"Okay!" said Burt.

"Ned and I will take that left trail into the woods," Nancy went on. "Mr Horn, will you come with us?" As he nodded, she said, "If any of you find our eavesdropper, try to nab him!"

When Nancy's group started off, John Horn said, "I know one thing you'll find. There's a cabin ahead of us that don't seem natural."

"How do you mean?" Ned asked.

"Nobody there, and it's locked tight and boarded at the windows. The right kind o' woods people always keep their cabins open for other hunters to use."

The three searchers followed the ski tracks until they disappeared about a hundred feet beyond the cab n the trapper described. Their quarry evidently had removed his skis and continued on foot.

"His footprints aren't like the ones the eavesdropper left at Aunt Eloise's cabin," Nancy remarked, "so we'd better turn back."

The trio stopped first to inspect the small cabin which was locked. At the door were lots of footprints.

"I wonder if they were made by hikers who stopped here to rest," Nancy said.

"Or by men who stay here," Ned replied. "By the way, that padlock hasn't been on the door long. It's brand new!"

John Horn nodded. "Reckon I won't go to the hotel yet. I'll just stay here and scout around a bit. You folks run along."

Nancy and Ned reached the Longview Inn about twenty minutes later. It was crowded with sports enthusiasts. George and Burt hurried across the lobby to meet them, and reported that neither they nor Dave had found anything of consequence.

Aunt Eloise beckoned her niece aside. "Your father and I are worried, Nancy," she said. "I talked with him on the telephone. He didn't send that telegram!"

"I wonder who did," Nancy mused.

"Someone who wanted to make sure you would be at the inn today," her aunt declared. "You will be extra careful, won't you?"

"Of course," Nancy promised. "But there's not much danger with so many friends around."

Although she pretended to take her aunt's news lightly, Nancy was aware that the telegram might indicate trouble. "The Channings must know by now that I'm responsible for Boyd's arrest," she thought. "They may try to trap me!"

Aunt Eloise continued to worry during lunch, and

ate very little. Chuck Wilson appeared while they were finishing dessert, and Nancy introduced him to her aunt and the others.

A short time later a bugle announced the opening of the afternoon programme. Everyone hurried outside to watch or participate in the contests.

"To start the afternoon's events," the master of ceremonies said, "the management is proud to present a special feature. Chuck Wilson, our new ski instructor, will make an exhibition jump from Big Hill."

There was a murmur of anticipation from the spectators as all eyes turned to the top of the slope where the blonde young man stood poised for the start. At a blast from the bugle, he was off.

Chuck raced down the incline, then soared into space, his arms spread out like a great bird's wings. For an instant he seemed to hang in the sunlit sky. A moment later he came swooping gracefully to earth.

The crowd burst into applause and Burt declared with a grin, "I'd give up college if I thought I could learn to do that!"

As he and the others skied over to congratulate Chuck, Nancy scanned the crowd of spectators. The Channings did not seem to be present.

Aunt Eloise came to her niece's side and spoke in a low voice. "I hope you're not planning to enter any of the events, dear," she said. "Your enemies may be waiting for your name to be announced."

Nancy agreed. She took off her skis and went to explain her decision to Ned. The young man was disappointed but said, "The important thing is to keep you safe, Nancy. Okay if I find another partner to enter the next event?"

"Of course," said Nancy. A few minutes later she watched as Ned and a pretty girl joined in the two-legged race.

Nancy left her aunt's side and pushed her way among the milling groups. She still saw no sign of the couple who had taken part in the stock swindles. "I'm wrong about their being here," she decided finally. "I should have entered the games after all. Hunches aren't—"

"Psst! Nancy!"

The urgent voice came from behind her. She whirled to face John Horn. The old man's eyes sparkled with excitement.

He beckoned with a calloused finger. "Follow me!"

· 18 ·

A Weird Light

NANCY looked anxiously about in hopes of seeing either Ned or one of her other friends. But none of them was in sight. John Horn tugged impatiently at her coat sleeve.

"I tell you we got to hurry, Nancy," he pleaded. "She's over on that pond in the woods right now. And skatin' around bold as you please!"

"Who's skating?" Nancy demanded.

"Why, that woman who sold me the fake fur stock," the old trapper snorted. "That thievin' Mrs Channing, of course!"

At the name Channing, Nancy hesitated no longer. "Lead the way!" she urged.

An instant later the two were running across the hotel grounds. They headed into the woods at the rear of the inn and trudged through the snow for nearly a quarter of a mile.

"There she is!" Horn pointed out. They slowed down and cautiously approached a small, cleared pond.

Nancy felt a tingle of excitement run down her spine. She stood on tiptoe for a better view and craned her neck. As Mitzi Adele ended a series of figures, she was facing Nancy directly.

The tall, slender brunette suddenly realized she had

134

"Fool!" said John Horn. "She'll break an ankle!"

been discovered. Like a flash she shot back towards the far bank. Without removing her skates, she raced off among the trees.

"Fool!" said John Horn. "She'll break an ankle!"

He was already taking snowshoes from his back, and quickly fastened them on to his boots.

"Looks like it's goin' to be a race!" he observed. "You follow as fast as you can, Nancy."

He soon outdistanced Nancy, who had tried sliding across the ice to save time. But she had fallen twice and wasted precious minutes.

Some distance ahead, the trapper saw Mitzi. She was seated on a log and had just finished changing into hiking boots. She leaped to her feet and fled further into the woods, but the old trapper was gaining with every step.

Nancy found their trail and sped after them as fast as she could through the deep snow. Suddenly she heard a scream, followed by:

"Let me go!"

A moment later she came in view of Mitzi and the trapper. The woman was kicking and scratching John Horn as he held her firmly by one arm. Mitzi's eyes blazed with anger.

"I'll have you arrested for this!" she panted.

"Oh, no, you won't, Mrs Channing," called Nancy, running up. "We're going to turn *you* over to the police."

Mitzi glared. "Why, if it isn't little Miss Detective herself!" she sneered. "And what have I done?"

"A great deal, Mitzi Channing. You've been selling fake stock certificates and you've stolen furs and jewellery. That should be enough."

"That stock is perfectly good," Mitzi snapped. "And I've never stolen anything. If this big gorilla will just —let—go—!" she added, trying to twist away from the trapper's grasp.

"Where's your husband?" Nancy demanded. "And where's Dunstan Lake?"

"*Wh-at?*"

The startled woman flung back her head. As she did so, her cap, loosened by her struggles, fell to the ground, disclosing a pair of sparkling earrings. They were shaped like small arrows with diamonds at each tip.

"Those are Mrs Packer's stolen earrings," Nancy charged.

"They are not. They're mine," Mitzi retorted. Then suddenly she clamped her lips tightly together and refused to say another word.

"Nancy, there's a couple of state troopers at the hotel," said John Horn. "If you'll hurry back and get 'em, I'll march our prisoner along and meet you halfway."

"I'll bring them as fast as I can," Nancy promised, and started off at a run.

She planned to tell her aunt and the others about the capture, but met the troopers first and decided to wait until the prisoner was in custody. She told her story quickly and led the officers towards the spot where she had left the captive and John Horn.

But when they arrived, there was no sign of Mitzi Channing. They saw only the limp body of John Horn, lying unconscious on the snow with a large welt behind one ear.

"Oh!" Nancy cried in horror, and knelt beside him. One of the troopers reached into his pocket for a tiny phial, removed the cap, and held the spirits of ammonia under John Horn's nose. Meanwhile, the other officer was inspecting the ground. He said that what had happened was plain. Footprints indicated that the trapper had been overpowered by two large men. Mitzi had vanished into the woods with her rescuers.

Fortunately, John Horn was not badly hurt and revived within a few minutes. He explained that he had been jumped from behind and had not seen his attackers.

"But I think I can identify one of those men," Nancy told the troopers. "He is named Channing, alias Jacques Fremont."

One trooper immediately set out to trail the men, while his partner hastened off to dispatch a radio alarm. Nancy and John Horn walked slowly back to the inn.

The old man protested that he was all right and that he needed no coddling. But Nancy insisted that he take a room at the hotel and have the house physician examine his injured head.

Nancy's aunt and her young friends were greatly upset by the incident. They concluded that the Forest Fur Company gang must be desperate. Nancy called State Police headquarters, but there was no word about Mitzi or the men.

Chuck Wilson was deeply concerned about his old friend and spent nearly an hour in John Horn's room. Because of this, he almost missed the special trapper's dinner which the guests enjoyed immensely. The management had provided a hillbilly orchestra, which played old-time ballads and lively polkas. Afterwards, the tables and chairs were cleared away for a series of square dances.

Nancy swung gaily through the "grand right and left," then promenaded with Ned as her partner. When it was over, Chuck Wilson came to join them.

"I'm going upstairs again to see how old John is feeling," he said. "Do you folks want to come?"

"Oh yes," Nancy answered.

They found the trapper pacing the floor of his room like a caged bear. "The Doc won't let me git outta here till mornin'," he grumbled. "He must think I'm a softy."

"Nothing of the sort," Nancy replied, and added affectionately, "You probably saved my life, Mr Horn. If I'd been standing guard over Mitzi, those men might have carried me off and dropped me down some snowy ravine."

"Don't talk like that!" Ned said severely.

While she had been talking, Nancy had walked to a window to gaze at the beautiful moonlit landscape. Suddenly her attention was caught by a glimmer of light along the ridge at the top of Big Hill. A moment later she could see the steady beam of a flashlight moving rapidly towards the ski run. It seemed very strange at this hour.

"Boys," she called, "why would anyone be up near the top of the jump at night?"

"I can't imagine," said Chuck as he and Ned joined her at the window. "Come on! Let's find out!"

The three young people waved a quick goodbye to the trapper and hurried downstairs to the cloakrooms. Hastily changing to ski clothes, they dashed outdoors.

For a moment there was no sign of the light. Then suddenly it showed up again at the top of the ski run and came hurtling downward, as the unknown jumper soared expertly at the take-off and landed below with a soft swish and a thud.

"Good grief!" Chuck cried. "What a chance he took! Let's speak to him!"

He and Ned raced off into the darkness, for already the light had disappeared and a cloud had cut off the moonlight.

Nancy waited until the cloud passed over, then tried to spot the jumper. She could not see him.

"Where could he have gone?" she asked herself. "That man wasn't just a phantom. He was flesh and blood!"

She turned towards the lake and the two giant snow statues which marked the end of the ski jump. Nancy's heart pounded at the sight she saw.

By a mere flicker of light that glowed, then vanished like a firefly, she could detect the shadowy outline of a crouching figure in a white sweater huddled behind the nearer statue. The person was cramming a bulky pouch into a hollow of the snowman!

As Nancy opened her mouth to call Chuck and Ned, a rough hand was clapped over her face.

"Quiet!" a harsh voice commanded. "*And don't try to run away or you'll get hurt!*"

·19·

Zero Hour

THERE was no escaping from the man's iron grasp. With her captor's fingers firmly gripping both arms, Nancy stood helpless, while the other man ran over from the statue. Roughly he stuffed a handkerchief into her mouth, tied her hands behind her, and bound her ankles together. Then the two men carried her swiftly towards the woods.

"If only Ned or Chuck had seen me!" Nancy thought. "Here I am with friends so close by and I can't even call for aid."

Although Nancy could not see the men's faces, in a few minutes she knew who her abductors were, for they began to talk freely.

"Say, Jacques, how much further is it to that cabin?" the shorter of the pair asked.

Jacques Fremont! The man whose other name was Channing! The man at the skating exhibition in Montreal! If only the police had not been forced to release him!"

"Just a little ways, Lake," he replied.

Nancy caught her breath. So Dunstan Lake was a man, not a place;

Channing gave a sardonic laugh. "All we need to do

is dump the Drew girl inside and lock the door. The place probably won't be opened again until summer."

"What a relief to have her out of the way!" growled his companion. "We had an airtight racket until Miss Detective began snooping around, asking for the Channings and Dunstan Lake. Although how she found out where we were, I'll never know."

"She's clever," Channing admitted. "But too clever for her own good. Now Miss Nancy Drew is going to pay for her smartness.

"Well, Lake, here we are. Suppose we see if this girl detective can solve the mystery of the locked cabin with both her hands and feet tied," Channing continued with a harsh laugh.

The cabin was bitterly cold, even worse than outdoors, Nancy thought, as her abductors flung her down on a bare bunk. Then, in the glare of a flashlight, Dunstan Lake, a squarish man with a bulldog face and beady eyes, made a mocking bow.

"Goodbye, Miss Drew." He smirked. "Happy sleuthing!"

"Come along! Let's get out of here," Channing snapped impatiently. "It's time we picked up Mitzi at the camp. She'll be tired of waiting."

Nancy shivered and closed her eyes despairingly as she heard the door slam and the padlock snap. She struggled to get out of her bonds, but it was useless. Already her fingers were becoming cold. With every passing minute the cabin grew more frigid. Nancy wondered desperately how long she could survive.

She knew that her only hope lay in exercise. She raised and lowered her bound ankles as high as she could until she was puffing with exhaustion. As she rested a moment, the fearful cold took possession of her again.

Nancy decided to try rolling on the floor. She managed to get off the bunk, and in doing so loosened the gag in her mouth. Crying loudly for help, she waited hopefully for an answer. None came.

She rolled, twisted, and yelled until she was bruised and hoarse. Finally her voice gave out completely. Her strength was gone. She became drowsy, and knew what this meant. Her body was succumbing to the below-freezing temperature!

Meanwhile, back at the slope, Ned and Chuck had completed a futile search for the mysterious jumper and were now walking to the spot where they had left Nancy. "I can't figure out why that fellow took off at night," said Chuck. "He could be arrested, you know. It's against all regulations."

"It was probably some crackpot who wanted to prove how brave he is." Ned shrugged. "Say, Nancy's gone!"

"I wouldn't worry." Chuck smiled. "She probably was chilled and went back to the hotel."

"Not Nancy!" Ned retorted. "She never gives up! If Nancy's not here, it's for a good reason. She probably spotted one of those swindlers she's been looking for and is trailing him alone!"

Nevertheless, Chuck persuaded Ned to go back to the hotel to look for Nancy. She had not come in, Bess reported. "What's going on?"

"Tell you later," Ned called as he and Chuck dashed off.

When they reached the ski slope, Chuck cried out, "Look, somebody's coming down Big Hill again! Two men with flashlights."

"But those fellows are descending like sane men," Ned observed. "They aren't taking any jumps."

The newcomers were state troopers. They said they were searching for the thief who again had stolen some mink pelts from the Wells Ranch. Chuck told them about the foolhardy jumper and they shook their heads in disgust. The men were about to go on when Ned stopped them.

"Have you seen a girl in a ski outfit?" he asked. "She was out here with us when we were looking for that crazy skier. Now she has disappeared and I'm afraid she's trailing the same thieves you are."

"Thieves?" the troopers echoed.

"Yes, thieves," Ned went on. "The girl is Nancy Drew, the one who captured that swindler, Mitzi Channing, this afternoon. But the woman got away."

"I heard about that over the police radio," one of the men said. "We'd better help you hunt for your friend. She may be in danger."

"We haven't much chance of trailing anyone," the other remarked. "There's been such a crowd around here, the place is full of tracks. How long has it been since you saw the young lady?"

"About twenty minutes," Chuck answered.

"Then she can't be far away," said the younger trooper. "Why not divide our forces so as to cover as much territory as possible?"

It was quickly agreed among the four that Chuck would search the hotel grounds while Ned followed the shoreline along the lake. The two troopers would examine the surrounding woods.

"Let's arrange a signal," said one of them. "The first man to find the girl will turn the beam of his torch towards the sky and wave it in an arc. In case of emergency, he will blink the light rapidly until help arrives. Is that clear?"

"Perfectly," Ned said impatiently. "Let's go!"

The next hour was torture for the searchers. The heavy snow made the going difficult, and a keen, arctic wind developed that knifed through their stout woollen clothing and sent the tears down their smarting cheeks. Added to this, their spirits were becoming low.

At the end of the hour the four met. No one had found a trace of Nancy. The troopers went back to their headquarters to report, while the two boys returned to the hotel. A frantic Aunt Eloise and the remainder of her house party rushed to meet them at the door.

"Where's Nancy?" Miss Drew demanded. "When none of you came back for the dancing, we all became worried and tried to find out what happened. But nobody knows a thing."

The two boys told the story of the strange skier and their separation from Nancy. Everyone listened in shocked silence. Then Bess offered a ray of hope.

"If John Horn is still upstairs, why don't we get his advice?" she suggested. "He knows more about the woods than all of us."

"Say, that's a great idea," Chuck agreed, rushing to the stairway. I'll ask the old fellow—" The rest was lost as he bounded up the steps.

In a few minutes he was back. With him was John Horn. The bandage on the old trapper's head was awry. He looked pale, but he insisted upon joining them in a new search.

"If those swindlers nabbed Nancy Drew, they wouldn't 'a' dared take her far off," he said. "I'll bet they took her to that empty cabin in the woods. Yes, sir. That's where they've left her. It's the only place around here where they could hide her without bein' found out."

"Oh, why didn't I think of that?" Ned chided himself, starting for the door. "If anything happens to Nancy—"

"Hold on!" Dave objected. "Burt and I are fresher and we can strike out faster. George and Bess can follow us with a Thermos flask of hot coffee and a blanket. But you and Chuck are in no shape to go."

"What do you mean?" Ned glared. "Maybe I can't go as fast as you, but what if there's trouble? I want to be there to help!"

"So do I," Chuck said firmly.

Nancy's friends and Aunt Eloise hurried through the night, determined to make a rescue.

· 20 ·

The Tables Turned

JOHN HORN trudged on as long as he could, then directed the others how to go. Dave and Burt, the first to reach the cabin, yelled Nancy's name. There was no answer.

Eagerly they charged up to the door. When they failed to open it, Burt said, "Focus your flashlight here, Dave.... Padlocked, eh?"

"We'll try a window," his friend suggested. "If necessary, we'll break the glass."

"Hey, is she there? Have you found Nancy?" George called as she and Bess came hurrying up to join the boys. Chuck and Ned were close behind.

"We don't know yet," Dave said. "This door is locked. We're going to try getting in a window."

"All of them are boarded up," Ned recalled. "But we'll get inside if I have to tear this shack apart."

George was using both fists to hammer on the unyielding door. "Nan-cy!" she shouted. "Nancy, it's George. Can you hear me?" There was no response.

Meanwhile, Burt and Dave were working on a window. "Here's a loose board," Burt yelled excitedly. "Pull!"

Snap! It came off so quickly they nearly lost their balance.

Burt played his flashlight inside the cabin. He could not see much in the clutter of furniture.

Dave was already pulling at another board. Together the boys yanked it off and broke the locked window just as Aunt Eloise came up.

"Nancy!" she called fearfully, but the hoped-for response did not come. By this time Ned was through the opening and flashing his light around. Suddenly the beam revealed the girl, lying on the floor, numb with cold and barely conscious.

"Nancy!" he cried.

"I'm—so—glad—you—found me," she whispered faintly. "I'm—so—terribly—sleepy."

One by one the others climbed through the window. Seeing Nancy, tears streamed down Bess's cheeks. "You're—you're all right, aren't you?" she sobbed.

Ned and Dave untied the robes that bound Nancy's hands and ankles.

"Of course she is," George told her cousin.

Aunt Eloise kissed her niece saying, "Don't worry, honey. We'll get you out of here right away. George, where's that Thermos flask?"

Nancy was given a few sips of hot coffee then wrapped in the blanket and carried out through the window. Burt and Dave insisted upon riding Nancy back to the hotel on a "chair" they made by interlocking their fingers.

A sense of relief, together with the stimulant, brought some warmth to Nancy's body. As the group neared the inn, she was able to talk again.

"As soon as we get inside," she said, "call the police. Tell them it was Channing and his friend Dunstan Lake who kidnapped me. Lake is a man!"

"Oh no!" George groaned. "But don't talk now. Save your strength."

"I must say this much," Nancy persisted. "Explain to the police that those men were going to meet Mitzi at a camp somewhere. Dunstan Lake's a short, ugly fellow with beady eyes."

"I'll tell them," Ned promised.

Aunt Eloise would not hear of Nancy's making the long trip to her house. Instead, she engaged a room for her niece and asked Bess to spend the night with her. Nancy was put to bed, and Miss Drew called in the house physician. After he had prescribed treatment, the doctor remarked:

"You had a narrow escape, young lady, but you'll be all right in the morning. Lucky you knew enough to keep exercising, or you might have frozen to death."

Nancy smiled wanly, and very soon was sound asleep. When she awoke the next morning, Bess, fully dressed, was seated beside her, and a breakfast tray stood on the bureau.

"I'm glad you're awake," she said. "How do you feel?"

"Fine. All mended." Nancy hopped out of bed.

After washing her face and combing her hair, she sat down to enjoy some fruit, cereal, and hot chocolate.

"Are you all set for some simply marvellous news?" Bess asked.

"You bet. Don't keep me in suspense."

At that moment there was a knock on the door, and Aunt Eloise walked in with George. They were happy to see that Nancy had fully recovered, and said the anxious boys were waiting downstairs.

"I was just going to tell Nancy the big news," Bess

said. "Listen to this, Nancy. The police have captured the Channings and Dunstan Lake!"

"Honestly? Oh, that's great! I was so afraid—"

"The troopers found their camp," George interrupted. "Nancy, do you realize what this means? That you've rounded up the whole gang, just as you hoped to do."

"With the help of all of you, including the state troopers," Nancy was quick to say. "Did Mitzi and the others confess to everything?"

George shook his head. "They won't own up to one single thing. The way that Channing woman plays innocent makes me furious!"

As Nancy continued to eat, Aunt Eloise remarked, "This place is full of excitement. The Wells Ranch was robbed again last night."

"What! Oh, my goodness!" Nancy cried.

She suddenly took the breakfast tray off her knees and jumped to her feet.

"That experience I had last night must have frozen my brains," she wailed. "Why, I've forgotten the most important evidence of all!"

"What evidence?" George wanted to know.

"The snow statue. Bess, hand me my clothes, quick! And, George, bring the boys up here in five minutes. There's not a moment to lose."

When the youths arrived, Ned demanded to know what all the excitement was about.

Nancy took a deep breath. "I'll tell you. Ned and Chuck, remember when we saw a man ski down Big Hill and wondered why?"

"I sure do. He was crazy."

"Maybe not so crazy as you think," Nancy replied.

"When you and Chuck left me, I saw the man in a white sweater conceal a bulky pouch in one of those big snow statues."

"You did?" Ned cried. "Nancy, why didn't you mention—"

"I was so cold and tired I forgot about it until just now," Nancy confessed. "Let's run down to the lake. Oh, I hope the pouch is still there!"

Before they could leave the room, the telephone rang. Aunt Eloise answered.

"It's police headquarters, Nancy. They want to speak to you," she said, handing over the instrument.

"Miss Drew, this is Chief Wester," came a man's voice. "We have those three suspects in jail, but they're a hard-boiled lot and refuse to admit a thing."

"I can identify them," Nancy said confidently.

"I know you can point out the men as your abductors," said the police chief. "But Mrs Channing demands her release and we haven't any charge against her."

"Just call Mrs Clifton Packer at River Heights," Nancy advised. "The diamond earrings Mitzi Channing is wearing were stolen from her. And the police at Masonville will tell you that Mitzi is wanted there for shoplifting."

"Thanks. You've helped a lot," said the chief. "And, Miss Drew, will you come to headquarters and be present when we question the trio again? I haven't told them that you were rescued."

"I'll drive over this morning," Nancy promised.

She repeated the conversation to her friends and added, "Now, about the snow statue. I suspect that the

Channing fur racket, which hasn't been cleared up, will be revealed in about ten minutes."

"How?" Bess asked, wide eyed.

"When we see what's in that hidden pouch. Why, where are the boys?" she asked, starting out the door.

Aunt Eloise smiled and put a restraining hand on her niece's arm. "They're acting as your deputies, dear. Let's sit here quietly until they return."

It was hard for Nancy to wait, but she knew her aunt was concerned about her. Twenty minutes later they heard pounding footsteps in the corridor and the boys burst into the room.

"*We found it!*" Dave cried.

"Yes sir-ree! Mission accomplished!" Ned said, grinning and waving a bulky, canvas-covered bundle at Nancy.

"Open it!" Bess urged. "I can't wait to see what's inside."

Tensely, the group gathered round while Nancy loosened the cord and peered inside.

"Furs!" George gasped. "Why, it looks like mink."

"It is," Nancy nodded, pulling several soft lustrous pelts from the bag. "We must turn these over to the police at once. I believe they belong to Mr Wells."

Nearing the bottom of the bag, Nancy gave an exclamation of glee. Sewn to one of the pelts was a small tag: *Wells Mink Ranch.*

"Oh, Nancy, you've done it again!" Bess shrieked.

Nancy hardly heard the remark. Her hand had touched a paper at the bottom of the sack. It proved to be one of the stock certificates to which was attached a note:

Jacques:
Made a neat deal on the earrings. Send Bunny Reynolds
a dividend to keep her from hollering when she finds out.
                                                    Sid

"This is all we need," said Nancy, rising. "Ned, will
you come to police headquarters with me?"

"You bet. I drove your car over here this morning."

It took only half an hour to get there. Nancy handed
the bag of mink pelts to Chief Wester at once and
explained what it held.

"Fine work, Miss Drew," he said as he shook hands
with her. The chief suggested that she go into his office
for the interview with the prisoners, and that Ned wait
for the right moment to bring in the loot.

"I got in touch with Mrs Packer and the Masonville
police," the chief went on as he closed the outer office
door. "They both confirm what you told us about
Mitzi Channing." He called to a guard to bring in the
prisoners through the rear-office door.

Upon seeing Nancy, the Channings and Dunstan
Lake looked at one another nervously.

"Miss Drew is here to identify you men as her
abductors last night," the chief said. "What have you to
say for yourselves?"

"Not a thing," Channing managed to say in a tense
voice. "I've never seen her before."

"Me neither," Dunstan Lake added, moistening his
dry lips.

"What about you, Mrs Channing?" the officer
asked.

"I could say a great deal about that meddlesome

little sleuth," Mitzi snapped, glaring at Nancy, "As for your outrageous charges, we deny every one of them."

"Miss Drew has just brought something that may refresh your memories," Chief Wester said coldly.

He flung open the front-office door. "Mr Ned Nickerson, will you come in, please?" he called.

The chief took the pouch from Ned's hands and laid it on his desk. The prisoners stared in stunned silence.

"The evidence in here is enough to convict you," Wester said. "Nancy Drew saw you put this bag in the snow statue not long after the pelts were stolen, Channing, or Jacques Fremont, which I believe is the name you use in Canada."

To Nancy's surprise, it was Mitzi who broke down first. Sobbing, she advised the men to admit their part in the racket.

"It'll go easier with us," she said. "But someday I'll get even with you, Nancy Drew, for what you've done."

The men finally confessed. Lake was the leader and had thought up the scheme of stealing the furs from the various ranches and secreting them in the snow statue while going for another haul.

"Ned and I must be leaving, Chief Wester," said Nancy. "Only I'd like to ask Mr Channing a question first." Turning to the dejected prisoner, she inquired, "Did you send me a telegram and sign my father's name to it?"

"Yes. You were always on our trail and we wanted to get rid of you until we could make our haul and escape. We hoped to catch you alone on your way to the hotel before you phoned your father."

"And one of you was eavesdropping at my aunt's lodge to find out if I was going to the inn?"

"I was," Dunstan Lake admitted as the prisoners were taken away.

The chief thanked Nancy again, then she and Ned started for Aunt Eloise's lodge.

"I guess this ends the *Mystery at the Ski Jump*," Ned remarked as he turned into the camp lane. "It was exciting, but I'll be glad to just sit and talk to you a while. In two days the old grind at Emerson begins again. Nancy, don't you dare get involved in another mystery before the winter carnival at Emerson."

"I promise," the young detective replied laughingly but secretly hoped another mystery would turn up very soon.

It did indeed, and came to be known as *The Spider Sapphire Mystery*.

Nancy and Ned had barely stepped inside the lodge when George cried, "Look! Someone's coming in a car. Could it be John Horn?"

"Not in a car." Bess giggled.

Their visitor was not the old trapper but Mr Drew. He and Nancy embraced joyfully.

"When Aunt Eloise telephoned me you were lost, Nancy," the lawyer said, "I took the first plane I could get. Poor Hannah was frantic too."

"Have you told her I'm all right?" Nancy asked.

"Yes. I phoned her from the inn. She was certainly relieved. And Hannah sent you a message, Nancy. Mitzi's skating partner Smith and that man Ben in New York who printed the Forest Fur Company stock have been arrested."

"Serves them right!" George stated firmly.

"And by the way," Mr Drew went on, "while I was at Longview, I talked to Chuck. John Horn came in too. You'll all be pleased to know that, with the old trapper's sworn testimony, Chuck is sure to regain most of his inheritance. His uncle had put the money into his own bank account, but hadn't spent much of it."

Then Mr Drew smiled at his daughter. "Chuck asked me to deliver a message. He thinks the successful outcome of his case and Nancy's calls for a celebration. He has invited all of you to be his guests at dinner at Longview tomorrow night."

"Hurrah!" Bess shouted. "A party!"

The next morning Mr Drew was obliged to return to River Heights. The young people spent the day enjoying winter sports, then changed to suits and dresses.

When they arrived at the inn they found that Chuck had engaged a small, private dining-room where places were set for ten persons. John Horn and Mr Wells were to join the party. There were colourful favours at each plate and a special menu, with the promise of dancing afterwards. When dessert was brought in, their host rose from his chair.

"This is a happy occasion for me," Chuck announced. "I've not only had gratifying news from my lawyer, Mr Drew, but I've made some grand new friends, among them one of the country's cleverest detectives."

Nancy found herself blushing as the others applauded.

"I've been given the pleasure of making some presentations. Mrs Packer has asked the police to present her diamond brooch to Nancy because of the wonderful way in which she tracked down the thief. And here it is!"

"Oh, Nancy, it's beautiful!" gasped Bess.

"B-but I don't deserve this," the embarrassed girl protested.

"Indeed you do." Chuck smiled. "You deserve it—and more."

As he spoke, the ski instructor laid a gaily wrapped box on the table before Nancy. "This," he told her, "is from Mr Wells, John Horn, and me."

There was a great hush as Nancy lifted the box lid. Inside were several glossy mink pelts—enough to make a lovely stole.

Nancy's eyes were moist with emotion. She did manage to thank them all, saying she would wear the lovely fur piece in remembrance of her adventure at Big Hill.

As the young people rose to attend the dance, Mr Wells called Ned, Burt, and Dave aside. There was a howl of laughter. Then Ned came walking forward with a deer head held in front of his face.

"For our fraternity house, girls. The old deer invites you to come to Emerson and help hang him over the fireplace!"

The Nancy Drew Mysteries

The Spider Sapphire
Mystery

Carolyn Keene

CONTENTS

Stolen Gem

NANCY Drew drove her convertible into the public parking lot and chose a space facing the far fence. There were few cars at this hour, since the early-morning shoppers had left.

As the attractive, titian-haired girl switched off the engine and took the key from the ignition lock, a car pulled in on each side of her. In an instant Nancy realized that they were parked so close she could not open either of her doors. The two drivers immediately jumped out and hurried away.

Nancy called to them. "Wait a minute! You've parked so I can't get out!"

The men paid no attention. She honked her horn loudly, but they did not turn their heads.

"How inconsiderate!" Nancy thought angrily. "And with the parking lot almost empty."

She caught a glimpse of the two men. They were dark-complexioned and she guessed they were from India. One looked to be about twenty years old, the other forty.

"Well," Nancy said to herself, "I'll just have to back out of here and find another place."

She put the key into the ignition lock and started the engine. At that instant a car came whizzing into the parking lot, turned sideways abruptly, and stopped directly behind her.

Nancy leaned out the window and called, "I want to get out of here!"

She could not see the driver, but she was sure he had heard her. Instead of moving his car, he jumped out and sped across the parking lot to the street. He was a large, well-built, dark-skinned man. She could not see his face.

With a sigh Nancy decided she would have to put down the top of her convertible and crawl over one of the cars. Then she remembered that before leaving home she had tried the mechanism and it had failed to work.

"I must stop at the garage on my way home," she decided.

Suddenly Nancy realized she was a prisoner. It also occurred to her that the whole episode had been planned by the three men.

"But why?" she asked herself.

Nancy sat lost in thought for a full minute. Her father, Carson Drew, a prominent lawyer, had recently taken an interesting case. There was a unique mystery attached to it. Was she being harassed to make her father give up the case? Nancy wondered. She had become well known as an amateur sleuth. Perhaps the people connected with the mystery had found this out and intended to keep her from helping her father.

"Whatever the motive, I'm stuck here right now," she told herself. "How am I to get out of this car?"

Nancy knew she would need help. She pressed the horn and let it blow continuously. Sooner or later someone would come to see about stopping the noise.

The person who arrived was a young policeman. Nancy did not know him, although she was acquainted with many of the men on the River Heights force. She had often worked directly with Chief McGinnis.

"What's going on here?" the officer asked cheerfully. "Somebody playing a joke on you?"

"I think not," Nancy replied. Quickly she told what had happened, and added, "I believe this was deliberate."

"My name is Orton," the policeman said. "I'll get you out of here as fast as I can."

He tried the doors of all three cars. Every one of them was locked.

Orton pulled a book from his pocket and began comparing numbers in it with the licence plates on the three cars. Finally he said, "Just what I suspected. Each of these cars is listed as stolen."

He said he would make a report to headquarters at once and a locksmith would be sent to open the doors. After he had gone Nancy fumed over the trick that had been played on her. In the future she must be more careful about traps.

About ten minutes later Orton returned with the locksmith and another policeman. While various keys were being tried, Orton asked Nancy for a description of the three men who had driven into the parking lot.

"I'm afraid it will be pretty sketchy," she replied, but told him what little she knew.

"They could be foreigners, especially the Indians," the officer stated. "Chief McGinnis will probably get in touch with the immigration authorities."

The three cars were finally moved and Nancy, relieved, stepped to the pavement.

"Thanks a million," she said to the three men. "I hope you catch those car thieves."

Nancy was convinced that the strangers were more than mere car thieves. She would talk the matter over later with her father.

She continued on to her destination, the River Heights Museum. Her father had told her about an amazing gem on display there. It was a huge sapphire with a spider embedded in it.

"To think that this rare piece of work is only synthetic," Nancy murmured. "Dad said it was made by Mr Floyd Ramsey, who fashions beautiful and unusual synthetic jewellery, right here in River Heights."

The mystery which her father had hinted at concerned Mr Ramsey and a wealthy Indian in Africa who owned a genuine sapphire with a spider embedded in it.

"I can't wait to hear the rest of the story," Nancy thought as she walked along Maple Avenue towards the museum.

She heard someone across the street whistle. Thinking it might be her friend Ned Nickerson, Nancy turned to look. At that instant someone banged into her from the rear, snatched her bag, and tried to knock her down. As Nancy teetered to regain her balance, the thief dashed down the street.

"He's the younger of the two Indians who penned me in!" she thought. Nancy started running after him, crying out, "Stop thief!"

A man, coming from the opposite direction, heard her. Seeing the bag clutched under one arm of the fleeing figure, he stopped the Indian and grabbed the bag, but it dropped to the pavement. He struggled to hold onto the thief, but with a neat judo shoulder throw, the bag snatcher tossed the man onto the sidewalk. Then the Indian fled round the corner.

Horrified onlookers were helping the man to his feet as Nancy ran up to him. "I'm dreadfully sorry," she said. "Are you hurt?"

The man smiled. "Only my pride." He picked up the handbag and handed it to Nancy.

A patrolman rushed to the scene and asked for the story. When Nancy stated that this was the second time within an hour that she had been annoyed by the same man, the officer took notes and he said he would telephone the information to headquarters at once. By this time the crowd had melted away.

The stranger who had come to her assistance refused to give his name. Smiling, he said, "I don't want any publicity. It was my privilege to help a young lady."

With a wave of his hand he strode off. As Nancy walked on, she reflected about people of good and bad intent who so often crossed her path.

Presently Nancy smiled to herself. "Hannah always says that things come in threes. I wonder what's in store for me now."

Hannah Gruen, the Drews' housekeeper, had lived with Nancy and her father since the death of Mrs Drew when Nancy was three years old. The warm-hearted woman was like a mother to Nancy and worried constantly about the strange situations which the young sleuth faced when solving mysteries.

"Poor Hannah!" Nancy thought. "She'll be so upset when I tell her what happened this morning."

By now Nancy had reached the museum. The

curator, Mr Sand, was standing in the entrance hall.

"Good morning, Nancy," he said. "Have you come to see Mr Ramsey's gem?"

"Yes, I have," Nancy replied. "I understand it's exquisite."

The curator nodded. "I defy anyone to tell the gem from an original. You'll find it in the room to the right of the one where the prehistoric animals are."

Nancy hurried through the big room and turned into the smaller one. A glass case stood in the centre. On a mound of white velvet lay the unique gem.

Before Nancy had a chance to examine it carefully through the glass, a homemade printed sign tacked to one corner of the case caught her attention. She read it and frowned, puzzled. The sign said:

THIS GEM WAS STOLEN

·2·

Missing Student

THE curator had followed Nancy to the spider sapphire case.

"Well, what do you think of—" Mr Sand began. He stopped speaking abruptly as Nancy pointed to the sign saying the gem had been stolen.

The man's face turned red with anger. "That is not true!" he cried. "Someone put the sign there—someone who is trying to cause trouble!"

He called to a guard standing near the door and quizzed him about recent visitors. "Everybody looked all right to me," the guard answered. He smiled. "Maybe some teenager put that up there for a joke."

"Maybe," the curator agreed, calming down.

Nancy was inclined to disagree, but did not voice this opinion to the others. She asked the guard to describe all the men who had been in the museum recently.

Her pulse quickened when he said, "One of the visitors looked to me like a native of India. He kept walking round and round the case and seemed mighty interested in the gem."

This was all the proof Nancy needed. The Indian visitor fitted the description of the older of the two men who had imprisoned her in the car.

15

After the guard had gone back to the door, she said to Mr Sand, "I don't trust that Indian. If he ever returns, watch him carefully."

The curator smiled. "You're mixed up again in some mystery and this time it involves an Indian?" he asked.

Nancy did not reply. She merely gave the man a wink.

The young detective rarely discussed her cases with anyone except her father, closest friends, or police and detectives. Mr Drew had given her this advice on her first case, and Nancy had followed his wise counsel in solving all her other cases.

Nancy now gave her full attention to the magnificent, almost round, inch-long gem in the case with the spider embedded in it. The sapphire, a shade darker than pale blue, sparkled brilliantly. The gem was transparent except where the spider lay. A card in the display case stated that Mr Floyd Ramsey had produced this sapphire synthetically.

"The gem is absolutely beautiful," she said to Mr Sand. "What gave Mr Ramsey the idea of embedding a spider in the sapphire?"

"He saw a picture of a similar gem—a real one—and decided to experiment to see if he could imitate it."

After a pause Mr Sand remarked, "You know, spiders are one of the oldest living creatures on earth. They appeared at least three hundred million years ago."

"Really?" Nancy asked, amazed.

The curator said that the study of spiders was intriguing. "The whole earth is covered with them. They're man's best friend. If spiders weren't around, we'd be overrun and eaten up with insects."

Amused by Nancy's frown, Mr Sand went on, "I read recently that a man in England made a study of spiders to determine how many there were in a certain area. A census of one acre was two and a quarter million spiders!"

Nancy gasped. Then she laughed. "Mr Sand, you make me feel positively crawly."

The curator's eyes twinkled. "Do you know how old the world's sapphires are—I mean the kind that Mother Nature fashioned?"

Nancy shook her head. "How old?"

"So far as is known they first appeared in the Carboniferous Era. That's roughly two hundred and fifty million years ago."

"So spiders and sapphires are much older than man," Nancy observed. "I believe human beings first appeared on the earth ten million years ago."

"That's right."

Mr Sand was summoned to the telephone and Nancy spent a few more minutes admiring the spider sapphire.

"I must go to Dad's office and ask him all about the spider sapphire mystery," she told herself, and left the museum.

She found tall, athletic Mr Drew dictating a letter to one of his secretaries, Miss Hanson. Nancy offered to wait in the reception room, but he insisted that both she and Miss Hanson remain.

"You never come here unless you have something important on your mind," he teased Nancy. "What is it this time?"

His daughter told about the "stolen" sign tacked onto the spider sapphire case.

"It may involve the ancient spider sapphire owned

by the Indian, Shastri Tagore," the lawyer said. "His agents are in this country. They revealed the theft of his gem. These agents, who are Indians, live in Mombasa, East Africa, where Mr Tagore has a home. They had heard about the gem Mr Ramsey claimed he made. The men don't believe his story and insist that the gem is Mr Tagore's stolen property."

"But you believe Mr Ramsey, don't you?" Nancy asked.

"Of course I do. I have known Floyd for a long time. There's not a more honest man in the world."

Nancy had not intended to tell her father about the bag-snatching incident, but he surprised her by saying, "I hear a man grabbed your handbag and almost knocked you down."

Mr Drew added that someone who had seen the incident had called him and related the story.

"I hope the person also told you about the nice man who retrieved my bag. And here's a story I'm sure you haven't heard."

Nancy told him of her experience in the parking lot and her suspicion that the man who had grabbed her handbag was one of the drivers. It was the lawyer's turn to look amazed, and Miss Hanson gasped.

"I'm sure the whole thing is bound up with the spider sapphire mystery," Nancy told her father.

"Then I'm glad you're going away so soon," Mr Drew said. "In the meantime I insist that you have someone with you whenever you leave the house."

Miss Hanson spoke up. "Oh, you're going away, Nancy?"

"Yes, on an African safari. Isn't it marvellous?"

"Will you be with a group?" the secretary inquired.

Nancy nodded. "You know that my friend Ned Nickerson attends Emerson College. The safari has been organized by some of the professors. Boys who are majoring in botany, zoology, and geology are making the trip. They're being allowed to ask friends to go at the students' rate. Bess and George and I have signed up. Burt and Dave, their boy-friends, will be along, too."

"It sounds thrilling," Miss Hanson remarked.

Nancy said that the leaders of the Emerson safari were Professor and Mrs Wilmer Stanley. "He's always called Prof and she's affectionately known as Aunt Millie to the boys."

"It certainly sounds like fun," Miss Hanson remarked as she picked up the telephone which had started to ring.

Mr Drew and Nancy stopped speaking. Miss Hanson said, "Mr Drew's office. . . . She's here. Do you wish to speak to her?" Then the secretary became silent. Presently her brow furrowed. Finally she said, "Thank you. I'll tell her."

Miss Hanson put down the phone and looked directly at Nancy. "The call was from Professor Stanley. He said he was in a hurry and wouldn't take time to speak to you. I'm terribly sorry to give you his message, Nancy. Ned Nickerson can't go on the safari after all."

Nancy's heart sank. What had happened? She forced herself to say, "That is bad news." She had talked to Ned only two days before and he was extremely eager to go on the safari. He had said, "Nothing in this world will keep me from going."

Mr Drew declared that it was strange Ned had not telephoned Nancy direct. Why should he have asked Professor Stanley to make the call?

Nancy's suspicions were aroused at once. She asked Miss Hanson to put in a call to the college and ask for Professor Stanley. It took some time to locate him, but finally the secretary reached the professor at his home.

"Miss Drew wishes to speak to you," Miss Hanson told him.

"Hello, Nancy," he said genially. "How are you? All ready for the trip?"

"Yes, I'm ready. But what's all this about Ned not going?"

"What do you mean?" the professor asked.

"Didn't you phone my father's office during the past few minutes?"

"Why no."

When she told what had occurred, Professor Stanley said of course Ned was going. Someone was just playing a prank.

Nancy doubted this but made no comment. She said she would be seeing the professor soon and hung up. Next, Nancy asked Miss Hanson to call Ned at the Omega Chi Epsilon Fraternity House at Emerson.

When the connection was made, Nancy learned that Ned was not there, so she asked for Burt Eddleton.

When he came on the wire, she told him what had happened. Burt was amazed at the story and also disturbed.

"Ned left the dorm yesterday afternoon. Later he phoned and gave someone a message that he was going home. I don't like this at all," Burt added.

"I'll call the Nickersons right away and see if he's there," Nancy said.

She spoke to Mrs Nickerson, who said that her son had not come home and she had not heard from him.

Because Nancy did not want to alarm his parents unnecessarily, she did not express the fear which was forming in her mind. Ned might have met with foul play!

·3·

The 4182 Code

ALTHOUGH Mrs Nickerson tried to remain calm, Nancy could tell that she was disturbed by the news. "It's unlike Ned not to be in touch with his father and me and his friends."

"I'll ask Bess and George to go with me to Emerson tomorrow morning and help search—if that's necessary," Nancy told her.

"I'm glad to know that," Ned's father said on their extension phone. "If you hear from him, please ask him to phone us."

Nancy promised to do so, then hung up and turned to her father. 'What do you think I should do now?" she inquired. "I have a strong hunch something is wrong."

"Why don't you telephone Burt and Dave? Ask them to make a thorough search of the campus to see if they can locate Ned."

Miss Hanson was already reaching for the telephone and again dialled the number of the Omega Chi Epsilon house. She asked for Burt Eddleton and Dave Evans. Both came on the wire and Nancy told them that Ned had not come home.

"I'm afraid he may have met with foul play," she said. "Would you make a thorough search of the campus and let me know what you find out?"

Neither of the boys answered at once and she could hear them whispering in the background. Finally Dave said, "That's kind of a large order, Nancy. Perhaps we should get all our fraternity brothers to help in the search. And maybe we should report this to the police."

Burt spoke up. "Personally I feel that Ned went off of his own accord to study. He'd be mighty embarrassed having a whole bunch of us burst in on him. You know we're all cramming for exams. We have a tough one coming up tomorrow morning."

There was another long pause, during which a plan was formulating in Nancy's mind. At last she said, "Would it help if Bess and George and I come up to help search—that is, if you don't find any trace of Ned this afternoon?"

Burt said this was exactly what the boys had hoped she might suggest. "We'll get busy at once and let you know at suppertime what we find out."

Nancy's next call was to Bess, who was astounded at the news. She agreed at once to go to Emerson. Her cousin, George Fayne, an athletic-looking girl was eager to help.

"Great," said Nancy. "I'll let you know as soon as I hear from Dave and Burt."

The afternoon hours dragged by. Nancy took her convertible to be repaired so that the top would lift and lower again. The mechanic said it had been tampered with and Nancy was sure the sabotage had been committed in the Drews' garage. "And by those men who imprisoned me in the parking lot!"

In her alarm over Ned, Nancy had forgotten about the African safari and the spider sapphire mystery. The whole thing came back to her as she packed a few clothes into a suitcase and talked to Hannah Gruen. The housekeeper was dismayed by the strange turn of events.

"No doubt about it," she said. "There are villains in this picture somewhere. The extent to which some people will go to gain dishonest ends is frightening. Please, Nancy, promise me that you will be very careful."

Nancy smiled and hugged the housekeeper, for whom she had a deep affection. "I promise."

At seven o'clock the telephone rang and Nancy ran to answer it. Burt was calling. There was a note of deep concern in his voice. Twenty-five boys had taken part in a thorough search of the campus. They had not found Ned.

"Nancy, do you think he has been kidnapped?" Burt asked.

She closed her eyes as if to shut out the dreadful thought and said, "It looks like it. I'll get in touch with the Nickersons immediately."

With a heavy heart Nancy dialled the number of the Nickerson home. This time Ned's father answered. Though he tried to keep his voice steady, it was evident he was apprehensive over his son's safety when he heard the upsetting news.

"Bess and George and I are driving up to Emerson early tomorrow morning," Nancy told him. "Will you be going too?"

After talking with his wife, Mr Nickerson said he thought not. They had concluded that if Ned had been kidnapped, a demand for ransom would come to the house. They wanted to be home to receive any messages.

"And we figure it's too soon to notify the police— at least before we get a ransom note."

Nancy said the three girls would make an extensive search of the area around Emerson. "Burt and Dave will join us in the hunt as soon as their exams are over. I'll let you know what we learn," she promised.

"And I'll call your father if we receive a ransom note," Mr Nickerson said.

No word came during the night and everyone in the Drew household arose early. Nancy did not feel like eating breakfast but her father and Hannah Gruen insisted.

"It's a long drive to Emerson and you'll need all your strength," the housekeeper stated.

Just before six o'clock Nancy stopped her convertible in front of Bess Marvin's home. At once the front door opened and the pretty, blonde-haired girl came out to the car, carrying a rather large suitcase.

"Hello, Nancy. Please forgive the big bag. No telling how long this mystery may last. Oh, isn't it terrible? I think this is the worst mission you've ever asked me to go on with you."

"I'm afraid it is." Nancy was grim.

There was little conversation for the next few blocks as they made for George Fayne's house. The slender, dark-haired girl ran down the steps, swinging a small overnight bag which she tossed into the back of the convertible, then hopped in.

Once on the highway, Nancy kept to the speed limit and the miles flew past quickly. By noon the three girls had reached Emerson and checked in at the Longview Motel.

"Let's start work right away," Nancy urged, as soon as they had eaten lunch. "I think we should go to the railroad and the bus station to ask if anyone saw Ned go out of town the day before yesterday."

When nothing was learned from these sources, the girls went to two rent-a-car agencies and made inquiries. No one answering Ned's description had rented a car the day he disappeared.

"I'm tired," said Bess. "Let's go back to the motel and rest, then start out again."

When the girls reached the Longview, Nancy said she would call the Nickersons. "I hate to report failure, but they may have some word by this time."

Ned's parents had heard nothing. Mr Nickerson said that if they did not hear from Ned by night-time, they would notify the police. They were almost certain that Ned had been kidnapped. But by whom and why?

"It begins to look as if the kidnappers were not after money," Mr Nickerson stated. "Nancy, have you any theories about the reason?"

"Yes, I have," she answered. "It may be a far-fetched idea, but there's a possibility that a mystery I might work on in Africa is the answer. The kidnappers may feel that by keeping Ned from going, I would stay home." In a moment she added, "And I would, too."

Presently Nancy said good-bye. As she came from the phone booth, Burt and Dave walked into the motel lobby. "Any luck?" they asked.

Nancy shook her head. "If we only had one little tiny clue—"

"We have!" the two boys cried together.

Burt said that a short while ago, when they returned to the fraternity house after the exam, they had received a phone call. The caller's voice was quick and muffled, but they were sure he had been Ned Nickerson.

"What did he say?" Nancy asked as Bess and George hurried up to the trio.

"The message sounded like 'Swahili Joe pair 4182.' "

"What does that mean?" Bess spoke up. "If Ned could talk to you, why didn't he tell you something you could understand?"

Nancy said that perhaps Ned was afraid the place where he was being held prisoner was bugged and he did not dare give the location except through this code.

"It's not going to be an easy one to crack," Dave remarked. "Who is Swahili Joe?"

"My guess," said George, "is he's the kidnapper."

Burt offered to telephone the local police and ask if they had ever heard of such a person. He soon returned to say that no one at headquarters had ever heard of a Swahili Joe.

"They thought he might be a restaurant owner or barber, but there's no record of anyone by that name."

"It's probably a nickname," Dave suggested.

The five young people talked at great length about the strange name and finally Nancy said she would get in touch with her father. "I'll ask him to contact the Immigration Department and find out if Swahili Joe is an African who entered the United States from some country where Swahili's spoken."

As she left to make the call, George came up with another theory. The numerals 4182 might be part of a phone number. "It will take us forever to go through the book but let's try."

When Nancy rejoined them she too started to look. The task seemed endless.

Bess sighed. "We're getting no place fast," she mumbled. "Nancy, what did your father say?"

"He's going to get in touch with the FBI as well as

the immigration authorities. He said he'd call me back, so I guess we'll have to stay here for a while."

It was three o'clock when the call came. Mr Drew told Nancy that no person nicknamed Swahili Joe was known to have entered the United States.

Nancy asked her father if there had been any more news about the case of the spider sapphire. When he answered No, she said:

"Dad, do you think there could be a fraud in connection with this whole thing?"

·4·

New Interpretation

THERE was silence on the wire for several seconds before Mr Drew spoke. "Do you mean that perhaps the real spider sapphire wasn't stolen?" he asked his daughter.

Nancy said that it might be an insurance fraud. The owner of the gem, working either alone or with some other men, might have reported to the insurance company that the jewel had been stolen.

"Then he'd collect a large amount of money for it," Nancy stated.

Later on the sapphire would be sold secretly to some unscrupulous person. The buyer might break up the huge gem into smaller stones and sell them.

"Your hunch is a very good one, Nancy," the lawyer answered. "At this stage no one really knows. Suppose I tell you the whole story."

"Please do," Nancy requested.

Mr Drew said that two men had come to call on Mr Ramsey.

"They said they were emissaries of the owner of the spider sapphire, Mr Tagore. Their names are Jahan and Dhan. They were born in India but live in Mombasa, Africa.

"Mr Ramsey was amazed and angry when the two men accused him of stealing the owner's gem and exhibiting it as a synthetic sapphire."

"The nerve of them!" Nancy burst out. "What did Mr Ramsey do?"

"He called in several of his company employees, who also vigorously denied the accusation, saying that Mr Ramsey was a genius and indeed had fashioned the synthetic spider sapphire himself."

"Then what happened?" Nancy asked.

Mr Drew told her that at this point Jahan and Dhan had apologized for being so hasty, but came up with a new theory. "They now accused Mr Ramsey of having borrowed the original from the thief and used it as a model for his own gem."

"That's even worse!" Nancy exclaimed.

Her father agreed. "Of course Mr Ramsey denied their claim, but Mr Dhan with a smooth sort of smile said, 'Mr Ramsey, if you will give us back the original gem, or the money it is worth, we promise not to say anything to the authorities. Certainly you want to avoid unpleasant publicity.' "

"That sounds serious," Nancy remarked. "What happened then?"

"By that time Mr Ramsey had become very suspicious. He said he would have to think over the whole matter and asked the men to return in a few days.

"Mr Ramsey came to me at once with the entire story. I decided to get in touch with the owner of the real spider sapphire, but was told he was away on vacation and his secretary, a man named Rhim Rao, also an Indian, was taking care of his affairs."

"Did he confirm Jahan and Dhan's story?" Nancy queried.

"Yes, he did." While he, too, had been polite, Rhim Rao insisted that Mr Tagore's spider sapphire had been stolen and suspicion most certainly pointed to Mr Ramsey. "I could not convince him that the synthetic gem had been made right here in River Heights," the lawyer added.

Mr Drew said that he had been in Mr Ramsey's office when Jahan and Dhan had returned. He, as attorney for Mr Ramsey, and to test the Indians' honesty, had insisted upon some kind of proof from the two foreigners before any discussion could take place. "They promised to bring some, but of course they never did. I engaged a detective to trail them, but unfortunately they managed to slip away."

Nancy asked her father if he thought this meant Jahan and Dhan had left the country.

"Possibly, but not under their own names—or at least the names of Jahan and Dhan. I checked with the immigration authorities."

Nancy continued to think about the strange story as she said good-bye to Mr Drew and returned to her friends in the lounge of the Longview Motel. They were so busy discussing how to go about finding Ned Nickerson that Nancy decided not to tell them her father's story now. Each one in the group made several wild guesses as to what the strange message from Ned could mean.

Suddenly Burt spoke up excitedly. "Hey, I just thought of something. Maybe we're figuring on the wrong pair. Ned could have meant *p-a-r-e*."

"You could be right," Dave replied, "but what's he going to cut off? It leaves us just as confused as ever."

"He could also have meant *p-e-a-r*," George stated.

"True," said Bess. "But what would he have meant by that?"

George could not resist the temptation to tease her cousin. "You love to eat. The answer should be easy for you."

Bess was used to George's gibes and invariably they piqued Bess into coming up with an answer. This time was no exception. With a toss of her head, she said, "How about a pear orchard?"

"Brilliant idea," Dave praised her. "But how are we going to locate the right pear orchard?"

"I might have an answer to that," Nancy spoke up.

"Then out with it," Burt urged. "The sooner we find Ned the better."

Nancy asked, "Wasn't Ned doing some map-making in connection with one of his courses?"

"Yes, he was," Dave replied. "How does that apply here?"

Nancy smiled. "In map-making you use latitude and longitude."

"Right," Burt agreed. "But what's the connection?"

Nancy's answer amazed the others. "Those numbers 4182. They might mean latitude and longitude."

"Boy, that's a brilliant idea!" Dave burst out.

"It sure is," George spoke up. "Let's find a map of this area."

The manager of the motel supplied one. The young people spread it out on a table in the lobby. Nancy ran her finger along the longitude line while George ran hers up the one for latitude. Their fingers met at a point several miles from Emerson.

"That's it!" Burt cried. "Let's go!"

The five young sleuths set off in Nancy's convertible. There were main highways only part of the distance. Then it became necessary to take bumpy, country roads. The last part of the journey was a long, very narrow stretch with a deep ravine on their side.

"I hope we don't meet anybody," Bess said nervously. "Whatever would we do?"

The words were hardly out of her mouth when they heard the roar of a motor round the bend just ahead. Nancy, who was driving, began to blow the convertible's horn. In a moment a truck pulled up in front of her and stopped.

The driver proved to be a farmer. Nancy got out and walked up to him.

"This is unfortunate," she said. "What are we going to do?"

The farmer scowled. "What are *we* going to do? You mean what are *you* going to do?"

Nancy stared at the unpleasant man. "I'm not familiar with this road. You must be. Is there a turnoff anywhere?"

"No," he answered. "I'll tell you what you're going to do. Get in that car of yours and back up."

By this time Burt and Dave had jumped out of the convertible.

"We're on the ravine side," Burt spoke up. "Couldn't you just pull your truck off the road a little so we can pass?"

"And maybe break a wheel or overturn?" the farmer cried out. "I should say not. Besides, I'm in a hurry. I've got to get to market."

"You're asking us to back up for a whole mile," Dave protested.

"That's exactly what I want you to do. And you'd better be quick about it!" the man shouted.

Nancy was dismayed. While it was not impossible for

her to back up a mile, it seemed unnecessary. She was sure that if the farmer would pull off the road a little, he would neither break a wheel nor overturn. He was being very unreasonable.

"Oh, this is dreadful!" Bess wailed.

The argument ceased when they heard another car coming along the road at the back of Nancy's convertible. The newcomer was a State Police officer. Quickly scanning the scene, he stepped up to the group and asked, "What's the trouble here?"

"These kids won't back up to let me pass!" the farmer growled.

Nancy was about to speak up when the officer said to the farmer, "I think it would be much simpler if you pull over and let these people pass."

The farmer, muttering under his breath, got back into his truck and pulled off the road. After thanking the policeman, the others returned to their car and continued their journey, with the officer following. At a crossroad the policeman turned off and waved to the young people.

"How much farther is it?" George asked.

Burt consulted the map. "Four-one-eight-two should be right ahead."

When Nancy pulled round a turn in the road past a little hill, Bess exclaimed, "A pear orchard!"

The trees were filled with white blossoms. On the other side of the road, a few feet below the edge, a brook gurgled along.

Everyone was tense. Which way should they go to search for Ned? Along the brook or through the pear orchard?

Before anyone had a chance to get out of the car, a

car suddenly roared up behind them. Two revolvers poked from the windows and shots were fired at the tyres of Nancy's convertible. The next moment four masked men leaped from the car and surrounded them.

One of the men ordered in a gruff voice, "Get out and follow us!"

·5·

Suspicious Initials

KNOWING that it would be foolhardy to resist the armed men, Nancy and her friends started walking down the road. Two of the holdup men were in front, the two with the revolvers in the rear. Burt and Dave exchanged glances, then looked at the girls.

All the young people understood the message: If there was any opportunity for them to attack their captors, they were to do it at a signal from Burt.

In a few moments the men with the revolvers put the weapons into their pockets and seemed to relax. Apparently they did not expect any trouble from their prisoners.

Suddenly Burt's hand went up in the air. Quick as a flash, he tackled the largest of the men. Dave took a tall man, while George in a surprise move towards one of the two shorter men used a judo twist on him. The mask fell from his face.

Nancy and Bess together had pinned the arms of the fourth man behind him. As they grabbed the mask from his face, Nancy gasped.

He was one of the men who had hemmed in her car! Out of the corner of her eye, she saw that the man George had swung to the ground was the other Indian!

In lightning moves the two suspects pulled away

from the girls and ran as fast as they could through the pear orchard.

"Let's chase them!" George urged.

"Better not," Burt mumbled between punches. "Don't forget—they're armed."

"Not now they aren't!" Bess exclaimed.

She pointed to the ground where two revolvers had fallen from the men's pockets. Nancy and George picked up the weapons and flung them down into the brook.

Although the boys had won the first round, they were having a struggle to keep from being beaten in the fight. At once George went to help Burt subdue his man. Then she ripped off his mask. He was about thirty years old, fair-skinned, and had blonde hair.

Nancy and Bess helped Dave. His assailant proved to be white also. "Who are you?" Nancy asked.

There was no answer. She put the same question to the other attacker, but he too remained silent.

"Nancy, have you any rope in your car?" Burt asked.

She nodded. "There's some in the boot."

"Will you please get it. I think we should tie these men up until we can get the police."

The hands of the attackers were tied behind their backs. Then the men's ankles were firmly bound together with rope.

Burt asked Nancy to drive to the nearest roadside phone and summon the police. She drove several miles along the country road but there was no place to make a telephone call. Finally she came to a farmhouse and asked the woman there if she might use the telephone.

"Yes. Come right in."

Upon hearing Nancy's report to the police, the woman was full of questions. Nancy answered as much as she thought advisable, then excused herself and hurried back to the group.

George told her, "We tried to catch these men off guard and asked them who Swahili Joe is. But they only looked blank. I guess they don't know him."

A few minutes later two State Police cars arrived with four officers. One of them, who said his name was Riggi, recognized the two prisoners as town thugs from nearby Landsdowne.

Nancy took Officer Riggi aside and told him about the two Indians who had escaped. "They may lead us to a friend of ours who was kidnapped," she added.

Riggi was amazed and said he and Officer White would join Nancy's group in their search. The other two officers would take the prisoners to Landsdowne.

The car which they had used belonged to one of the thugs. Riggi ordered that the gas be drained from it, the air let out of the tyres, and the key taken so that if the two Indians came back to use it, they would find this impossible.

"What about your car?" Officer Riggi asked Nancy. "The men might steal it."

"I'll fix that," Nancy replied. "There's a secret switch under the dash that locks the wheels." She turned it, then locked all the doors.

"And now let's go," said Riggi.

He and Officer White looked for footprints of the two escapees. Presently they picked them up and the group quickly went through the pear orchard. At the far end of it stood a cabin which appeared to be abandoned. The police tried the doors and windows. All were locked.

"*Here's a clue!*" *Nancy cried out*

At the top of his voice, Riggi ordered anyone inside to come out at once. No one appeared and there was utter silence.

"I guess we'll have to force open a window," Officer White said. He did this and reported that there was no one inside the building.

Meanwhile, Nancy hurried down the stepping stones which led from the rear door of the cabin. At the end of the path, Nancy found what she suspected might be there—four sets of footprints in the dirt beyond.

"Come here, everybody!" she called.

The others hurried to where she was pointing and Officer Riggi said, "Hm! You're quite a detective."

Nancy smiled her thanks. "If my friend Ned Nickerson was being held here, I believe those two Indians took him away. Let's hurry!"

The prints were easy to follow. Everyone was excited. Were they near the end of the search? Dave had just expressed this thought when the footprints ended abruptly at a wide brook.

"Oh dear!" Bess exclaimed. "Now what do we do?"

"I believe," said Nancy, "that if it was Ned who was here, he would have tried in some way to leave a sign to tell us which direction to take."

"But how could he if he was a prisoner?" George asked.

Nancy did not answer. She was examining the ground and the trees in the area. Suddenly she cried out, "Here's a clue on the trunk of this tree."

Crudely marked but plain enough were the initials SJ. Underneath was an arrow pointing to the left.

"Those aren't Ned's initials," said Dave. "Whose are they?"

The three girls chorused, "Swahili Joe's."

Dave shook his head in bewilderment. "I'm more confused than ever. If Ned did this, why would he put Swahili Joe's initials here instead of his own? And how would he know which way they would head?"

"You're really asking me a hard one," said Nancy. "All I can do is guess. When the three men got here, the two Indians tied Ned to this tree while they refreshed themselves in the brook and talked over their plans. Ned felt that it would not be safe to scratch his own initials, but we'd recognize SJ if we were able to follow his clues."

The two police officers looked at her admiringly. "You know, Miss Drew," said Riggi, "you ought to be a secret agent."

"I'd love that," Nancy said quickly.

"But we wouldn't," Bess spoke up. "You get into enough trouble just being a girl detective."

The group wasted no more time. Following Nancy's hunch, they turned in the direction of the arrow and hurried along the brook. The kidnappers they were trying to overtake had apparently walked in the water with Ned because there were no more footprints. The searchers had covered nearly two miles and still had found nothing to indicate where Ned might be now.

Bess said her feet hurt. She had not worn suitable shoes for tramping in the woods and had turned her ankle several times.

"Take off your shoes and walk in your stocking feet," George suggested. But Bess paid no attention.

Suddenly, just ahead, a stone hunting lodge loomed up. Riggi suggested that Officer White and the two boys surround the building while the girls knocked on the door. No one came to answer.

A feeling of panic overtook Nancy. Ned just had to be in here. She cried out loudly, "Ned! Ned Nickerson! Are you in there?"

She listened intently. No sound came from inside. Finally she shouted again. Then she listened. Her pulse quickened. Had she heard a noise, or were her ears playing tricks on her?

"No, I'm right!" she said aloud. "Listen, everybody!"

There was a muffled cry from inside the building. *"Help!"*

·6·

The Rescue

"It's Ned!" Nancy cried. "We must get in at once!"

Officer Riggi ran to her side. "Just a minute. This may be a ruse," he told her. "We don't want any more captures. I suggest that you girls stay here. We men will break in and see what's going on."

"All right," Nancy conceded, although she chafed under the restraint.

Bess and George hurried over to her and Bess said, "Oh, I hope it's Ned and he's all right!"

The others did not comment. They waited breathlessly as the two policemen forced open a window and climbed into the hunting lodge. In a few seconds the front door opened and Riggi called out, "Come in!"

"You go first," Burt suggested to Nancy.

She fairly leaped inside. The two officers had just whipped a pillowcase from the head of a bound-up young man lying on the floor, his face pale, his dark, wavy hair dishevelled.

"Ned!" Nancy cried and ran to his side.

"Boy, am I glad to see you all," he murmured weakly. Then he grinned. "I sure could use something to eat. Anybody bring along lunch?" This broke the long tension over Ned's absence.

The others burst into laughter and helped him to his

feet. In a moment Ned's hands, which had been tied behind his back, were freed and his ankles unbound. He wavered a little as he tried to walk but Nancy supported him until he regained his equilibrium.

Bess opened her large handbag and brought out a box of biscuits and a candy bar. She gave them to Ned, saying, "I always carry a little snack for emergency. I guess this is an emergency." She looked sideways at George as if expecting to be either teased or chided about her penchant for snacks, but her cousin said nothing.

"As soon as you feel like talking, Ned," said Officer White, "tell us what happened."

"But please make it snappy," Riggi added. "Your kidnappers will probably be back. It would be best if all you young people are away from here before their return."

It did not take Ned long to tell his story. He had been walking across the Emerson campus towards the library when a car with two men in it had stopped and the dark-complexioned driver had asked directions to the main gate.

"I walked over to tell them and a moment later a handkerchief with something sweet-smelling was put under my nose. The next thing I knew I woke up in a cabin."

Ned said that when he awakened, a tall well-built African negro was standing over him. "He spoke very little English and said that his language was Swahili. He told me to call him Joe."

"Swahili Joe!" Nancy murmured excitedly to herself.

Ned quickly continued. "Joe was my guard and evidently felt he could manage me without my being bound up, so I wasn't tied and could walk around."

Ned grinned. "I didn't test his strength, but I did keep alert for some chance to escape. I discovered that there was a telephone in the cabin and once when Joe turned his back, I lifted the receiver to see if it was connected. There was a dial tone and this gave me the idea of trying to get in touch with you people."

Ned went on to say that while waiting for a chance to call, he figured out the latitude and longitude of the cabin's location by a mountain he could see in the distance. "It's where we go skiing sometimes."

"Nancy broke the 4182 code," Bess spoke up proudly.

Smiling his thanks, Ned continued his story. Joe had told him he was going outside for a minute, but that if Ned tried to escape he would get a good beating.

"So I didn't try it. Instead I dialled the number of our fraternity house. By the time you fellows came on the wire, I could hear Joe coming back, so I talked as fast as I could and hung up. Joe never suspected what I had done, because I was across the room by the time he came inside."

"Very clever," Officer Riggi put in. "And now I think you young folks should leave. White and I will stay here. Just two more questions before you go, though. Ned, do you know who your abductors were and what was the reason for the kidnapping?"

"I can answer your first question in the affirmative. My two abductors were a father and son from Mombasa, Africa. They are Indians. The father is Dhan, the son is named Jahan. They never talked so I have no idea why they kidnapped me. What little information I picked up about them came from Joe.

I'm sure Nancy's involved, though, because Jahan and Dhan raced in and said you were coming. So the men moved me here."

By this time Ned had finished the box of biscuits and eaten the candy bar. He declared he felt a hundred per cent better and would like to get back to Emerson. "I hope the dean will let me take the exam I missed. I'd hate to flunk the course."

Officer Riggi smiled. "If you have any trouble convincing him, just let me know."

"Thanks," said Ned.

After glasses of delicious water from a well just outside the lodge, the six young people started their trek back along the brook, past the cabin where Ned had first been taken, and on through the pear orchard to the road. By this time it was dusk. Fortunately the shots fired at the tyres on Nancy's car had not punctured them. She slid behind the wheel while the others climbed in.

"I hope I can find my way back to Emerson," she said. "Ned, what's the latitude and longitude of your fraternity house?"

The others laughed. They knew that Nancy had a sixth sense for direction and did not need any instruction.

Silence had fallen over the group when Nancy spoke up. "Well, one mysterious disappearance solved."

"*One?* How many are there?" Bess asked.

"Have you been keeping something from us, Miss Drew?" George put in.

Nancy's friends had quickly discerned from the tone of her voice that there was indeed more mystery in the wind!

The girl detective revealed the curious story of the

two spider sapphires and a definite connection between that mystery and Ned's kidnapping.

"You mean, in other words, that our African holiday is going to be a really *hot* one!" Ned quipped.

Nancy merely smiled. It was dark by the time they reached the Longview Motel. Ned immediately telephoned his parents and told them of the rescue. Nancy in turn called her father and asked him to notify the Faynes and Marvins.

When Nancy and Ned rejoined the others, Bess said, "I hope the dining room is still open. It's been a long time since lunch."

To their relief, dinner was still being served. "I'll have roast turkey with all the trimmings," Bess announced as they sat down.

When they had finished dessert, Ned remarked, "This day certainly didn't turn out the way I planned. There's a concert tonight at the university and a reception afterwards for the soloist. She's an African by the name of Madame Lilia Bulawaya. I understand she has a marvellous voice." He looked at his wrist watch. "Would you girls like to go? We're late but we could hear part of the concert."

Nancy asked, "Do you feel up to it, Ned?"

"Of course. Let's go! I guess you girls will want to change your clothes. Suppose we fellows go back to the fraternity house and make ourselves presentable. May I borrow your car, Nancy?"

"Go ahead. We'll be ready by the time you get back."

Nancy was dressed before the boys returned and put in a telephone call to State Police headquarters near Landsdowne. The officer who answered said he had little to report. The two prisoners had refused to talk.

Jahan and Dhan had not appeared at the hunting lodge yet.

"We did get one little clue," the officer stated. "Our men found a letter on the floor of the prisoners' car. It was written to 'Dear Joe,' postmarked Mombasa, and was in Swahili. Unfortunately there was no return address and no signature."

"So the strong man was probably from Mombasa!" Nancy thought. Aloud she said, "Thank you for the information."

By this time the boys had arrived. Nancy quickly told them about the police report, then the young people set off for the concert. Madame Lilia Bulawaya was an outstanding performer. Not only was her voice sweet but she had a charming personality.

In her repertoire were several delightful songs in Swahili. She announced that she was singing these in honour of the Emerson student safari to Africa. When she finished, the applause was thunderous.

"Isn't she lovely?" Nancy said. "I'm so glad we'll have a chance to meet her later."

When the concert was over, there was a long reception line. On it were Professor and Mrs Stanley who were to head the safari.

While Nancy stood in line waiting, she began to hum one of the Swahili songs. When she was introduced to Madame Bulawaya, the woman's eyes sparkled. "Didn't I hear you humming one of the songs I sang?"

Nancy nodded. "It is lovely. What do the words mean?"

"It's a lullaby. My mother used to sing it to us children. Would you like to learn the words?"

"Indeed I would," Nancy answered.

"Then as soon as I have met everyone, I will teach them to you," the singer said. "I'll meet you at that table where the bouquet of carnations is."

She turned to shake hands with the next person in line and Nancy moved off. She was thrilled by Madame Bulawaya's offer and waited for the singer to come. It was not long.

"Shall we first hum the melody together?" the woman asked.

Nancy was embarrassed but followed the suggestion.

"You have a very sweet voice and well-suited to singing in Swahili," Madame Bulawaya said. "You probably noticed that the language has a soft, musical quality."

It did not take long to learn the strange words of the lullaby. Nancy sang it softly phrase by phrase after Madame Bulawaya. Then the artist asked her to try it all the way through alone.

Nancy did so and the woman smiled. "You are an apt pupil," she said. "Now let us sing it together."

Nancy looked at Madame Bulawaya in astonishment. She was to sing the song with this great artist!

As she demurred, George spoke up. "Go ahead, Nancy. You can do it."

Madame Bulawaya smiled. "Of course you can."

She began singing and nodded for Nancy to make a duet of it. Finally she did and this time the voices were loud enough to be heard throughout the reception room. At the end everyone clapped and Nancy's face turned red with embarrassment.

Ned came dashing across the room. "That was great," he said. "Thank you so much, Madame Bulawaya, for teaching the song to Nancy. Now when we go to Africa, we'll get her to sing it once in a while."

Nancy laughed. "You'll do nothing of the kind," she told him. "I might just sing it for the six of us, but don't you ever dare ask me to do it in public!"

Ned merely grinned and made no comment. Bess spoke up and told the singer that Nancy had many talents. "She's a marvellous detective along with other things."

Madame Bulawaya looked amazed. "A detective? Then maybe you would do something for me while you're in Africa."

"I'll do anything I can," Nancy replied. "What is it you wish?"

Sadly the woman said that the song Nancy had learned was a favourite of a brother of hers named Tizam. "Once in a while he acted as a guide on a safari. About a year ago he took some white tourists from the United States into lion country. Tizam suddenly disappeared and the others thought he had been attacked and killed by a lioness."

"How dreadful!" said Nancy.

"Recently," Madame Bulawaya went on, "I had a dream that my brother is still alive. I'm making this concert tour to get enough money to send an expedition out to find him."

She turned pleading eyes to Nancy and her friends. "Perhaps you can pick up a clue. I would be eternally grateful to you if you could find Tizam."

·7·

A Warning

"I'll do all I can to find your brother," Nancy assured Madame Bulawaya.

"Oh, thank you," the singer replied.

"Where did Tizam's safari start from?" Nancy asked.

"Nairobi."

Nancy told the woman this would be the first stop in her safari and she would make some inquiries. Madame Bulawaya gave a description of her brother. He was tall, slender, and very dark. The singer smiled. "He has a lovely smile. I miss him very much and wish you the best of luck in finding him for me."

In a short time the reception ended and good-byes were said to Madame Bulawaya. The boys escorted Nancy and her friends to the Longview Motel. Ned said that he had been in touch with the dean about the exam he had missed that morning. He had obtained permission to take it the following afternoon.

"In the meantime I'll have to catch a little shut-eye and do some heavy studying."

Nancy told him that the three girls would leave early the next morning. "We'll meet you boys at Kennedy Airport in New York two hours before take-off time."

"Perfect! We'll be seeing you day after tomorrow!"

Ned, Burt, and Dave departed and the girls went to

bed. They were up early the following day and were among the first diners in the restaurant. Before leaving for River Heights, Nancy telephoned State Police headquarters near Landsdowne again.

"I want to find out if there is any news of Jahan and Dhan."

The report was discouraging. The two kidnappers had not returned to the hunting lodge and the man called Swahili Joe had not been there either.

When Nancy told this to her friends, Bess burst out, "That horrible Joe! He left Ned there to starve!"

"Maybe not," George spoke up. "Swahili Joe may have been coming back when he discovered Ned had been rescued. In fact, he could have been the one to tell Jahan and Dhan that they'd better flee."

A little while later the three girls were on their way to River Heights. They discussed the problem of what clothes to take to Africa so they would have enough but not be overweight in their baggage.

Later Nancy talked it over with Hannah Gruen. "I don't want to have to pay excess baggage."

The housekeeper smiled. "I'll help you avoid it. You put out everything you want to take and I'll weigh them on the bathroom scales."

Nearly all the next day was spent sorting, picking out, discarding. As the afternoon wore on, Nancy, tired of this job, began to talk about the two mysteries she was going to try solving in Africa.

"They both sound dangerous," Mrs Gruen remarked. "But if I had to make a choice, I'd take the spider sapphire. Going into lion country after Mr Tizam sounds really scary to me."

Nancy's eyes twinkled. "It might be exciting."

"Too exciting," the housekeeper said. Then she shrugged and put an arm around Nancy. "All I can say for the millionth time is, 'Please be careful.' "

At last the packing was finished. Late in the afternoon Mr Drew drove Nancy, Bess, and George to the River Heights Airport where they were to board a plane for New York. He smiled fondly at them. "You know, I'm really envious. Your trip sounds like a lot more fun than staying in my law office working on briefs."

Nancy hugged him. "If I hit a snag, I'll cable you to come and join us." She gave him a wink. "Shall I make the opportunity?"

"I'll let you know," he countered.

The plane to New York was announced over the loudspeaker and the girls climbed aboard. An hour later they reached Kennedy Airport in New York. Ned, Burt, and Dave were already there with the Stanleys. The professor was of medium height and had greying hair. He was very serious-looking in contrast to his plump, smiling wife.

"Madame Bulawaya told me, Nancy, that you're going to try locating her brother," Aunt Millie said. "I love mysteries." She chuckled. "Call on me if you need any help."

"I surely will."

Other members of the safari group arrived in twos and fours. Nancy and her friends knew all the boys but had never met any of the girls who were going along.

One tall, slender blonde stood out in the group. She was overdressed for travelling, and it was quite evident that she wore a blonde wig. Gwen Taylor greeted the others in a rather supercilious way and almost at once nobody seemed to care for her.

"She looks like a freak!" George whispered.

Bess came to Gwen's defence. "Maybe she's just shy and underneath it she's a nice person."

Her cousin did not agree. "She's too artificial."

There was a long wait before plane take-off, so Nancy and Ned walked round the airport building, looking for Jahan and Dhan. It was possible that if the men had not left the country, they had followed the young people and would try to cause them harm again. The couple saw nothing of the Indians, however, and returned to their group in the main lobby.

At that moment a voice came over the loudspeaker "Message for Miss Nancy Drew. Please come to your airline ticket office."

Nancy had jumped from her seat. She hoped that the message was not bad news from home. Ned went with her to the ticket office.

"Miss Drew?" a clerk asked.

When she nodded, he said that Nancy was to telephone her father immediately. He himself put the call through and the lawyer came on the wire.

"Nancy, don't worry. Everything is all right here. But I'm not so sure it will be all right for you in Africa. I want you to watch your step very carefully. Our police got a tip that Jahan and Dhan took off for Africa. They haven't been apprehended because apparently they were using passports under assumed names."

"Where did they go?" Nancy asked.

"The police haven't received a reply yet from the immigration authorities on this point. I thought I should warn you, though. I know it's almost take-off time, so run along. Hannah sends her love and of course you have mine, and promise me you won't go anywhere alone."

"I promise, Dad, and don't worry. I aim to solve both mysteries without being kidnapped." She laughed gaily to reassure her father, then said good-bye.

Before long, the chattering, laughing Emerson group hurried aboard the chartered plane. When they were airborne, small groups began singing songs, some of them college numbers, others from musical comedy hits. Once in a while someone would call out a wisecrack and set everyone laughing.

"This is such fun," said Bess to Nancy.

The three girls were seated together. Ned, Burt, and Dave were across the aisle. Dinner was served and presently lights were turned low and everyone was expected to sleep. The young people were in too exuberant a mood for sleep and it was past midnight before they settled down.

At three A.M. New York time the voices of the stewardesses could be heard saying, "Good morning! Would you care for some orange juice?"

Each of the Emersonians blinked open one eye, confused for the moment as to where they were. But presently they sat up and drank the juice. Rolls, scrambled eggs, and a beverage followed.

"I'm still confused and sleepy," said Bess. "What time is it?"

George giggled. "Which country will you have it in? In London where we're heading it's eight A.M."

Nancy told Bess there would be time for a nap later. The safari schedule included a day's stop at a motel near the airport. "You can sleep for a few hours, Bess."

Ned's group arranged to meet in the lobby at

lunchtime. Nancy arrived ahead of the others and decided to put a question to the desk clerk.

"I'm sure you have many Indians from Africa stopping at your motel, but the group I'm with is looking for two special gentlemen. I wonder if by any chance they may have stopped here."

"What are their names?" the man asked.

"Jahan and Dhan."

The clerk consulted his list of recent guests, then shook his head. "No men by those names have been here."

Nancy was about to walk off when it occurred to her that if the men were using passports with fictitious names, they naturally would have had to use these.

She said to the clerk, "The men may be travelling incognito," and gave a full description of the father and son.

The clerk smiled. "I believe your friends have been here, but they've gone."

"To Nairobi?" Nancy queried.

The man at the desk shrugged. "Or possibly Mombasa," he said. "At least that is where the Prasads are from."

Nancy thanked him for the information and walked off. "So Prasad is the name Jahan and Dhan used on their passports!" she thought.

Soon her friends came downstairs.

"Boy, did I sleep!" Burt burst out.

Everyone admitted having slept well and all had ravenous appetites. In the dining room they were seated at a table for six. Bess ordered two kinds of fruit, soup, baked fish, and a whipped cream dessert.

"If all you do is sit in a plane and sleep and eat,

they're going to charge you for being overweight," George teased her.

Bess endeavoured to defend herself and finally told the waitress she would skip dessert.

As dusk came on, Professor and Mrs Stanley gathered the members of the safari and engaged taxis to take them to the airport. Although the group was as merry as on the previous evening's flight, the gaiety did not last so long. By ten-thirty everyone was sound asleep.

Nancy did not know how much later it was when she was suddenly awakened by all the lights being turned on brightly.

In a moment the captain's voice came over the loudspeaker. "Please fasten your seat belts! Turbulence ahead! I repeat, please fasten your seat belts immediately!"

The sleepy students did so almost automatically. They wondered why the order had been given because the plane seemed to be rushing through the night without trouble.

The stillness was abruptly shattered by Gwen Taylor exclaiming, "I hate seat belts! They make me positively ill! I'm not going to put mine on!"

She was standing defiantly in the aisle when the plane made a sickening drop. Gwen grabbed the back of the seat and eased herself down.

A few moments later the plane began to roll sharply to left and right. The craft sank again as if it had suddenly lost all of its lift. This time the plane seemed to be going completely out of control. Tensely the passengers clutched the armrests of their seats.

·8·

The Lemur Cage

ALTHOUGH everyone became more alarmed as the plane continued to lose altitude, they all managed to remain quiet except Gwen Taylor.

Again she stood up in the aisle. Her friend Hal Harper tried his best to make her sit down but she refused.

"If I'm going to be killed," she exclaimed, "it's going to be standing up, not tied to a seat!"

She pitched forward and almost fell. Hal grabbed her and pushed the hysterical girl into her own seat.

At the same moment the pilot's voice came clearly over the loudspeaker. "Will the young lady who is standing up please stay in her seat and put on her belt? This is an order from your captain."

Gwen did not adjust the seat belt, but she was quiet for several seconds. Then suddenly she got up again and lurched forward. "I'm going to have my father sue this airline!" she cried out.

Within seconds she had yanked open the door to the pilot's compartment, jumped inside, and slammed the door. Hal Harper unfastened his own belt and started after her.

From the rear of the cabin the steward yelled frantically, "Sit down! Put on your belt!"

As Hal obeyed, there came a scream from the pilot's compartment. The next moment the plane went into a dive!

Those in the cabin waited fearfully, but the pilot seemed to be a magician. No matter how violently his craft was tossed about, he seemed able to get it back under control.

The plane climbed rapidly and in a few moments levelled out in smooth air. Everyone uttered groans of relief, then turned their eyes towards the door of the pilot's cabin. What was going on inside?

Presently the door flew open. Gwen came out, looking very dishevelled. Her wig was awry, giving her a comical look.

As Gwen half stumbled towards her own seat, Bess called out, "What made you scream, Gwen?"

The unruly girl stopped short and said haughtily, "If you must know, the flight engineer grabbed me."

Bess's eyes lighted up. "How exciting!"

"Well—uh—I screamed because I didn't think this was quite fair to Hal," Gwen said lamely.

George burst into laughter. "Better straighten your wig, Gwen, or Hal won't love you any more."

In disdain Gwen quickly pulled her false hair into place and went to her seat.

"For Pete's sake," said Hal, "what were you up to?"

"I was trying to put some sense into that pilot's head," Gwen answered defiantly.

Nancy, Bess, and George exchanged glances and George remarked, "Do we have to put up with that pain on this whole trip?"

Nancy grinned. "How would you like to try changing her?"

"No thanks. I'll leave that to you and Bess. You're better at that sort of thing than I am."

Aunt Millie Stanley came forward and stood beside Gwen. "I'm terribly sorry you were so frightened," she said. "I guess everyone was. Do you feel all right now?"

"Yes, thank you. I lost my head. Sorry."

The Emerson students and their friends went back to sleep. A few hours later the pilot announced that they were approaching Nairobi.

When the group entered the airport building, Nancy looked around to see if Jahan and Dhan might be spying on them. As she and Ned waited in line to go through Immigration and Customs, she said, "I have a feeling we're being followed."

Ned grinned. "Don't let your imagination run away with you." Then he said seriously, "I guess you and I had better be on our guard at all times."

There was no sign of the two Indians here or at the attractive hotel where the group was to stay. The Stanleys announced that they were all to meet in an hour for a bus tour of the city.

Nancy found the trip fascinating. The Emerson group was divided among three buses that were painted with black and white zebra-like stripes. The buses were camouflaged so that when travelling in wild animal country, from a distance they would look like a small herd of zebras.

The bustling city of three hundred and fifteen thousand inhabitants was international in character. There were Africans, Europeans, Indians and Arabs.

"Don't you love the Indians' native dress?" Bess asked Dave.

"They sure are colourful," he replied, "but I'd just as soon wear American-type clothes."

The men wore white turbans and a fringe of beard, but English business suits. The women's saris were made of several layers of veil-thin pastel materials. Scarfs covered their hair. Some of the women had a jewel embedded in their foreheads.

In contrast the Arab women were sombrely swathed in black. Some had the lower part of their faces covered.

Professor Stanley, who was seated in the front of the bus, rose from time to time and gave statistics about the city. He said that the Arabs and Indians spoke their own languages and English. The Africans spoke Swahili.

"Some of them have learned English and for this reason are able to obtain better jobs."

The bus stopped in front of a Moslem mosque. To reach it one had to cross a long flagstone pavement. A guard told the group that they must remove their shoes before walking on it.

George exclaimed, "Ouch! These stones are boiling hot!"

Nancy grinned. "Don't forget we're not far from the equator."

The inside of the building was like a large lobby with niches and a place for the priest to stand. In one corner a man lay asleep on the floor. When Burt expressed surprise at this, a guard said that all Moslems were welcome to come in out of the midday heat and take a nap.

Back in the bus again, Professor Stanley told the students, "It is believed that the Arabs were the first foreigners to set foot on African soil. They went pretty far inland and became traders. It is through them that African art was brought to the outside world."

After a restful lunch and a short stroll, the young tourists were ready to start on a trip to Nairobi National Park, a wildlife game preserve.

Professor Stanley announced, "All the animals roam loose. The park covers forty-four square miles and has twenty miles of roads."

The buses had barely entered the vast stretches of grassland when Bess exclaimed, "I see a giraffe! Wow, is he tall!" The animal stood higher than the tree from which it was eating the top leaves. "I've seen giraffes in zoos but never one that tall."

Burt laughed. "Maybe they come bigger in the open."

As they rode along, Nancy and her friends saw graceful eland, sturdy hartebeest, dignified marabou storks and ostriches. All the animals seemed friendly and unafraid. Several of them came close to the buses. The drivers turned off the road and started through a bumpy field.

"Oh, this is horrible!" Bess cried out. She was swaying from side to side and banged her elbow hard against the window. Dave put an arm around Bess to keep her steady.

"Where are we going?" she asked.

Professor Stanley turned round in his seat and called back, "Our driver has spotted some lions. It is against the rules to get out of the bus and should one of the beasts start towards us, close your windows immediately. Lions do not attack unless provoked, but one never knows what may provoke them."

George said in a low voice, "I wonder how Gwen likes all this."

The driver pulled round a small clump of high bushes near a tiny stream and stopped. He spoke to Professor Stanley, who in turn called out in a loud whisper, "It is advisable that we do not talk. It might disturb the lions. If you will look ahead in a grassy depression near the water you will see a lion family. Papa is stretched out asleep. By the way, Papa sleeps seventeen out of the twenty-four hours every day."

Ned grinned. "No time to be the aggressor."

Professor Stanley smiled. "Not normally. The lioness does the killing for food and drags the antelope or gazelle back to Papa. He is the first to eat. After he has gorged himself, Mama eats her share. The cubs take what is left."

By this time everyone was standing up and training their eyes hard on the area Professor Stanley had indicated. Presently the lion raised his head and looked sleepily at the bus.

"What a regal creature he is!" Nancy whispered.

The others agreed. Suddenly they saw something moving a little nearer the water.

"The cubs!" Nancy said.

The next moment she spotted their mother, who also seemed to be sleeping. Professor Stanley said that no doubt the whole family had just finished a big good meal.

The other two buses pulled in nearby. Gwen Taylor poked her head and shoulders far out of a window and pointed her camera at the beasts. The lion raised its head again and this time gave a loud roar. The noise unnerved Gwen and she dropped her camera.

"Oh!" she screamed. "Somebody get my camera!"

Professor Stanley called across to her, "It's against the

rules for anyone to get out of the bus in lion country."

Gwen became petulant. "That camera is very special. It cost a great deal of money. I'm going to get it back."

"Stay where you are!" the professor said sternly.

The driver of the bus Gwen was in refused to open the door. The girl protested so loudly that the commotion disturbed the animals. Both the lion and lioness stood up and looked balefully at the visitors.

"We'd better leave," Professor Stanley told their driver. He called across to the other two drivers to do the same.

Mrs Stanley, who was in the bus with Gwen, said she would try to rescue the camera. She had brought along an umbrella with a curved handle. With it she reached out the window and caught a leather strap attached to the camera. In moments she retrieved Gwen's property. The buses backed up, turned around, and went on to other sections of the park.

George was extremely annoyed by Gwen's actions. "If I were running this tour, I'd make her go home."

"Oh, she'll probably change," Bess prophesied.

When the buses reached the hotel, Professor Stanley announced that the Emerson safari had been invited to supper at the home of an American couple, Mr and Mrs Northrup. Everyone was to be ready to leave at six o'clock.

The Northrup home was situated on the outskirts of the city. It was a large English-type house, set in a beautiful terraced garden. Huge poinsettia plants, two storeys high, grew against the walls. All the other flowers in the garden were of massive size. An attractive swimming pool was ringed with bright-red and white hibiscus.

The Northrups were a charming couple. Their host was connected with the American Embassy in Nairobi and related many interesting stories about this former British Protectorate, now being governed entirely by Africans.

The visitors divided into groups. Mrs Northrup took Nancy and her friends down to the lowest terrace to show them a pet lemur. The animal paced back and forth in a small, barred cage.

"It's an intriguing-looking animal," Nancy remarked. "It has a face like a fox, a body like a cat, and a long, ringed, striped tail."

"The only place in the world where there are lemurs is on the island of Madagascar," Mrs Northrup told her guests.

The Americans stayed for several minutes to watch the animal. Then all of them except Nancy went back up the steps to the house. She was too fascinated by the pet to leave.

"I'd love to own one of these," she thought. "But I suppose it would be cruel to—"

Nancy's thoughts were suddenly blotted out when a sack was pulled down over her head and quickly tied around her neck. As Nancy tried to grab her attacker, a piece of paper was thrust into her hand. Then she heard running footsteps.

Nancy began to suffocate. She realized that the sack was lined with plastic. She must get it off at once! But this was impossible. The knots which held the cord tight were firmly tied. Nancy knew that in a moment she would black out!

·9·

Baboon Thief

FRANTICALLY Nancy tore at the cords which held the plastic-lined sack over her head. She could not do without air much longer, but her struggles to free herself were in vain.

"I must get help!" she thought wildly.

Feeling as if her lungs were ready to burst, Nancy stumbled towards the steps of the terrace. Then she collapsed to the ground. The next moment she felt hands working at the knots and the sack was ripped from her head.

"Nancy, whatever happened?" she vaguely heard Ned say.

Then, dazedly, she realized that he was massaging her back and she was gulping in fresh air. Nancy was still too weak to open her eyes, but she could hear Ned's voice as if coming from a far distance.

"Nancy! Nancy! Wake up!" he pleaded.

Seconds later she opened her eyes.

"You all right now, Nancy?"

"Yes, I guess so," she answered softly.

Ned told her not to try talking until she felt stronger. Finally she was able to tell him what had happened.

"Who was the rat who did it?" he asked. His eyes blazed with anger.

67

"I don't know," Nancy replied. "I didn't see anyone. The sack was pulled over my head by someone who crept up behind me."

Just then she remembered the paper which had been thrust into her hand by the unknown assailant. She asked Ned to look for it.

He found the crumpled paper near the lemur's cage and brought it to where she was sitting on the grass. They looked at it together. Both gasped. The warning message read:

Nancy Drew: Give up the spider sapphire case or worse harm will come to you.

Ned stared at the paper a moment, then looked at Nancy fondly. "I agree with the writer about giving up the case."

Nancy did not reply at once. Finally she said, "Ned, you know I never give up on a mystery."

"But, Nancy, if anything should happen to you on this trip, how could I ever explain it to your father?"

"But you wouldn't be responsible," Nancy countered.

Ned looked directly at her. "Leaving all that aside, I personally don't want anything to happen to you. Hereafter I'm going to stay close to you whether you want to be guarded or not."

"Thanks. With you nearby I know I'll be safe," she said with a smile. "Well, I feel all right now. Let's go back up to the party."

Nancy brushed her dress. Then she tidied her hair with a comb from her handbag, which had not been disturbed by her attacker.

The couple walked up the steps. As they reached the top terrace, they were met by their friends. George inquired why Nancy had not joined them. When they heard what had happened, Bess, George, Burt, and Dave became alarmed.

"It seems," said Bess, "as if you aren't safe anywhere, Nancy. Somebody must be following you every minute, waiting for a chance to harm you."

Nancy smiled and said, "I hereby appoint all of you as my bodyguards. Surely no one could get at me with you five brave people surrounding me."

George grinned. "Not with us facing outwards at all times!"

Bess looked at Ned. "I think we'd better put you inside the ring too. I haven't forgotten yet that you were kidnapped and left to starve."

Nancy noticed Mr and Mrs Northrup coming towards them. "Let's not say anything to them about what happened," she begged, and the others nodded.

"I'm fascinated by your lemur," Nancy told the couple. "Did you bring it from Madagascar?"

"No, a friend brought it. She travels a great deal. She is particularly keen on safaris."

This gave Nancy an idea. "By any chance have you or your friend ever heard of a guide named Tizam?"

Mrs Northrup looked surprised. "Did you know him?"

"No," Nancy replied, "but I had the pleasure of meeting his sister Madame Lilia Bulawaya. We heard her sing at Emerson College and she told us about her brother."

Mrs Northrup said that her friend, Mrs Munger, had mentioned the sad fate of the guide. "The story is he was attacked by a lion."

"Yes," Nancy answered, "but Tizam's sister believes

he may still be alive. She asked us to try to find out what we can while we're travelling round Kenya."

"Would you like to meet Mrs Munger and learn more about what happened on the safari?" Mrs Northrup asked.

"Yes, indeed," Nancy replied.

Mrs Northrup offered to telephone her friend immediately and make an appointment.

"Our group," said Nancy, "is leaving tomorrow morning for Treetops Inn. We'll be staying there overnight. May we see Mrs Munger when we come back?"

"I'll try to arrange a meeting two days from now," Mrs Northrup said. She went off to telephone but soon returned. "Mrs Munger has invited you and your friends to tea that day." Nancy thanked her for making the arrangements.

A few hours later she and the others said good-bye to the Northrups, thanking them for their delightful hospitality. Everyone slept soundly and was up early for the next part of their safari. All of them looked forward to staying at Treetops Inn, built into the branches of enormous fig trees. From there, they would watch wild animals come to the nearby water hole.

The drive was long and hot. A stop was made at the Outspan Hotel, where they had lunch and deposited their main baggage in a large room. Only flight bags were allowed to be carried for their overnight stay at Treetops.

In the middle of the afternoon, the three black-and-white-striped buses travelled up a winding road through a wood and came to a halt at a fence. Everyone climbed out and a tall gate was opened for the visitors. Some little distance beyond stood a man in a belted khaki suit, a stout rifle slung over one shoulder.

"This is Mr Zucker, our White Hunter," Professor Stanley called out.

"Please form a circle," said the man, who had an English accent.

The Emerson group gathered in front of him.

"We have between quarter and half a mile to walk to reach the inn. I must caution all of you to be as quiet as possible. Otherwise you will scare away the animals."

Bess, looking nervously at the rifle, asked him, "Do you have to use that very often?"

"Not often." The hunter held out the rifle to show that it was larger than the type usually carried by hunters. "This is the only rifle," he said, "which can pierce the hide of a rhino or an elephant."

"You mean they attack sometimes?" Bess queried.

"Sometimes. Keep your eyes open, and again I ask all of you not to talk. When we reach the inn, you are to go up the stairway and remain inside the building until tomorrow morning. It would be too dangerous for you to be on the grounds."

George glanced at Gwen Taylor. Hal had hold of her arm and was whispering into her ear. No doubt he was reassuring her and warning the girl to do exactly as she had been told.

The hunter turned and the Emersonians followed him in silence. Their eyes darted to the partly grassy, partly wooded area on either side of the path. They saw nothing scary—merely timid gazelles.

Treetops Inn was the most unusual hotel Nancy and her friends had ever seen. There were extra supports besides the tree trunks to hold the weight of the large building. A small wooden stairway led to the first floor, leaving the ground area free for the animals to wander beneath.

The visitors were amazed at the size of the place. There was a centre section containing a lobby, a lounge, and a large dining room. To left and right were corridors and here and there a tree branch blocked the path, forcing guests to climb over it to continue down the hallway. The inn had two storeys, with long porches on both levels and an observation roof.

As soon as the girls had been assigned rooms, they took their cameras and went to the lower porch. In front of it was a large water hole. Professor Stanley, walking by, told them it was saline and this was one reason the animals came there to drink. The girls chose front-row seats a little distance from one end of the porch.

"Look who's here," George whispered.

Seated in a wicker chair at the very end of the porch was Gwen Taylor. Next to her was a wooden partition which separated the porch from the front bedroom area. She was alone and was reading a book which lay on her lap. Apparently Gwen had no interest in the animals that came to the water hole.

"She's probably sulking because Hal scolded her," George guessed.

At that moment two warthogs appeared from among the trees. They went directly towards the water, but instead of drinking it and retreating, they waddled in.

"Ugh!" Bess said.

"That's how they clean themselves," George said in a whisper.

Nancy was amazed at the silence of the place. Not

The baboon snatched off Gwen's wig

only the people on the porches, but the beasts that
came to the water hole were very quiet. Each breed of
animal waited until the ones already there had finished
drinking or bathing.

A group of wildebeest had just left, when Nancy said
in a low voice, "Get your cameras ready! Here come
some water buffalo."

George grinned. "They have bowed hind legs!"

The girls' attention was distracted by a baboon
which scampered along the railing in front of them. It
stopped briefly to grab candy from Bess's hand.

Then it went on to where Gwen still sat reading. He
gazed at her a moment, then Nancy saw one of his
great arms suddenly reach out. In a moment he had
snatched off Gwen's wig!

"Oh!" she screamed.

Gwen tried to grab the hair piece but the baboon
drew back and slapped her arm. The next moment he
scooted up the side of the building, carrying the wig
with him.

Nancy leaned out to look up and saw that the animal
was seated on the railing of the flat roof. She jumped
out of her chair, dashed through the lobby of the inn,
and up an outside stairway that led to the top of the
building. No one was there. The baboon was swishing
the wig back and forth across the floor.

"He'll ruin it!" Nancy thought.

She hurried forward, but just before reaching the
animal, he jumped to the railing and scooted to the far
side of the roof. As Nancy dashed after him, he raised
his upper lip, baring his teeth. She knew now that the
only way to get the hair piece away from the baboon
was to use kindness and coaxing.

Nancy took a piece of candy from her handbag and held it in the palm of her hand. The baboon looked at it, then turned back to the wig and began pulling the hair from it.

Nancy laid the candy on the railing and waited. Quick as a flash the baboon ran towards it, grabbed it in his mouth, and ran off without dropping the wig. The next moment he jumped towards a tree and started downwards.

· 10 ·

A Doubtful Robbery

NANCY could reach neither the baboon nor the wig. All she could do was try some strategy.

"Nice boy!" she called to him in a soft voice. "I shan't hurt you. Come on over here."

The animal eyed her without flinching and did not move. Then, as if trying to tease her, he reached up and hung the wig on a high branch of the tree.

At that moment a waiter came up the stairs carrying a tray of pineapple slices, cakes, and teacups. He was followed by a man with the tea service. Behind him walked the White Hunter with his rifle. He stationed himself at the far end of the roof, while the waiters set the food down on a long table.

"Tea, miss?" one of the waiters asked Nancy.

"Not now, thank you," she replied, "but is it against the rule to feed the baboons?"

"Oh no."

"Then may I have a couple of cakes for my friend up there in the tree?"

A waiter handed some to her and she walked over to the railing. Nancy called to the baboon, "Cake in exchange for the wig!"

The animal did not comply. He jumped to the railing and put out a hand for the titbit.

"First get the wig," she said, holding back.

The baboon had other ideas. With a quick swoop of his arm, he took the cake out of her hand and jumped back to the tree.

Guests began to troop up the stairway. Bess and George appeared first, then the three boys.

"Where's the wig?" Bess asked.

Nancy pointed and said, "I have half a mind to jump over to that branch myself and get it."

The boys said that if anyone was going to get the wig, one of them would. Again the baboon outwitted them. Grabbing the hair piece in his hand, he scooted down the tree and out of sight.

George spoke up. "Who'd want to wear that now anyway?" she asked. "It's ruined and probably full of fleas!"

The others nodded but Bess said sympathetically, "I feel sorry for Gwen. That wig meant a lot to her."

"Too much," said George crisply.

"Someone will have to tell her," Nancy remarked. "As soon as I have a piece of this delicious-looking pineapple, I'll do it."

"Please let me," Bess begged. "I have an idea what to say to her."

As soon as Bess had eaten, she excused herself and hurried off. She found Gwen in her room. It was evident she had been crying. Bess went up and put an arm about the distressed girl.

"Gwen, don't let an old baboon get you down. You know something?"

"What?" Gwen asked.

"It's foolish of you to let a hair piece spoil your whole safari. Gwen, you have beautiful dark hair and just between you and me it's a lot more becoming to the colour of your eyes and skin than blonde hair is. Tell you what! Let me shampoo and set your hair. I'll bet you'll love it—and Hal too."

Gwen looked at Bess for several seconds before she said, "I've been so horrible on this trip I don't see how anybody would want to bother with me."

Bess hugged her. "Don't be a silly, Gwen. You just be yourself and everybody will love you."

"You mean it?"

"Sure. I'll go for the shampoo and we'll get to work."

Gwen smiled at her new-found friend. "Okay," she agreed. "You're a darling, Bess."

Up on the roof, Ned suddenly called out, "Here come the rhinos!"

"I can't say they're beautiful," George remarked.

Nancy laughed. "Unless you make yourself believe that everything in the world is beautiful."

The two-tusked, beady-eyed animals sauntered in and at once took charge. The White Hunter walked over and told the group that next to the lion, the rhinos are the most feared animal in the jungle.

"They're very powerful and unpredictable," he said. "They've been known to turn over a bus!"

Nancy noticed that the rhinos seemed to stay in a family group. As they approached the water hole, all the warthogs, gazelles, wild pigs, and water buffalo left.

Presently Nancy detected a disturbance among the rhinos. A male and his mate seemed to be having an argument. Mama Rhino began to hiss and snort at Papa Rhino. He put up no resistance. Instead, he turned and walked towards the inn. There he began to cry piteously.

George chuckled. "The big sissy!"

Nancy grinned. "That's one of the funniest things I've ever seen. A great big fat dangerous rhino crying like a baby!"

Papa remained in the spot until Mama came for him. She chucked him in the neck with the longer of her two tusks. As if he had had sufficient punishment, she led the way back to the water hole. He followed meekly.

Hal Harper came to join the group. "Have any of you seen Gwen?" he asked. "She's been gone for ages."

Nancy's eyes twinkled. "She'll be here presently. Bess has her in tow."

"Why?"

"You'll see."

Suddenly a pleasant voice behind them said, "Hello, everybody! Here's a new Gwen! Done over by a big baboon and a girl named Bess Marvin."

The others turned and looked in astonishment. The old Gwen Taylor was gone. Here stood a beautiful, smiling girl with dark wavy hair becomingly arranged in a modern hairdo.

"Gwen!" Hal cried out and dashed forward. "You're absolutely stunning!" He gave her an affectionate hug. Gwen blushed, and as other compliments came her way, looked happily at the group.

George more than anyone else was taken aback by the transformation. She whispered to Nancy, "Gwen's positively blooming."

Supper was announced and everyone went into the attractive rustic dining room with its long tables. In the centre of each was a deep groove into which trays of food could be inserted and passed along. The Emerson boys and their friends became a bit noisy and Mr Zucker was forced to ask for silence.

"We're hoping that elephants will come to the water hole tonight," he said. "But if you make too much noise, they may jolly well be discouraged."

The young people ate the delicious roast beef meal almost in silence.

After supper Nancy talked with Mrs Zucker, the wife of the White Hunter. She in turn introduced the girl to two men guests.

"Miss Drew, I should like you to meet Messrs Ramon and Sharma. They come from Mombasa. Miss Drew is from the States."

"Charmed to meet you," Ramon said, and Sharma added, "I am delighted to make your acquaintance."

Both men wore European sports clothes, but Ramon had a large, beautiful ruby ring on the first finger of his right hand.

He caught Nancy looking at it admiringly and said, "We Indians like precious stones. This ring has been in my family for many generations."

"It is handsome," said Nancy.

Sharma spoke up. "If you admire fine, precious gems, you ought to see the fabulous spider sapphire. But unfortunately it has disappeared."

"I've heard about it," Nancy replied. "I understand it was stolen."

The two Indians exchanged glances, then Ramon said, "Perhaps, but I doubt it."

Nancy asked what made him think this.

Ramon smiled and said, "Oh, just personal reasons.

But, Miss Drew, please do not put any credence in my—what you Americans call hunch."

She merely smiled. It was an amazing coincidence that she herself had had the same hunch, but she did not mention this to the Indian.

The conversation ended when the White Hunter came to announce that elephants were arriving at the water hole. All the guests hurried to the porches. The large lumbering beasts appeared from the woods and lined up in front of Treetops.

"Why don't they go to the water hole?" Nancy whispered to Mr Zucker, who was standing next to her.

"They are afraid of the rhinos. They will stand here and wait patiently until the other animals go away."

The interested watchers seated on the porch chairs did not mind the wait. It gave them a chance to take flashlight pictures of the great animals.

After a while George became restless. She got up and began pacing back and forth behind the chairs. As George reached the far end of the porch, she became fascinated by a dark shape climbing up the side of the building.

"It looks like a baboon," George said to herself. "But they're not usually out at night."

She went near the railing and watched, fascinated. Yes, it was a huge baboon. Perhaps she should return to her chair.

Before George could back away, the beast grabbed her and pulled her onto the railing! George was in a panic. Did he intend to drop her to the ground? She could be seriously injured—perhaps killed!

George struggled to free herself, but the baboon's

grip was like iron. Was this the same animal which had taken the wig? Was he just being playful?

George decided not. She tried to cry out for help but a great paw was clamped over her mouth.

The helpless girl was swung from the railing and quickly taken to the ground. The baboon ran off with her towards the woods!

Jungle Clue

"WHERE's George?" asked Burt, walking up to Nancy and Ned. He had gone inside the inn to get more film.

"Why, I don't know," Nancy replied, looking along the dark porch. "Last I noticed she was walking up and down."

The group continued to watch the elephants. The rhinos had left and now the big beasts went to the water hole to suck up the saline water through their trunks.

"Aren't their babies cute?" said Bess, shooting a flash-bulb picture of two who had waded into the hole and were spraying water over their backs.

Presently Nancy became uneasy over George. Quietly she left her chair and searched throughout the inn for her friend. George was not in sight.

"Is it possible she disobeyed the White Hunter's orders, went down the steps, and onto the ground?" Nancy thought worriedly. She came back and mentioned it to her friends.

Bess spoke up in defence of her cousin. "George wouldn't do such a foolish thing," she said.

Her friends agreed but wondered why she had disappeared. Nancy decided they had better tell the White Hunter. They found him talking to his wife.

"This is serious," he said. "I will go downstairs and

take a look." Swinging his rifle over a shoulder, he hurried off.

Just as he reached the top of the stairs, he met George coming up. The White Hunter said sternly:

"It is the rule here that no one leaves these premises."

"Please, Mr Zucker," George pleaded, "I didn't go of my own will. Let me tell my story."

She went into the lounge, and when everyone was seated, related how the baboon had carried her over the railing and down to the ground. "Then he ran off with me."

Bess gave a cry of dismay. "That's horrible! How did you get away?"

George said that when they were a little distance from Treetops, suddenly the baboon had begun to talk.

"I couldn't understand him, but I knew then that he was a man in disguise and not a baboon."

Burt's face was livid. He declared that he was going out to "find that human beast and give him what he deserves."

Mr Zucker put a stop to this idea at once. "It would be extremely dangerous," he said. "The jungle is alive at night with preying animals. You might easily be a victim."

George looked at Burt. "Thanks a lot. But since I'm safe, let's call it quits."

"Tell us how you got loose," Nancy begged.

George said that as soon as she realized the baboon was a man in disguise, an idea came to her. If the headpiece were twisted, he would not be able to see.

"So I gave it a sudden yank sideways. He was so surprised, he let go of me. I ran back here as fast as I could."

"Thank goodness you are safe," Mrs Zucker said. "George, can you remember any of the words the man said to you?"

"I don't think he was talking to me," George replied. "He seemed to be muttering to himself." She thought a moment, then repeated a few of the words she could remember.

"That's Swahili," Mrs Zucker said. " '*Glw a heri*' means good-bye."

The White Hunter said to his wife, "Do you remember that man from Mombasa who was a combination strong man and acrobat in the travelling circus?"

Mrs Zucker nodded. "You mean the one they called Swahili Joe?"

Nancy and her friends were startled when they heard the name. If the man in baboon disguise had been Swahili Joe, then he had followed the young people to Treetops and intended to harm them.

"Tell us more about him," Nancy requested.

Mr Zucker said that Swahili Joe had been a fine person and an excellent performer. "Unfortunately he had a bad fall and it was reported he was not well co-ordinated after that and had to leave the circus."

Nancy thought, "Then he'd take orders from Jahan and Dhan, not realizing what harm he's doing."

"I wish I had seen this baboon fellow," said Ned. "He and I would have recognized each other."

Professor and Mrs Stanley had heard rumours of George's absence and now came to learn more about it. They were thunderstruck and alarmed by the story.

"I had no idea," said Aunt Millie, "that this trip would involve any of you in so much danger."

"I know it's all my fault," Nancy spoke up. "I'm dreadfully sorry."

George came to Nancy's defence. "You had nothing to do with that baboon man coming here and carting me off."

Nancy was unconvinced. She had felt for some time that to hunt for her enemies would not be necessary because they would come after her.

"Maybe I should take the initiative," she thought, but did not express this idea aloud for fear of alarming the others.

Bess could see that Nancy was upset. To dispel the tenseness of the situation, she said, "O to be an elephant, with no worries!"

"That's where you're wrong," Professor Stanley told her. "Did you ever hear what happens to the ex-leaders of herds?"

Bess shook her head. The professor went on, "When a bull elephant becomes old, and a young buck wants to become the leader, he fights his way to the top and forces the old fellow out. No one in the herd dares come to his defence. It seems to be the law and nobody breaks it."

"What happens to the poor old elephant that's out of a job?" Bess asked.

Professor Stanley said that he had to become a lone wanderer. "They often grieve so much that they don't eat and starve to death."

"Oh!" Bess exclaimed. "That whole system is very cruel."

"Nature," said the professor, "often does seem cruel. But we must remember the natural laws which bring about a balance of life on this earth. If there weren't such a thing, the whole world would be in chaos."

He stopped speaking as a horrible, screaming laugh from somewhere in the jungle reached their ears.

"What's that?" Bess queried.

"A hyena," the White Hunter replied.

He and his wife looked at each other. Nancy was sure they were wondering how Swahili Joe had fared. Had some wild beast got the man's scent and come for him?

Although Nancy disliked Swahili Joe intensely, the thought of such a horrible death for him made her shiver. Then, thinking of what he had been guilty of, she began to reflect who was more cruel and cunning— the wild animals or man?

Ned interrupted her train of thought and said, "Let's watch the elephants some more. I want to take a few more pictures."

They returned to the porch and watched. It seemed to the young people as if the elephants would never get enough water to drink. They moved around very little and only once in a while did they trumpet. This happened when one of them was annoyed by another elephant.

Although Nancy enjoyed the mystical scene in front of her, lighted only by the dim yellow glow of subdued searchlights, her mind kept reverting to the spider sapphire mystery. Here she was in the middle of the jungle and yet the mystery had pursued her on two occasions. First she had been told by one of the Indian guests that he believed there was a fraud in connection with the reported theft of the gem. Then the man believed to be Swahili Joe had suddenly appeared.

"It's all very weird," she thought.

The following morning Nancy and the rest of the

Emerson group were up early. At breakfast they recounted the various activities of the animals which they had seen. Nancy hardly took part in the conversation. Her mind was still on the mystery. Now she was going back to Nairobi to hear the strange story of Tizam's disappearance.

That afternoon Nancy and her friends went to have tea with Mrs Munger. Their hostess proved to be a charming woman who was very well informed on the subjects of African history and jungle lore.

After tea had been served, she began her story. The guide Tizam had been an unusually intelligent and helpful one. Her safari had reached a rest camp and Tizam had gone off by himself.

"Unfortunately he never returned," Mrs Munger said. "We felt very sad about it. After we waited a couple of days for him, we interviewed some other guides and then moved on with one of them, named Butubu."

The new guide had told of seeing a native defending himself against a lioness. From a description of him, she was sure he was Tizam.

Butubu had screamed and beat on trees to distract the beast's attention. This had given him a chance to throw his spear and kill the lioness.

"Butubu himself was nearly set upon by another lioness, so he ran off to safety. Later he and his friends returned to the spot. The man was not there and they found no trace of him. Apparently he had not been killed because there was no evidence of this."

"How amazing!" said Nancy. "Then where did he go?"

Mrs Munger replied, "Perhaps he was found by

members of some tribe and taken to their village to be cared for."

"But he'd be well by this time and could have returned," Nancy said.

"That's true," Mrs Munger agreed. "That is part of the great mystery surrounding Tizam."

·12·

Surprise Meeting

"THEN there is a good chance that the guide Tizam is alive," said Nancy. She was excited at the thought of how happy Madame Lilia Bulawaya would be if Nancy succeeded in locating him.

"I hope he is alive," Mrs Munger replied. "He's a very nice man and I understand talented. I did not find out what it is he does. Acting as a guide was just a sideline."

When tea was over and the young guests were saying good-bye to their hostess, she asked where they were going next.

"To the Mount Kenya Safari Club early tomorrow morning," Nancy told her.

"That is a beautiful spot," Mrs Munger remarked. "With magnificent snow-capped Mount Kenya in the distance and the grounds— Well, you'll see for yourself."

The Safari Club and the surrounding country were as beautiful as Mrs Munger had said. The extensive grounds were attractively laid out, with beautiful gardens and inviting play areas. At the foot of a grassy slope was a series of ponds. One was a swimming pool for guests; the other ponds were homes for various kinds of birds. Crested cranes stalked about the lawns. Swans, both white and rare black ones, swam serenely among water lilies on one of the ponds.

"It's heavenly here!" Bess remarked. She was admiring the view from the girls' first-floor bedroom window.

The room was large and had three beds in it. Living-room furniture, attractive curtains, and a fireplace at one end gave the place a cosy atmosphere.

There was a knock on the door and a smiling African entered, his arms full of logs. With a pleasant "Good morning," he knelt down and built a fire. Because of a slight chill in the air, the girls were delighted to have the fire. The boy bowed and went out.

"Since we're going to be here a little while," Bess spoke up, "I'm going to hang up my dresses. They really can stand an airing."

The girls hung up their suits and dresses. They left the rest of their clothes and jewellery in the suitcases.

"It would be fun to have our breakfast in front of this fire," George remarked, "but we promised to meet the boys, so we'd better go."

"Actually this is our second breakfast," Nancy reminded the others. "But I must admit I can use it after that drive up here."

As usual, Bess said, "I'm starved!"

While the girls were walking through the attractive club to the dining room, Bess remarked, "This looks like a safe place for us to be. No villains, baboons, or anything else to bother us. We can just have fun and forget all the mysteries."

Nancy made no comment, but she thought that surely her enemies knew the Emerson itinerary. It was doubtful they would leave her and her friends alone.

"I just hope I see them first," Nancy said to herself.

The breakfast hour was jolly and at the end Nancy

suggested that they all put on bathing suits and go to the swimming pool.

"Great idea," Burt agreed.

"And I can do some sun-bathing," said George.

Bess warned her cousin to be careful of the strong African sun. "I hear it will give you a terrible burn without you realizing you're turning to a crisp."

When the young people left the dining room, Ned and Nancy were last in line. As they strolled through the lobby, Nancy whispered to him, "See that Indian over there in the corner reading a newspaper."

Ned looked in the direction which she indicated. The man was elderly. He was handsome with his shock of white hair and wore his European suit well.

"That's some ring he's wearing," Ned remarked.

On the little finger of the Indian's left hand was a ring with a large flashing diamond.

Nancy was more interested in a name pencilled in an upper corner of the newspaper. "Ned, it says Tagore! Do you suppose he's Shastri Tagore?"

"Maybe."

"Let's ask the receptionist," she suggested.

"Why don't we just introduce ourselves?" Ned proposed.

Nancy was tempted to follow his suggestion, but on second thought changed her mind. "If it is Mr Tagore, why don't I ask when he made his reservation? It's just possible he came here because of us."

Ned agreed and went with her to the desk. To the couple's surprise, they learned that indeed the man was Mr Shastri Tagore from Mombasa and that he came here year after year at exactly this time.

The man at reception seemed somewhat amused at

Nancy and Ned's interest in Mr Tagore. "Would you like to meet him?" he asked.

Nancy blushed but said, "Yes, I would."

The desk-clerk escorted the couple to where Mr Tagore was reading. As soon as introductions were made, he excused himself and returned to his desk.

Mr Tagore had risen and it was evident at once that he was a very polite and cultured man. "You are from the United States? How interesting! Won't you sit down? I should like to ask you some questions about your country."

For several minutes the conversation remained general. Every subject which was touched upon was one with which Mr Tagore seemed very familiar, even sports in America. He talked with Ned for several minutes about football and then with Nancy about tennis.

"Do you ride?" Mr Tagore asked them. When both nodded, he said, "If you are ever in Mombasa, I wish you would come to see me. I have horses which I believe you would enjoy riding."

All this time Nancy was thinking, "How could this fine-appearing gentleman possibly be part of a jewel fraud?" It was some time before it seemed opportune to mention the subject uppermost in her mind but finally the opportunity came. "I understand that you own a fabulous spider sapphire which disappeared."

"Yes. It was stolen, I am afraid." Then a puzzled frown crossed his forehead. "But you are from the States. How did you know about this?"

"Because I'm from River Heights," she answered.

At this, Mr Tagore looked blank and said, "I do not understand."

Nancy felt sure that if he did know about Mr Ramsey's synthetic gem, he would not have placed much value on it. She was not ready yet, however, to give up trying to find out all she could from him.

Nancy asked, "How would one tell a real spider sapphire from a modern synthetic one?"

The Indian smiled. "I greatly doubt that anyone could fashion such a gem, but if he were clever enough to do so, there would be a sure way to tell the difference."

Nancy and Ned waited for Mr Tagore to continue. Here was a marvellous clue! If he chose to tell them—

Mr Tagore went on, "Millions of years ago the spiders on this earth had no spinnerets. The one in my sapphire has none."

"How amazing!" Nancy remarked.

She was tempted to tell Mr Tagore about the Ramsey synthetic gem. No doubt the modern spider in it did have spinnerets. But she decided to find out more about this man before revealing what she knew. Nancy asked him why the ancient spiders apparently did not need to spin threads and weave webs to trap their food.

"The original spiders lived on the water," Mr Tagore replied. "Later, when some of them became land arachnids, they developed spinnerets." He paused for a moment and looked quizzically at Nancy. "I have a feeling, Miss Drew, that there is something of greater interest to you on this subject than the history of spiders."

Nancy smiled and said, "I heard a rumour that your stolen gem is in the United States."

Mr Tagore looked surprised and shook his head. "That is not the truth," he said. "It is still somewhere in Africa."

Ned asked, "Where do you think it went?"

The Indian looked round, making sure that no one could hear him. He whispered, "I believe it was taken by a guide who later disappeared."

"A guide?" Nancy repeated. "You mean a guide on a safari?"

"Exactly. The guide was reported to be looking for a relative of his who was captured by a raiding tribe in the jungle."

"But you do not believe this story?" Ned queried.

Mr Tagore thought a moment. "I do not know what to believe. So many theories have come to me that I am utterly confused. But this story about the guide seemed the most likely. I think he is in hiding."

"What were the names of the guide and the relative he was looking for?" Nancy asked.

"Chotu was the relative—and let me think. Oh yes, the guide's name was Tizam."

· 13 ·

A Disastrous Fire

TIZAM was suspected of being one of the thieves involved in the stolen spider sapphire mystery! Nancy and Ned could not help but show surprise.

Mr Tagore looked at them puzzled and asked, "You know these men?"

"Not Chotu," Nancy replied. "But we have heard of Tizam. He has a sister who is a singer. She's in America. When she learned we were coming to Africa, she mentioned her brother."

"Did she tell you that he was reported to have disappeared?" the Indian asked.

Nancy felt that she should reveal no more and merely said, "She mentioned something of the sort. Have you any idea where he is?"

"No," said Mr Tagore. "If I had, I would send the authorities after him."

Nancy's mind was in a whirl. What a strange combination of stories there were about Tizam's trek into the jungle! He was reported to have been mauled and killed by a lioness. He was supposed to have been rescued but disappeared. Now he was being accused of theft and staying in hiding!

Nancy said to Mr Tagore, "I certainly hope that the person or persons who took your spider sapphire will be found."

The couple said good-bye and went off. They continued to discuss the strange turn of events, but presently Ned asked, "What's next on our programme, Nancy?"

"We're all to meet at the swimming pool," Nancy reminded him.

"Then I'll see you in a few minutes," Ned said, and hurried off towards his room.

By the time Nancy had reached hers, Bess and George were already in their suits. Nancy quickly changed and the three girls went outside. The day was sunny and very warm.

"How beautiful Mount Kenya is!" Bess exclaimed, looking into the distance. "Just think! Snow all year round near the equator!"

Tables with umbrellas were set up around the pool. Gwen, looking extremely attractive, came over with Hal to join the girls.

"Water's wonderful!" she said.

Hal remarked, "Gwen's a real nymph." She blushed, but it was evident she enjoyed the compliment.

In a few minutes Ned, Burt, and Dave joined the group. There was a lively exchange of teasing and witty wisecracks.

Presently Ned said, "Fellows, how about a race to the end of the pool and back?"

"Sure thing," Burt responded and took his place at the edge. Dave swung into position alongside him, Hal next, and Ned fourth.

George was elected to call out the start and to be the judge of the winner. She stood behind the boys and said:

"Ready! Get set! Go!"

The four swimmers dived in. Each one made a long underwater swim. When he rose to the surface, the racer ploughed madly along to the opposite end of the pool, gave a quick push with one foot, and started back. Each of the four girls egged on her particular friend.

"Go!"

"Hurry up!"

"Swim, swim!"

"Give it to 'em!" George cried out, rooting for Burt, although she was supposed to be an impartial judge.

Whether it was her cry of encouragement, or because Burt was the best swimmer, no one could say, but he did come in first and was pronounced the winner.

As he climbed from the water, shaking his head to get the water off, he said with a grin, "I like Africa! This is the first race I've won in a long time!"

By now most of the others in the Emerson safari had gathered and soon the pool was full of swimmers. There was some horseplay, then finally everyone came to sit in the chairs or on towels spread on the ground. One of the boys had brought a transistor radio. When he turned it on, they could hear an American record being played.

"That music makes it seem as if we weren't so far away from home," Bess spoke up.

Record after record of American-composed songs and dances followed. Presently a waltz came on.

Ned stood up and called out, "How about you girls putting on a show? A water ballet?"

"Good idea," said Gwen. "Come on, girls!"

Without time for any rehearsing, the performers were forced to make up their own ballet. From the enthusiastic clapping, they judged it was good. It was evident to the watching boys, however, that Gwen

Taylor far outshone the others. She was grace personified in the water and Hal's remark about her being a nymph was true.

As the record ended and the girls pulled themselves up over the side of the pool, the boys clapped loudly. Then Ned said, "We didn't call this a contest and we have no prize, but I'd like to tell you, Gwen, that you're a beautiful dancing swimmer."

"Oh, thank you, but I thought everybody else was marvellous," she said.

Some in the group who were not yet aware of Gwen's change of attitude looked at her in amazement. Many of them crowded around her and she knew from this that she was now "in".

Someone called out, "It's almost lunchtime. Meet you all on the patio." The meal was to be served here.

The swimmers rose and walked towards the club. Nancy, Bess, and George, towels around their shoulders, went up the slight incline of the beautiful green lawn and entered the main building. They got the key to their room from reception.

As Nancy unlocked their door, Bess remarked, "Phew! What a horrible odour!"

The three girls walked through the short hallway and stepped inside the room. They looked round. Suddenly all of them gave a gasp of dismay.

Heaped in the fireplace were the remains of their burned clothing and suitcases!

The girls rushed forward disbelievingly. In a moment Bess burst into tears. "My lovely dresses!" she wailed.

George's face turned red with anger. She went to the closet and opened it. Every dress was gone.

"This is an outrage!" she stormed.

Heaped in the fireplace was their burned clothing!

Nancy was grim. For several moments she said nothing. What vandal had been in here and done such a sadistic thing? "Our enemies!" she decided.

Turning on her heel, Nancy went out the door and hurried to the manager's office. She told him what had happened and asked him to come and see the damage. Upon looking at the still smouldering fire, he stood still in amazement.

Then he turned to the girls. "Why would anyone do such a thing? I'll get the room boy at once and see if he knows anything about this."

He telephoned the employees' quarters and in minutes the room boy arrived.

"Roscoe, do you know anything about this?" he asked.

When the boy saw the mess in the fireplace he stared at it blankly, and denied any knowledge of the vandalism. Roscoe said he had brought in more wood, tidied up the room, then gone out and locked the door.

"Someone must have come in through the open window," Nancy said to the manager.

He excused the room boy, who went off. "I'm sure Roscoe is honest," he said. "And anyway, what would he have to gain by burning your belongings?"

The girls agreed. Finally Nancy told the manager that she was trying to solve a mystery here in Africa.

"I think that certain people who don't want me to learn the facts perpetrated this outrage."

The thought went through her mind, "Could it possibly have been Mr Tagore?" It seemed unlikely, yet from the beginning she had wondered if he might be involved in the theft.

The manager offered to send someone to town

immediately to purchase clothes for the girls. "Thank you," said Nancy, "but I think we can borrow enough from our friends to last us until we get to Nairobi."

Bess spoke up. "Let's ask Gwen first. She has lots of clothes."

The manager and Bess left together. She returned in a few minutes saying that Gwen was delighted and would herself take charge of asking for donations from the other girls. Within fifteen minutes she knocked on their door and came in with her arms loaded. Behind her were two other girls, one of them carrying a suitcase which contained underwear and shoes.

"Oh my goodness!" said George. "I couldn't wear all these clothes in a week!"

"This is like Christmas," Bess added. She had spotted a frilly white dress and said, "Nancy and George, do you mind if I take this one?"

"No," Nancy replied. "It looks just like you."

The various articles of clothing were distributed. As the three from River Heights gazed at themselves in the mirror a few minutes later, George grinned and said:

"Who am I?"

Gwen giggled. "I think you're Dot Bird. Nancy, you look lovely in the light-blue linen that used to be mine."

By the time the River Heights girls reached the patio, the story of the fire in their room had spread among other guests. Mr Tagore left his table and came over to speak to Nancy. She introduced her friends.

"I am sorry to hear about your loss," he said. "Only someone with a criminal mind could have done such a thing. I regret that Africa has treated you so badly."

"It was a great loss indeed," Nancy answered. "But our friends kindly shared their clothes with us."

Mr Tagore asked whether the three girls had also lost the jewellery they had brought.

"Yes, we did," Bess replied. "It was in the suitcases and the fire ruined everything."

"Perhaps," Mr Tagore suggested, "the jewellery was not burned but was stolen."

Nancy had not thought of this possibility and agreed that it could be true.

Mr Tagore had evidently finished his lunch because he said good-bye and went into the hotel.

Nancy and her friends found two tables under a flame tree overlooking the large grassy area, which was surrounded by other small, tree-shaded tables. To one side were spits on which turkeys, squabs, and pigs were roasting. In front of these stood long tables loaded with a variety of food, including tropical fruits. Smiling chefs were in attendance to help serve the buffet.

Bess was ecstatic and started to heap her plate. One dark glance from George and she put back a luscious-looking pork chop.

Halfway through the meal, Ned said, "Here come the dancers."

Members of the Choku tribe, all men, appeared from a rear garden. Their gay costumes included short, fringed skirts, large shaggy headdresses, and anklets. They carried bongo drums between their knees and moved in a circle as they played and danced. Each motion was part of a story. At times the men swung the drums under one arm. Every so often they would squat.

"The rhythm is great," said Dave. "And the dance is not very different from some of ours. Now at our next fraternity dance maybe I'll get a costume, a bongo drum, and—"

"Dave Evans," said Bess, "if you dare show up in a brief costume like these men are wearing, I—I won't let on I know you!"

An hour later the group left the patio. The plan was to take a walk and later go swimming. Nancy, Bess, and George decided to change their clothes and went to the desk for their room key.

The clerk handed each girl a gift-wrapped package. Smiling, he said, "These are with Mr Tagore's compliments."

·14·

Into Lion Country

PUZZLED and amazed by the gifts from Mr Tagore, Nancy, Bess, and George hurried to their room and tore off the wrappings. In each box lay a necklace of African semi-precious stones.

"They're beautiful!" Bess exclaimed. "I guess Mr Tagore's pretty nice after all."

George, who rarely wore jewellery, clasped her necklace round her neck and looked in the mirror. "Hm! This will go well with sports clothes."

Nancy was very pleased with her necklace. It was a little more elaborate than that of the other girls and had bold beads between African jade stones. She had seen it in the window of one of the club's shops.

Suddenly George turned round and said, "As long as we suspect Mr Tagore of being implicated in the spider sapphire disappearance, I think we should return these gifts."

"Oh no!" Bess cried. "I don't believe he's a crook. He has a real nice face. I don't care what you do, but I'm going to keep my necklace."

Nancy smiled. "Whatever we do, let's not be hasty. Even if Mr Tagore sent this gift to throw us off the scent, we ought to have a little more proof that he's not an honest man."

"How do you hope to do that?" George asked.

"By making a few discreet inquiries among the hotel personnel," Nancy answered. "I'll begin at the desk."

Bess pleaded with her not to start her investigation now. The girls had promised to meet their friends at the pool. "Once you get to sleuthing, no telling how long it will take. Ned will be furious."

Nancy laughed and agreed to wait until after the swim period was over.

It was close to six o'clock before the girls returned to their rooms. Nancy dressed at once, this time in an intriguing print of African animals donated by a girl named Beth Jones. The young detective walked out to the desk and began talking to the receptionist about the hotel's evening entertainment. Gradually she turned the conversation to Mr Tagore.

The clerk said, "He's a very fine gentleman. Been coming to the club for six years. He's a great lover of birds and enjoys our collection very much."

"And he's very fond of jewellery too, I assume," Nancy said. "He wore a beautiful diamond ring and gave us three girls necklaces."

"That's just like him," the clerk said. "Always doing thoughtful things for other people."

At that moment an arriving guest took the clerk's attention and Nancy went to her room. She reported the clerk's high opinion of Mr Tagore.

"That settles it," said Bess. "If we try to return these necklaces now, we'd only hurt his feelings. I think all we should do is thank him."

The other two agreed. But when they looked for Mr Tagore in the dining room, he was not in sight. Finally the girls wandered back to the desk and asked the clerk where he thought they might locate him.

"Mr Tagore has checked out," the man said. "He left here about two hours ago."

"For Mombasa?" Nancy asked.

"Yes."

The girls turned away and Bess said, "I guess we'll have to call on Mr Tagore in Mombasa to thank him."

Two mornings later the Emerson group left the Safari Club. There was not a single clue to the person who had burned the suitcases and clothes of Nancy and her room-mates. After checking in at their Nairobi hotel, the three girls went shopping. First they bought suitcases, then went from shop to shop filling them.

Everything proved to be easy to find except shoes. They bought some for rough walking but saw nothing for dressy wear except styles with extremely high, narrow heels. They did not want these.

"I guess we'll have to keep wearing the borrowed ones," George said finally. "I'm tired of shopping. Let's go home!"

They took a taxi back to the hotel. At once they changed to some newly purchased attire, and called the laundry service for a quick cleaning job before returning the borrowed apparel.

At that moment Gwen wandered into the room. When she heard the plan, she refused to take back anything she had given and said the other girls in the group felt the same way.

Nancy laughed. "You're all wonderful. Anyway, if you want to borrow any of your own clothes, let us know!"

Nancy telephoned Ned and asked if he would accompany her to the agency for which Tizam had worked.

"Meet you in five minutes," Ned replied.

The agency was within walking distance of the hotel. When Nancy and Ned entered the office, the staff was busy with clients who were planning safaris. Nancy noticed that one of the men was free, so she and Ned approached him.

"Won't you both sit down?" he said. "I'm Mr Foster."

As they seated themselves, Nancy said, "We'd like to get some information about a guide you used to have named Tizam."

Mr Foster heaved a sigh. "I wish I could give you some definite information but really I have none."

Nancy looked disappointed. Mr Foster went on, "Since you are asking about Tizam, I suppose you know he was lost on a safari. Rumour has it that he was mauled by a lioness."

Nancy told him of the other theory that Tizam might still be alive. "I understand another man saw him being attacked, but killed the lioness before she had mauled Tizam to death."

Mr Foster nodded. "Yes, there was that story, but we at this office thought it was probably exaggerated."

Ned asked Mr Foster what kind of man Tizam was. There was an immediate enthusiastic answer. "A very fine guide and a most trustworthy man. Everyone spoke highly of him."

After a pause, Nancy asked, "He wouldn't be the kind of person to steal any jewels?"

"Oh no," Mr Foster answered. "He was a very upright young man. His loss to us has been great. We have never found anyone to replace him."

Nancy told Mr Foster about having met Madame

Lilia Bulawaya and of Nancy's promise to try locating her brother Tizam. "Have you any suggestions as to how I might go about this?"

Mr Foster looked into space for several seconds. Then he said, "I could arrange a safari for you."

"Would it be very expensive and how long would it take?" Nancy queried.

Mr Foster smiled. "Since your errand has to do with Tizam I would give you a special rate. Y u could go by Land Rover to the spot where he was attacked and be back in one day. I could supply a driver."

"Ned, do you think we should do it?" Nancy asked. "I'm sure the Stanleys would agree if all our crowd could go."

Reluctantly Ned reminded her that they were to fly the next morning to Mombasa. To change the schedule would upset sightseeing plans for everyone.

Nancy sighed, but already a plan was formulating in her mind. She would ask Professor and Mrs Stanley if her group of six might stay over one day in order to make the trip.

' She mentioned this aloud to Mr Foster. "If I obtain their permission, could you get the Land Rover for tomorrow?"

"Yes, and I could arrange for Butubu to go with you, if you like."

"That would be perfect." Nancy was thrilled. "Ned, let's hurry back to the hotel and find the Stanleys."

First Nancy and Ned approached Burt and Dave and then Bess and George to see if they wanted to make the somewhat dangerous trip.

"I'll go," Bess said, "but I certainly hope we don't meet any lions."

Professor and Mrs Stanley did not give permission at once, but a little later decided that Nancy and her friends could be relied upon to take care of themselves. With promises of acting with extreme caution, the young people thanked their chaperons.

Early the next morning a large black-and-white-striped Land Rover came to the hotel. The driver introduced himself as Butubu. He had a good-natured smile and was very pleasant. In addition to this, Nancy knew from what she had heard about him that he was fearless and brave in the jungle.

The Land Rover zipped along at a good pace, and though the road was rough, its passengers made no complaints. After a while Butubu announced that he was going to stop at the hippo pool.

"There are two good things to take pictures of," he said. "Have your cameras ready."

He stopped the bus and walked forward to where two Africans stood in uniform. The men spoke to one another in Swahili.

The Americans noticed the unusual ear lobes of one of the men. There was a large hole in the centre of each one and the flesh hung down in a long loop. Attached were earrings that almost touched the man's shoulder. Bess took their picture. The two guides led the way through woodland to a large pool at the foot of a grassy, stubbly hillside.

"Watch carefully and you may see a hippo come out of the water," Butubu said. "By the way, these guides belong to the Masai tribe. Formerly it was a custom to treat the ears this way, probably as a tribal identification."

"I don't see any hippos," Bess complained.

She was holding her camera ready to shoot at an instant's notice. Bess turned to Butubu.

"Would you mind standing beside these guides and I'll take all three of you?"

The men lined up. Bess looked into the finder and decided she should stand a little farther back. Inadvertently she stepped too far back and the next moment lost her balance. She began rolling down the hillside!

In an instant Dave went after her. It was evident from his long strides that he would soon overtake Bess.

But the camera had flown out of Bess's hands. Now it was bouncing downhill. Nancy rushed after it, but the chase seemed hopeless. In another few seconds the camera would drop into the water!

With a final sprint Nancy reached the camera just in time. At the same instant she saw a huge hippo rising out of the water almost directly in front of her. Quickly adjusting the camera she snapped a picture. Then she climbed the hillside.

As Nancy handed the camera to Bess, she said, "I hope this wasn't broken and I got a good shot for you."

Bess examined the camera and it seemed to be all right. "Thanks a million," she said. "I never would have made that good shot myself."

The young people and their guides walked back to the bus and climbed in. No more stops were made. Soon Butubu turned into an area which had no visible road, merely very tall grass and here and there some trees.

Wary of lions, Butubu ordered the group to stay in the Land Rover. Slowly he wound his way along, then finally drew to a halt.

He pointed ahead to the shelter of some trees. "Over there is where I saw Tizam and the lioness," he said.

At that moment six Africans rose up from the tall grass. They held spears ready to throw and advanced towards the Land Rover.

·15·

Native's Help

IN an instant the whole Emerson group dropped to the floor of the bus. Would the native warriors try to break in upon them?

"This is terrible!" came Bess's muffled wail.

The Americans could hear Butubu calling out in Swahili to the oncoming men. There was a long conversation, which did not sound hostile to Nancy. In fact, she heard a couple of the spearmen laugh.

Cautiously she raised her head and looked out the window. The tribesmen stood with their spears pointed towards the ground and did not appear at all menacing now. Finally Nancy stood up and spoke to Butubu.

"Everything is all right," he said. "No danger."

Somewhat sheepishly the young people got up from the floor and took their seats. Butubu explained that these men were stalking a roving lioness. She was reported to have killed a child in one of the villages.

"How horrible!" Bess exclaimed.

Butubu nodded. "These men were amused that you thought they meant to harm you."

"It wasn't so funny," Bess complained.

Nancy asked the guide to find out if the natives knew or had heard of Tizam. He questioned the men, then translated the answer.

"A year ago a man dragged himself into their tribe's village. He had been mauled by a lioness but had survived the attack."

"Did they find out who he was?" George asked.

Butubu shook his head. "The man had lost his memory. He had developed fever and it took a long time for the medicine man to make him well. After a while his body was all right, but he could not remember who he was or where he came from."

"Is he still at their village?" Nancy queried.

Butubu questioned the natives, but the answer was No. The stranger had disappeared one night and they had no idea where he had gone.

Nancy and her friends were dismayed and alarmed to hear this. If the man was Tizam, there was no telling where he might have wandered. He might even have lost his life. In any case, it would account for his never having communicated with his sister or Mr Foster's agency.

George said in disappointment, "Just when we were getting within reach of solving the mystery, it slips right through our fingers!"

Nancy continued to ask questions, hoping to elicit some clue to Tizam's whereabouts. She learned that several times, in somewhat lucid moments, Tizam had said in Swahili, "I must get to Mombasa and report those thieves to the police."

"What do you think he meant?" Dave queried. "Something to do with the spider sapphire?"

Nancy requested Butubu to ask the tribesmen if Tizam had carried any gems with him.

"No, he had nothing in his pockets and no identification."

Burt spoke up. "I doubt that we can learn any more. Don't you think we should start back for Nairobi?"

Butubu nodded, but when he told this to the spearmen, they objected. The guide translated that the men insisted the visitors come to their village for a meal and a ceremonial dance.

"I am afraid you cannot deny them this pleasure," Butubu said.

The natives started their trek to the village and the bus followed slowly. No one saw any lions, but Butubu pointed out graceful elands and kudus. They resembled American deer but their horns were quite different. Those of the elands were long and straight and pointed slightly backwards. The kudus' rose straight up from the forehead and curved in such a way that from a distance they resembled snakes.

Suddenly Butubu stopped the bus. "Look!" he said, pointing towards a tree-shaded area. "There's a family of hyrax. In Africa we call them dassies."

"Aren't they cute?" Bess exclaimed. "Are they some kind of rabbit?"

"No," Butubu replied. "If you will look closely, you will see that they have no tails. People used to think they belonged to the rat family. But scientists made a study of their bodies and say their nearest relatives are the elephants."

"Hard to believe," said Burt. "Think of a rabbit-sized elephant!"

The small, dark-brown animals were sunning themselves on an outcropping of rocks. Three babies were hopping about their mother. Butubu explained that they were among the most interesting African animals.

"The babies start walking around within a few

minutes of their birth and after the first day they're on their own. They return to the mother only long enough to be fed, but they start eating greens very quickly."

Butubu drove on but continued to talk about the dassies. "There is an amusing folk tale about these little animals. It was said that in the days when the earth was first formed and animals were being put on it, the weather was cold and rainy.

"When all the animals were called to a certain spot to be given tails, the dassie did not want to go. As other kinds passed him, he begged them to bring him back a tail."

Nancy laughed. "But none of them did."

"That is right," Butubu answered. "And so to this day they have no tails that they can use to switch flies."

As they were now approaching a village of grass-roofed huts everyone rushed to look out of the bus windows.

The spearmen called out to some of the villagers, and men of all ages and women and children came running from the huts. When the visitors were announced, some of the natives hastened back inside.

"They are putting on their ceremonial dress," Butubu said.

The visitors got out of the bus and were asked to sit on the ground. The meal would soon be served to them. It was not long in arriving and consisted of wildebeest stew and mealies, a sort of coarse cornmeal mush.

Bess looked askance as her bowl was heaped with the steaming stew and the mealies put on top of it. Nancy and George were amused by the expression on her face. For once Bess was not saying, "This looks delicious!"

Nancy was the first one to dip her crude wooden spoon into the food. She announced that it was delicious, although salt-free and rather flat. Everyone was hungry and soon all the bowls were empty. The handsome native children smiled shyly as they served wild grapes for dessert. The fruit was sweet and tasty.

In a few moments several men appeared, drums hanging from their shoulders. They stood in front of the guests, then began swaying left and right as they beat on the instruments. There were several different songs. With some, the men moved forwards and backwards; with others, they remained in a kneeling posture.

Presently they sat down, laid their drums on the ground and beat upon them softly as they began to sing the next song.

Startled, Nancy sat upright. It was the tune she had learned from Madame Lilia Bulawaya! Unconsciously she began to hum it, then sang the words with the men.

When the dance was over, the men stood up. A tribesman, whom Butubu said was the chief, came over to Nancy. He said something to her in Swahili, which Butubu translated.

"We are charmed that you know our song. Please stand up with the dancers and sing it."

Nancy blushed a deep red. "Oh, I couldn't. I don't know it that well," she protested.

The natives would not take No for an answer. The chief took her hand and raised Nancy from the ground, then escorted her forward to the dancing group.

To herself Nancy was saying, "Oh, I hope I don't muff this! I suppose it is the least I can do in return for the meal."

The drums began to beat softly and the men hummed

just above a whisper. This was Nancy's cue. Raising her voice, she sang the lovely lullaby just as Madame Bulawaya had taught her.

At the end the natives were enthusiastic. They beat on the drums, stamped on the ground, and shouted their applause. Nancy bowed several times, then sat down with her friends.

"That was great!" Ned praised her. "I expect they will make you a princess of this tribe."

Nancy's eyes twinkled. "And have me become one of the chief's wives?" Then she became serious. She knew that while tribal customs were kept, the men, women and children were being educated and polygamy was fast becoming a thing of the past.

When the entertainment was over, Nancy and her friends stood up and asked Butubu to thank the chief for the friendly hospitality and to tell him it was an experience they would never forget. The leader grinned broadly and hoped they would all come again—they would always be most welcome.

The visitors returned to the bus and drove back to Nairobi. They discussed the new clue to Tizam and asked Nancy what she intended to do next to solve the mystery about him.

"It's only a hunch, but I have a strong feeling that he's still alive and I'm going to work harder than ever to find him."

"In Mombasa?" Ned asked.

"Probably. Now I can hardly wait to get there."

She and her friends reached the hotel in time for a very late dinner. As she stopped at the desk to get her key, the clerk said that two men, one older than the other, had called on her that morning.

"They wouldn't leave their names, but said they were most eager to get in touch with you," he reported.

"What time were they here?" Nancy asked.

The clerk said he did not remember exactly, but that it was before the rest of the Emerson group had left for Mombasa. "The men seemed very annoyed to learn that you were not here."

Nancy asked for a description of the two men. It was possible they were Jahan and Dhan! From what little the clerk could remember, however, it was hard to tell.

"One of the men mumbled something about having to wait all day for you to return," the clerk said. "Oh, I forgot to mention that they'll be back this evening."

Deep in thought Nancy walked to the elevator, where her friends were waiting for her. On the way upstairs she told them what she had just learned.

"I don't like this," Ned commented. "Nancy, please don't see those men alone. I'll stick around and make sure that you're safe!"

"And I'll certainly be glad to have you." Nancy smiled.

It was decided they would not spend much time dressing, as everyone was hungry. Besides, the dining room would soon close. They hurried and met downstairs. The young people had just finished dinner when one of the hotel boys handed Nancy a small silver platter. On it lay a note signed by the desk clerk. It read:

"Messrs Brown and Ross who came earlier today to see you are waiting in the lobby."

As Nancy rose from the table, her heart began to beat a little faster at the thought of what might lie ahead of her.

·16·

Swahili Joe

NANCY and Ned hurried into the lobby. The clerk nodded towards two men near the door. They were not Jahan and Dhan, but they definitely were Indians.

"Miss Drew?" one of them said. "I'm Mr Brown. This is Mr Ross."

Nancy introduced Ned Nickerson but the Indians did not put out their hands to shake Ned's. She quickly sized up the two callers. Her intuition warned her that these men had hard, cruel characters.

"Miss Drew," said Brown, "we understand that you have a great interest in Mr Tagore's spider sapphire."

"An interest?" Nancy replied. "I have heard it is very beautiful and I think it's too bad that the gem is missing."

"Indeed it is," Mr Ross agreed. "We would like your honest opinion about the gem we read about on display in the River Heights Museum."

Both Nancy and Ned were thinking the same thing: Why would these men be interested in a synthetic gem fashioned so many thousands of miles away, unless they were somehow connected with the loss of Mr Tagore's property?

"There is little I can tell you," Nancy said. "My father personally knows the man who created the gem in the museum. It is synthetic. I have been told that Mr Tagore's gem was formed by nature millions of years ago."

There was a slight lull in the conversation while Brown and Ross seemed to be trying to decide what to say next.

Ned broke the silence. "How did you men learn about Mr Ramsey's gem?"

Ross answered, "From the newspaper."

"But what is your interest in it?"

Ross's eyes snapped. "What's yours?"

Ned did not reply. Instead he turned to Nancy and said, "Come on! Let's go!"

Nancy hesitated. Looking directly at the two Indians, who, she felt sure, were using assumed names, she asked, "Where is Swahili Joe now?"

Ross was taken off guard. Before realizing it, he replied, "In Mom—" Then he stopped short.

A frightened look came over Mr Brown's face. Tugging at Ross's sleeve, he urged him to leave. The two men dashed from the hotel.

For a second Nancy and Ned stood looking after them. Then suddenly Ned turned and hurried towards Bess, George, Burt, and Dave, who had just reached the lobby. He said excitedly, "Come on, fellows!"

"What's up?" Burt queried.

"Tell you later," Ned replied, and ran from the hotel. The other two boys were right behind him.

Nancy knew what Ned had in mind. He wanted to overtake Brown and Ross and find out the real reason for their coming to see Nancy. The thought worried the young detective and she called out:

"Don't go!"

But Ned and his fraternity brothers paid no attention. Soon they were out of sight.

The boys spotted Brown and Ross running down a side street. The men sped down the next block and turned into a business section where the shops now were closed. There were neither pedestrians nor traffic at the moment.

In a few minutes the three boys overtook the men. "Stop!" Ned called out.

Brown and Ross did as he suggested. But before Ned could speak to them, the men lashed out at the three boys. The Indians' muscles seemed to be made of steel.

Burt received a punch on the forehead which made him see stars, but it angered him so much he retaliated like a prize fighter. Dave was punched in the stomach and he doubled up with pain. Ned was trying to tackle both opponents at once.

The tide of battle became one-sided when reinforcements arrived for Ross and Brown. Two more men joined the melee with fists flying.

One of them was a black and powerful. Ned just had time to cry out, "Swahili Joe!" when the man caught him with a swift uppercut to the jaw that knocked him unconscious.

The tussle continued, but Burt and Dave were fast losing ground. Then Brown, Ross, and one of the others suddenly sped off. Burt and Dave were puzzled until they turned and looked the other way. Approaching at a run were four policemen!

Swahili Joe saw them too. In a swift move he picked Ned up and swung him across one shoulder, then leaped down the street.

Burt and Dave, though almost exhausted, ran after

the big fellow and yanked Ned from him. Swahili Joe did not protest. He took to his heels and was out of sight before the police arrived.

The four officers asked what had happened. Quickly Burt explained.

"I see you do not need us," one of the men said. "Your attackers have gone. Did they get anything?"

Dave answered. "Those men aren't ordinary thugs. They didn't try to rob us. But our friend here was kidnapped and the big man was the guard."

At that moment Ned sat up, shook his head, and said, "He sure was—back in the States."

This announcement surprised the policemen, who said they would try to find him. "What is the man's name?" one of the officers asked.

Ned answered, "His nickname is Swahili Joe. We think he's connected with the thieves who stole the spider sapphire."

Burt took up the story. "Those men who ran away first are also part of the ring, we think."

The leader of the police team said that one man would accompany the boys back to the hotel to be sure they were all right and would not be attacked again. The other three would start an immediate search for the assailants.

The trek to the hotel was slow and painful. The boys were bruised and their muscles ached.

"A fine lot of fighters we look like," said Burt, managing a grin.

"Just the same," Dave spoke up, "I'll bet Nancy, Bess, and George will be glad to see us."

The policeman asked, "By any chance are you speaking of Miss Nancy Drew?"

The boys' surprise was evident. "You know her?" Ned asked unbelievingly.

The officer grinned. "Miss Drew is the one who telephoned headquarters. She was fearful you would be attacked."

"And she was right!" Ned said ruefully.

When the four reached the hotel, Nancy, Bess, and George were waiting for them. The girls were aghast at their friends' dishevelled condition, and amazed when they heard that Swahili Joe and another man had joined Brown and Ross.

"It must have been pre-arranged," Nancy said. "Oh, how can I ever thank you for risking your lives?"

"As fighters I don't think we rate very high," Burt spoke up. "I'll bet those men, Brown and Ross, are ex-prize fighters!"

The boys went upstairs immediately to get a long sleep before taking off for Mombasa in the morning. The girls went to their room, but talked a long time about the new turn in the mystery. George was particularly interested in the fact that Swahili Joe was in Nairobi when Ross had indicated that he was in Mombasa.

"He and the other man with him must have planned to meet Brown and Ross on that street. They were to be told what the Indians had found out from you, Nancy, about the spider sapphire."

Bess was sure they had more dire motives than that. "I hope the police catch them."

Before Nancy left her room the next morning, she telephoned police headquarters to find out if the four assailants had been captured. To her disappointment the men were still at large.

Bess was worried. "This means that strong-man Joe can keep on harming us," she said.

"We'll just have to keep our eyes open," George retorted. She grinned. "He won't dare try another baboon trick on me!"

Nancy and her friends met in the lobby. The three boys looked refreshed but carried a few battle scars. Ned had a slightly blackened eye, Burt's forehead wore a lump, and Dave had a bandage on his left hand.

"Our heroes!" George teased.

The ride to the airfield and in the plane to Mombasa proved to be uneventful. There was no sign of their enemies. The young people hoped that for a time at least they had left their troubles behind.

When the plane landed, the Emerson group went at once to claim their baggage. Due to the large number of passengers, there were a great many suitcases rolling along the conveyor belt.

Finally Nancy spotted the large suitcase initialled ND. As her fingers reached for it, she noticed that a paper had been tied around the handle with a cord.

It occurred to Nancy that this might be a warning note! She grabbed the bag from the conveyor belt, set it on the floor, and immediately untied the paper. To her surprise there was nothing on either side of it.

She held the paper up to the light to look for any hidden writing. Apparently there was no message on the paper, so she tossed it into the nearby waste-paper basket.

By this time Ned's bag had come along and he removed it from the conveyor belt with his left hand and grabbed Nancy's in his right.

They went outside and found a large taxi to accom-

modate three couples. It had a big luggage compartment
in the rear. Their bags, as well as those of Bess, George,
Burt, and Dave, were put into it, then the six
Emersonians started for the hotel.

They had not gone more than a mile when Nancy's
hands began to burn and itch. She scratched them
instinctively, but this made them smart furiously.

"My hands are all red and they burn," she told the
others.

"Mine too," said Ned as he held them up.

Suddenly a thought came to Nancy. "Somebody
must have put acid on the handle of my suitcase! It's
eating into our hands!"

· 17 ·

Telltale Film

IN another minute the pain in Nancy's and Ned's hands became unbearable. She leaned forward and spoke to the taxi driver, requesting him to stop at a chemist. He put on speed and soon parked in front of Albert's Pharmacy.

Nancy and Ned jumped out of the taxi and ran inside. A short, energetic Englishman, seeing them rush in, hurried up behind the counter.

"I'm Mr Albert," he said. "Is something wrong?"

"Yes. We got acid on our hands by accident," Ned told him.

"Please," Nancy spoke up, "may we have some oil quick to put on our hands?"

Mr Albert looked at the reddened hands.

"Are you sure it is oil that you want?"

The couple's hands hurt so badly they could hardly stand still. Fidgeting about, Nancy pleaded with the proprietor. "We don't know what the acid is, so I figure oil is the best thing."

"Well, perhaps you're right," Mr Albert conceded. "Once when I was a boy—"

Nancy lost patience. "Please, please bring us any kind of oil at once!"

The man blinked, then reached up to a shelf behind

him and brought down a bottle of mineral oil. He opened it for them and the suffering couple poured it liberally on their hands.

By this time Mr Albert looked a little worried. "I will give you the name of a good doctor," he said. "Nobody should ignore a dreadful condition like that. Where have you been?"

Nancy and Ned hardly heard the loquacious man. Though the pain in their hands had eased a bit, both felt that if they could only douse them into oil up to the wrists, there would be a better chance of it penetrating the skin and offsetting the effects of the acid.

"Mr Albert," said Nancy, "would you please bring us basins so that we can put our whole hands into oil?"

The chemist seemed loth to do this. He acted as if he were afraid to have them in his shop.

"Listen, Mr Albert," Ned said, "I know we are a lot of trouble to you but this is an emergency. No telling what might happen to us before we could get to a doctor."

The man gazed at Ned for several seconds, as if reluctant to accede to his request. Finally he invited them into a back room and brought down two small basins from a shelf. He poured large quantities of mineral oil into each. Nancy and Ned submerged their hands.

Mr Albert continued to make pessimistic statements. "That acid could be poisonous and already be going through your system," he said dolefully.

"I'm sure it hasn't," Nancy said. She took her hands out of the oil. "All the burning has stopped."

Ned tested his. "Mine seem to be all right."

By this time Bess and George had come to see what

was happening. They were relieved to hear that Nancy and Ned were better and ready to go.

Ned paid the chemist for the oil and Nancy thanked him for his kindness. Once more the group set off.

The main part of Mombasa was situated on a large island and was reached by crossing a causeway. There was a large harbour with ocean liners and cargo vessels from many countries tied up.

The taxi went directly to an ocean-front hotel, with beautiful gardens and a swimming pool.

"Isn't this attractive?" Bess exclaimed.

Professor and Mrs Stanley and the rest of the group were waiting for them on the steps of the portico. Nancy and Ned did not mention what had happened.

Burt insisted upon staying behind to take care of the baggage. He wrapped a newspaper round the handle of Nancy's bag before picking it up and refused to let either the taxi driver or porter touch it. Burt carried the suitcase to his own room and scrubbed the handle thoroughly with soap and water before delivering it to Nancy's room.

As he came in with the bag, Burt said, "Nancy, who do you think put the acid on the handle?"

"I can't name any one person," she answered, "but I'm sure it was one of the people connected with the spider sapphire mystery."

George spoke up. "It must have been done in Nairobi. Let's hope the villains have been left behind!"

Nancy was sure they had not been, but she did not intend to let this latest vicious act of her enemies deter her from continuing her detective work.

The Stanleys had arranged that the Emerson safari be given an early lunch so they could have a full afternoon for sightseeing. The incident of the suitcase had not been told to anyone but the Stanleys, who were solicitous and worried. Nancy and Ned assured them their hands felt all right.

"I have arranged separate tours for you young folks," said the professor.

He explained that several taxis had been hired. Nancy, Bess, George, and Gwen would go in one.

Aunt Millie Stanley smiled. "The professor and I thought that the girls might be interested in different things from the boys. Your drivers have been instructed where to take you."

In a short time the taxis arrived. The four girls climbed into the first one and the driver set off. He was a pleasant, smiling African, who spoke Swahili and perfect English.

"First I thought you would be interested in seeing our many fruit markets," he said. "You know Africa is noted for its melons, pineapples, and berries."

He drove to a wide thoroughfare with fruit stalls on both sides of the street.

"Look!" Bess exclaimed. "I've never seen such big oranges in my life!"

Presently Nancy asked the driver if it would be permissible for her to take a couple of snapshots of a street scene. She knew that some African peoples often did not like to have their pictures taken.

"I think it will be all right."

Nancy stepped out of the car and took one lengthwise picture of the street and one of a fruit stand. As she got back into the taxi, a tall, muscular man came racing across the street. He began waving a fist at her and speaking rapidly in Swahili.

"Give me film or I have you arrested!"

"What is he saying?" she asked the driver.

"He is demanding your camera, because you took his picture."

"But I didn't," Nancy replied. "I snapped the whole fruit stand from over here."

The tall man continued to gesticulate and talk rapidly. By this time a crowd had gathered round the car.

"Why does he want the camera?" George asked.

The driver explained that people who belong to certain tribes believe that if their picture is taken it will take away their soul.

"I see," said Nancy. "But I didn't take this man's picture."

The tall man shook his fist at her again and said in halting English, "You give me film or I have you arrested!"

"Don't you do it, Nancy!" George cried out, but Bess and Gwen were terrified and begged her to turn the film over to him.

At that moment they all noticed a tall, handsome police officer hurrying towards them. He wore a white suit and helmet.

Smiling, he listened to the protestor's demand, then said to Nancy, "Please tell me your side of the story."

She explained. Apparently he believed her, for he turned to the tall man, spoke a few sentences in Swahili, and dismissed him with a wave of his hand.

The fruit dealer was reluctant to give in, but was finally persuaded to go back to his stand. The policeman scattered the crowd and the taxi drove off.

"Oh my!" said Bess. "I was scared silly. I think I'm going to faint!"

George turned to her cousin with a withering look. "Don't be a ninny," she said.

As they drove through one street after another, the girls were intrigued by the costumes of the Indian and the Arab citizens. Some men were wearing turbans with feathers stuck in them, others red fezzes. Nearly everyone wore sandals, but many were barefoot.

Their guide stopped near a Hindu temple. It was a beautiful white, gold-domed building. A long courtyard led to a high-roofed portico with several steps leading up to it. A sign reminded the visitors to remove their shoes.

"Oh, look ahead!" Bess whispered.

As the four girls walked through the portico, they stopped to admire a large oblong pedestal on which rested the image of a white cow. It was gaily decorated with garlands of flowers and scarfs. Gwen asked the meaning of this.

"I've read," Nancy told her, "that in the Hindu religion the cow is a sacred animal and is never killed or eaten."

At the end of the portico and down several steps was a small room. Here were priests and worshippers, bowls of what looked like grain, and pots of incense. Since the visitors did not understand the significance, they bowed politely to those inside and turned away.

The next stop was in a commercial area where ivory auctions took place twice a year. Buyers came from all over the world. The warehouse manager showed the girls round. Tusks of elephant and rhino ivory lay on the floor.

"Is this made into jewellery and figurines?" Bess asked him.

"No, Kenya ivory is too soft. Most of it is used for billiard balls. Hard ivory comes from Uganda. It goes to Hong Kong and Japan for carving."

Nancy stepped among the great tusks. Near the end of the building were two huge elephant's feet. Nancy felt them and was surprised that they were covered with long bristly hairs.

When she returned to the entrance, George was just saying, "What would a rhino tusk be worth?"

"In an auction the price varies," the manager replied. "But the last one I sold brought seven hundred dollars."

"Whee!" George exclaimed. "When I saw those rhinos at Treetops Inn, I had no idea they were worth so much money!"

Bess giggled. "You'd have to pay me a lot more than seven hundred dollars to capture one."

The girls thanked the warehouse manager and returned to the taxi. Their driver took a side road which led to a village of wood carvers.

The villagers lived in attractive wooden houses, beyond which was an open-air, thatched-roof "factory" where carved figures of animals and ceremonial masks were made from mahogany tree trunks.

Groups of men were chipping out the rough statuettes, others were doing the more delicate carving. Some workers were sandpapering and still others doing the final polishing. The results were satin-smooth, graceful figures of wild animals and every type of mask from pleasant-looking to the most grotesque.

Nancy went up to one of the series of small shops where the objects were displayed on rugs on the ground. "My father would love this," she said to the other girls, picking out a rhino. She also bought a duiker for her Aunt Eloise and an eland for Hannah Gruen.

Nancy paid for the articles. As the shopkeeper gave her change, he suddenly stared at Nancy and said, "You follow me!"

Nancy was startled. She had thought these people friendly. What was going to happen now?

The man, as if sensing her surprise, added, "All girls come! I make you death mask!"

·18·

A Trick of Memory

"A death mask!" Bess shrieked. "Nancy, this is another threat! Let's get away from here as fast as we can!"

It was the shopkeeper's turn to look startled. "You are afraid of something?" he asked. "I mean no harm. I want to give gift to this nice young lady. She has lovely face. I have special artist to make likeness."

"But you said death mask," Bess told him.

The man shrugged. "Our people make them so relatives can enjoy the face after people are dead. Maybe your papa would like to have this if something happen to you? No harm come to you in this village."

Reassured, Nancy and the other girls followed the man to a tree-shaded area where a lone wood carver sat cross-legged on the ground working. He was an old man with an ingenuous smile.

He requested Nancy to seat herself on the ground, to raise her chin and hold very still. The other girls watched in fascination as the man's light fingers carefully chipped at a block of wood. In a short time the likeness to Nancy's features could be seen plainly. Soon he indicated he no longer needed her as a model and she was free to roam about until the mask was finished.

"He's very talented," Gwen remarked.

The others thought so too. Now they wandered

about the village. The children were very good-looking and grinned most of the time. Nancy inquired if it was all right to take pictures and was told Yes. Once she started, the children crowded around, each one wanting to be in every picture. In a short time Nancy's film was used up.

The girls walked through the various areas, watching the deft fingers that produced the beautiful handiwork. Several times Nancy asked the workers if they knew a guide named Tizam. Each one shook his head.

Finally the old artist beckoned to them and they hurried over. He said the mask would be ready soon— a worker was giving the piece its final polish.

When Nancy queried him about Tizam, the wood carver's eyes lit up. "I know Tizam. He is very fine wood carver."

"Really?" Nancy was surprised that no one had told her this before. Perhaps he was not the same Tizam whom she was trying to find. "Was he also a guide?"

"Yes. Last time I hear of him he take party out from Nairobi."

"What became of him?" Nancy inquired.

The old man said he did not know. He had not seen or heard of Tizam in a long time.

Nancy was excited by the idea that if Tizam were a wood carver this might be a real clue to his whereabouts. She asked the old man whether Tizam specialized in any type of figures.

"Yes. He always make statue of three gazelles together."

"That's unusual," George spoke up. She thought she knew what was racing through Nancy's mind.

"You're going to start hunting for some of Tizam's work?"

As Nancy nodded, a boy brought her finished mask to the old man. He smiled.

"You like this? You are satisfied?"

"Indeed I am," Nancy replied. "Of course one never knows what one looks like. What do you girls think?"

"It's an amazing likeness," Bess told her.

The elderly wood carver examined his work inside and out very carefully before summoning Nancy to his side. "I want to show you special secret thing I put in."

He turned the mask over and pointed to the eye sockets. They had been covered with tiny wooden doors. Now the wood carver lifted up each one with a fingernail. A tiny spring with a miniature wooden peg held the doors in place. The sockets were empty.

"This good hiding place," he said. "You keep money or jewellery in here. Nobody think to look and steal."

Nancy congratulated him on his ingenuity, and expressed her appreciation for the extra effort e had put into making the marvellous mask. Nancy took it from him and asked how much she owed.

A hurt look came over the artist's face. "I take no money for this. It is gift for you. Enjoy it. Maybe you give it to your papa and tell him I once had daughter like you. She older now. Have eight children." He pointed towards some whose pictures Nancy had taken.

"You are very fortunate and very kind," Nancy said. "Since you will not let me pay you for the mask, at least I can send you copies of the pictures I took of your grandchildren."

He smiled. "That very nice reward."

The girls said good-bye and walked back towards their taxi. When they passed the shop where Nancy had made the purchases, she showed the mask to the owner. The man grinned broadly.

"I am glad the old man did such good work," he said. "Did he put in the secret eye sockets?"

Nancy showed him and he said this custom was still followed by some African tribes. A mask was put over the face of the deceased person and precious belongings inserted into the sockets.

When the girls reached their taxi, Nancy held up the mask for their guide to see, then slipped it into her large shopping bag. As they continued their tour of the city, she asked him to take them to various shops where wood carvings were sold. The driver looked a little puzzled, having just taken them to the best one. But he merely nodded.

They returned to the heart of the city and stopped at one shop where a variety of gift items were sold. The girls thoroughly combed the shelves and counters but saw no carved pieces of three gazelles together. The searchers went into several other shops.

Finally in one George exclaimed, "Nancy, here are three gazelles!"

The girl detective ran over to look. At almost the same time Bess and Gwen discovered two others. They were exquisite pieces, but there was no artist's name carved into the bottom.

Nancy approached a clerk and asked if she might see the store owner. She was taken to a little office at the rear of the shop. The owner was a very pleasant English woman.

"I am very much interested in these pieces of three gazelles," Nancy said. "Would you mind telling me who the artist is?"

The woman said, "I do not remember but I will look it up."

She took a ledger from a shelf and began to turn the pages. After checking her list of purchases, she pointed to one entry. "The man's name is Huay, and like so many of his people a very fine wood carver."

"I will buy this," Nancy said, indicating the one in her hand. "Does Mr Huay have a shop near here?"

"Right around the corner. There are some old stone buildings. You'll see a lane with a gate. It's the only one on the block. Mr Huay's shop is at the rear."

Nancy paid for the figurine and the girls hurried outside. They told their driver they were going to a shop round the corner and would return soon.

The girls found the gated lane easily, let themselves in, and walked to the rear. A fine-looking African sat cross-legged on the floor near the doorway of his shop. He was carving gazelles. At the girls' approach, he looked up.

"Mr Huay?" Nancy asked.

The man laid down his work and stood up. "Yes, miss. May I help you?"

Nancy was trying not to stare at the man, but instinct told her she had found Tizam, using an assumed name. He looked very much like Madame Bulawaya!

Many thoughts raced through her mind. Was he hiding because of something he had done? If not, then he must be suffering from amnesia. Could she startle him into a confession or recollection?

"I have just purchased one of your beautiful pieces, Mr Tizam," she said.

The wood carver looked at her blankly. "Yes, that is one of my pieces, but my name is Huay."

The other girls looked at Nancy, wondering how she would proceed. They too were convinced that this man was indeed Tizam and that he had lost his memory.

"Have you been here long?" Nancy asked him.

"I am not sure," the wood carver replied, and a frown crossed his forehead.

"As you have probably guessed, we girls are from the United States. Just before we flew to Africa, we attended a concert by Madame Lilia Bulawaya."

Nancy paused and carefully watched the effect on the man.

"Oh yes, Lilia," Huay said. Then again his eyes clouded. There was no mistaking the fact, however, that there had been a flicker of recognition at the name.

Nancy now tried a new tack. Softly she began to hum the Swahili lullaby which Madame Bulawaya had taught her. In a moment Mr Huay began to hum with her.

Bess thought excitedly, "I just know something is going to happen!"

When Nancy finished the tune, she began to sing it again, this time with the words. Mr Huay smiled and joined her. The light in his eyes became clearer and clearer.

When the song ended, he said, "Where did you learn those Swahili words?"

"From your sister, Madame Lilia Bulawaya."

"Yes, yes of course," the man said.

Bess could not refrain from asking, "You remember her, don't you, Mr Huay?"

The wood carver turned puzzled eyes on the girl. "You called me Mr Huay? That is not my name. It is Tizam."

The girls could have jumped for joy. They had found the guide, long supposed dead but only suffering from amnesia!

As memory fluttered back to Tizam, he was besieged with questions. But he remembered nothing from the time a lioness began to maul him and he had blacked out.

"Perhaps you girls can tell me more about my recent life than I can," he said.

Nancy told what little she knew, including the fact that a guide named Butubu had saved Tizam's life by killing the lioness before she had a chance to maul Tizam to death.

"I shall go to Nairobi some day and find this Butubu to thank him," the wood carver said. "I am curious to know how I got to Mombasa and rented this shop. Perhaps I can find out from my neighbours. But the most important thing now is to get in touch with my sister. Do you know where she is?"

Nancy said she did not know exactly, but thought her friend Ned Nickerson could find out through the college where Madame Bulawaya had given a concert.

"I'll ask Ned to cable as soon as we get back to our hotel," she promised. "Mr Tizam," Nancy added, "when we visited the tribe that befriended you, they told us that a couple of times you had made a certain remark. It was 'I must go to Mombasa at once and report those thieves to the police.' What did you mean?"

Tizam looked puzzled. To jog his memory, Nancy asked, "Could it have had anything to do with the famous spider sapphire?"

The wood carver stood up very straight and his eyes blazed.

·19·

The Dungeon Trap

FOR a few moments Nancy began to wonder if she had
undone all the good she had accomplished in restoring
Tizam's memory. His eyes continued to stare into space
and smoulder with anger. The girls glanced at one
another and waited in fear for him to speak.

With a deep breath Tizam finally said, "It all comes
back to me now. Just before I was attacked by the
lioness I was keeping watch, I heard two men speaking
in English. They were evidently spying on me, but
thought I did not understand the language.

"I could not see either man and did not hear them
call each other by name," Tizam went on, "but I
judged they were from India, because every once in a
while they would slip in an Indian word."

"Were they talking about you?" Nancy queried.

"Yes. They said they were going to take a valuable
spider sapphire in Mombasa and then start a rumour
blaming the theft on me!"

"And they did just that," George spoke up, recalling
Mr Tagore's accusation.

Although Tizam was still angry over this injustice,
he spoke softly to the girls.

"I was sure those two men intended to kill me, so
that I could never report them. I turned to confront

them, forgetting the lioness. At that moment the animal attacked. The two men apparently thought I had been killed and in order to save their own lives I guess they ran away."

George told Tizam that the guide Butubu who had saved his life had spotted a lioness, evidently the companion of the one he had killed. It sprang at him so he too had run.

"By the time he got back to help you, Mr Tizam, you had disappeared."

When Nancy revealed that the spider sapphire was gone, and told how she had become involved in the mystery, the wood carver looked amazed.

"Did those men say where they intended to take the gem after they had stolen it?" Nancy asked.

Tizam thought a moment. "They mentioned something about a dungeon and Vasco da Gama. He was a Portuguese explorer who came here many years ago. A street was named after him."

"Then it's probably in an old part of town," Nancy surmised.

"It is," Tizam replied.

Nancy said she would investigate the dungeon as soon as possible. In the meantime her friend Ned Nickerson would cable the college to try to find out Madame Lilia Bulawaya's address.

"Are you sure you will be all right here alone?" Bess asked the wood carver.

He smiled. "I think so. But perhaps, until the mystery is solved, I had better remain as Mr Huay." The others agreed this was a wise decision.

When the girls returned to the hotel, stories of the day's events were exchanged with Ned, Burt, and Dave, but none could compete with the astounding adventure of finding Tizam.

"I'll cable the college at once," Ned offered, and went to do this.

The others sat in a quiet corner of the lobby, discussing how to go about locating the spider sapphire. "I think we should alert the police," Bess said positively.

George did not agree. "Wouldn't it be more sensible to go to Mr Tagore? He seemed honest to me, and after all the spider sapphire belongs to him."

Nancy, who had been deep in thought, spoke up. "I now suspect not only Jahan and Dhan, but Mr Tagore's secretary Rhim Rao. I suggest that we go right to that dungeon."

Gwen, in the meantime, had asked to be excused and had gone to her room. Nancy asked the desk clerk where Vasco da Gama Street was and was directed to a section some distance from the hotel.

"You had better take a taxi," he said.

Nancy went back to her friends and there was more discussion on how to proceed. Finally it was decided that Bess and Dave would pay a friendly call on Mr Tagore. The couple would not mention what they had learned or what their group suspected. The main reason for their visit would be to check on the secretary, Rhim Rao.

The other four would go directly to Vasco da Gama Street. If they could find the dungeon, George and Burt would stay outside and act as lookouts. Nancy and Ned would enter and search for the missing spider sapphire.

One taxi carried Bess and Dave to Mr Tagore's home. Another took the others to the old part of the city where Vasco da Gama Street was located. They got out and dismissed the driver. Smiling, Nancy approached a small, barefoot boy. She asked him if he knew where there was a dungeon on this street.

The grinning little native said, "Americans ask me funny questions. Yes, I know where a dungeon is. I show you."

Ned handed the boy a coin and the four followed him down the street. On either side were ancient stone buildings. The boy stopped in front of one.

"No one inside," he said. "You go to dungeon alone. Many sightseers do. I will not enter. Evil spirits might be in there."

He scampered off. George and Burt took up posts on opposite sides of the street. George walked across while Burt remained near an unlocked basement door. Nancy and Ned knocked. Receiving no answer, they stepped inside.

The place was dank and dark and at once the searchers turned on their torches. A steep incline led them to a door which opened into a wine cellar with a great many kegs. It was apparent that the place had not been used in some time.

"I'm sure nobody would hide a precious gem in one of these kegs of wine," Nancy remarked. "It might mar the lustre."

Nevertheless, Ned shook each keg to be sure of this. He and Nancy heard nothing but the sloshing of wine.

Next, they began an examination of the walls, which had once been covered with plaster, but now most of it had crumbled away, revealing the rock foundation. There was no noticeable hiding place in the wall Ned was examining.

Nancy had turned her attention to another wall

where the upper section was set back about six inches making a narrow earthen shelf. As she beamed her light along it, Nancy saw that in one spot the dirt and plaster had been dug out, then replaced. She called softly to Ned.

He held both torches as Nancy quickly removed the soft dirt with her fingers. At the bottom of the hole lay a gold box. The two young detectives held their breath. Had they solved the mystery?

Hoping against hope, Nancy opened the box. Inside lay a gleaming sapphire and in its centre rested a spider!

"This is it!" she whispered excitedly, and asked Ned to hold the light closer. "The gem's not synthetic! See, that spider has no spinnerets!"

The couple continued to stare at the magnificent gem, which sparkled like a weird, unearthly fire.

Finally Ned said, "Nancy, you've done it again! You've solved a very puzzling mystery!"

She smiled at him, then said, "I think we had better get out of here as soon as possible and take this to Mr Tagore."

"You're right."

Still carrying the box, Nancy led the way to the door. It would not open.

Ned yanked and pulled at the latch but it did not budge. "Someone has locked us in!" he said.

Nancy's heart sank. Any minute their enemies might come in and take the spider sapphire away from her!

"I must hide it," she thought. "But where?" There was no likely place in the dungeon.

Just then she thought of the mask which was in her shopping bag. Handing it to Ned, she whispered, "Help me!"

She handed him the jewel box, then reached into the bag and pulled out the mask. Quickly she lifted the little door behind one of the eye sockets and slipped the precious gem inside it. Then she tucked the mask back into her bag.

At the same instant she and Ned heard a sliding door scraping open. They looked towards the sound which came from the opposite side of the room. A concealed door was slowly being opened. Two men in Indian dress walked in.

Jahan and Dhan!

The latter was carrying a whip which he began to brandish.

"So you thought you would spoil our little game!" Jahan said. "You underrated us."

He reached towards Ned's hand and grabbed the jewel box. Nancy had a fleeting hope that he would not open it, that the men would leave, and she and Ned escape.

But her hope was shattered when Dhan ordered excitedly, "Open that box!"

Jahan did so. He gave a cry of dismay upon finding it empty. He screamed at Nancy and Ned, "Where's the spider sapphire?"

The couple made no response. The two Indians were furious. As Dhan snapped and cracked the whip, it came within inches of the couple.

"Search them!" he cried.

Jahan carefully went through Ned's pockets, then he turned to Nancy's shopping bag. Her heart almost stopped beating. Would he discover the hiding place of the spider sapphire?

She and Ned gave no sign by the expression on their

faces that they were worried. Though Jahan searched carefully, he hardly looked at the mask and did not even turn it over.

"The jewel's not here," he reported to his father.

The older man, his face livid with rage, cracked the whip several times. Finally he faced Nancy.

There was a cruel, unrelenting look in his eyes as he said to her, "Tell us where the spider sapphire is or I'll use this whip on your friend here!"

· 20 ·

A Double Cross Backfires

ALMOST speechless with terror and yet determined not to give up the spider sapphire, Nancy jumped in front of Ned.

"Don't you dare strike him!" she cried out.

Jahan and Dhan were taken aback by the young detective's defiance. As Ned stepped in front of her so she would not be harmed, Nancy began to talk fast.

"No matter what you do to us," she said, "it will not keep you from being arrested. Your whole scheme has been found out!"

Dhan stopped the whip in mid-air. As he was trying to make up his mind whether to strike Ned, the squeaky sliding door opened a bit farther. Swahili Joe walked into the room.

He spoke to the men in Swahili, then advanced towards the prisoners.

"Stand back, Nancy!" Ned ordered. "I'm not going to let this big baboon pull another kidnapping!"

Nancy went on, "There's a police net around here. All three of you will be caught."

"They can't arrest us," said Dhan, "because we have not done anything."

"Oh no?" said Ned. "You nearly smothered Nancy with a plastic-lined sack and stuck a warning note in her hand. And you burned all the clothes and suitcases of Miss Drew and two other girls. You even stole their jewellery. After you kidnapped me, you sabotaged Miss Drew's car and tried to keep her from flying to Africa by phoning her father's office that I wasn't coming. And you put acid on the handle of her suitcase to delay her work. It might have scarred her for life!" The men did not deny the accusations.

Nancy's eyes snapped. "You men stole the spider sapphire from Mr Tagore," she said. "Then you came to the United States and tried several ways to get the synthetic gem in the River Heights museum to bring back here and put in place of the original—even hoped to blackmail Mr Ramsey with a sign saying his gem was a stolen one."

"It was not our idea," Jahan spoke up.

"We suspected that," Nancy continued. "It was Mr Tagore's secretary, Rhim Rao, who engineered the whole scheme. He paid for your trip to our country. You came there under the false name of Prasad."

The two Indians stared in amazement. Swahili Joe stood looking blankly at Nancy. Apparently he did not know what she was talking about.

Ned took up the story. "You used Swahili Joe as your strong-arm man. The poor fellow is under your domination. After his bad fall in the circus, he became an easy dupe for you people. I don't know what the penalty is in your country for kidnapping, but he has a count against him up at Treetops for carrying off one of our girls."

The three men stared speechless at Nancy and Ned. They translated a bit of the conversation to Swahili Joe, who suddenly looked frightened. Nancy went on with her accusations, to gain time until she and Ned could be rescued. She mentioned that Ross and Brown were part of the gang and the Indians did not deny this.

"Tizam—whom you planned to kill and who you thought was killed by a lion—is alive," Nancy said. At that, Jahan and Dhan actually jumped in astonishment.

She asked suddenly, "Do you trust Rhim Rao?"

The two Indians exchanged glances, then Jahan finally admitted that Rao had thought up the whole scheme. "He was going to collect the insurance for Mr Tagore and later sell the spider sapphire. But the company has been making a thorough investigation, and he became a little worried. When he heard about the synthetic gem in the United States, he thought if he could hand it to his employer as the real sapphire, he would be safe and Mr Tagore would not know the difference."

Nancy thought, "So Rhim Rao doesn't know about the spinnerets! Mr Tagore would have detected the substitution at once!"

Dhan now seemed ready to talk. "Rhim Rao never told us where he hid the spider sapphire. He promised us our share when he sold it."

Ned spoke up. "He couldn't have sold it. The gem would have been traced too easily."

"He was going to break it up into smaller stones," Jahan explained.

Dhan said, "We have been following you people. When you came into this building, we thought you had found the hiding place of the spider sapphire. Both of us know this old building well. We locked the outside door to this dungeon and then went round to the inside and came down here."

His son's face took on an angry expression. "Since you didn't find the spider sapphire, I guess Rao hid it somewhere else. Maybe he has already sold it and is going to cut out my father and me."

Nancy and Ned did not comment, but it served their purpose to let the men think this. Now maybe they would release their prisoners.

Dhan spoke up again. "Rhim Rao is a thief. He steals from Mr Tagore, his employer, all the time. This is how he got the money to send us to River Heights. Mr Tagore doesn't suspect his secretary. In fact, it was Rhim Rao who told him Tizam had taken the spider sapphire."

Suddenly Dhan said, "We have talked too much. If we let this girl and her friend go, they'll tell the police. Let's leave them locked in and get out of here!"

The two Indians and Swahili Joe were about to depart through the sliding door when there was a commotion outside. Several police entered the dungeon. They quickly arrested the three Africans and explained that when George and Burt had seen them enter the building, George had notified the authorities.

As Nancy and the others reached the street, George and Burt rushed up, relieved to see that she and Ned had not been harmed.

"When I saw that whip, I wanted to go right in after those men," said George, "but Burt wouldn't let me." She smiled. "And I wouldn't let him go either. We might all have been trapped and unable to summon the police."

"You did the right thing," one of the officers told her. "Do I understand other people are involved in the theft of the spider sapphire?"

Nancy quickly told what she knew and said that two friends of hers had gone to the Tagore home to keep an eye on Rhim Rao.

"I think we should go there," she said, "and give Mr Tagore his spider sapphire."

"And arrest Rhim Rao," Ned added.

At that announcement Jahan's and Dhan's eyes bulged. "You found it?" Jahan screamed. "Rhim Rao didn't double-cross us after all?"

Nancy did not reply. Instead, she told the police where she had found it and they agreed she should be the one to return it. Two detectives would go to the Tagore home with her and arrest Rhim Rao if he were there.

"In order to avoid suspicion," said one of the detectives, "I think you four young people had better go in one taxi. We will follow in another. If Rhim Rao suspects the police are after him, he will certainly try to get away."

Taxis were summoned. When Nancy and her friends reached the Tagore home, they saw Bess and Dave just coming out. They were followed by an Indian about forty-five years old.

Ned paid the taxi driver and the visitors walked forward. "Hello!" Bess called cheerfully. The others knew she was eager to ask them how they had made out, but her expression gave no sign of this. "I would like you to meet Mr Rhim Rao," she said, and presented him to her four friends.

Nancy kept up a running conversation until she saw the detectives' taxi coming. As soon as the policemen got out, she introduced them. Rhim Rao looked puzzled, but the expression on his face changed when the detectives announced that he was under arrest.

"This is preposterous!" Rao shouted.

His further protests were interrupted by the appearance of Mr Tagore. He bowed to the callers, then asked what the trouble was.

"These men are trying to arrest me and I have done nothing!" Rhim Rao exclaimed.

During the conversation, Nancy had taken the mask from her shopping bag. Now she turned it over and lifted the tiny door at the back of one eye.

"Here is your missing spider sapphire, Mr Tagore," she announced, and handed it over. The owner stared disbelievingly. "You found it? Where?"

"Perhaps you should ask Mr Rhim Rao where he hid it," she answered.

The thief became bold in his reply. "Me!" he cried out. "I know nothing about the disappearance of this gem. I am delighted that it has been recovered."

Ned gave him a dark look. "Your friends Jahan and Dhan have confessed," he said. "They are in jail."

Hearing this, Rhim Rao lost all his bravado. He changed into a snivelling, pleading individual, assuring his employer that no harm had been intended. Mr Tagore stared at him in disgust. "Your defence can be brought up in court. Take him away, men."

When the excitement had died down, Mr Tagore invited his callers to enter the house. He led them through a richly carpeted hall to a rear garden. It was filled with beautiful flowers, and had a large pool partly filled with water lilies. At the end of it stood an attractive white summerhouse.

"Let us go over there and talk," their host suggested.

"Isn't this picturesque?" Bess whispered as they followed Mr Tagore.

A servant, wearing a white tight-fitting suit and a bright-red turban, entered the summerhouse, carrying a huge tray. Tea was served and with it delicious pastries and a bowl of fruit. As they ate, Mr Tagore asked for full details of the young people's adventures since meeting them at the Mount Kenya Safari Club.

At the end he said, "I must talk with Tizam. You say he is not far away. Perhaps I could send for him."

Ned offered to go for the wood carver. While he was gone, the others continued to exchange stories about the mystery. Nancy asked Mr Tagore if he had ever heard of men named Ross, Brown, Ramon, and Sharma.

"I do not know the first two, but they are probably part of Rhim Rao's gang. I think we should ask our police to get in touch with the authorities in Nairobi and find out if the men have been picked up yet.

"Ramon and Sharma are friends of mine. They advised me some time ago not to put so much trust in Rhim Rao. Unfortunately I did not take their advice."

As Bess finished her second cup of tea, she said, "Mr Tagore, do you know that at one point in solving this mystery we all distrusted you? Please forgive us."

George grinned. "We were even going to give back the necklaces you left for us."

Mr Tagore chuckled. "I don't blame you one bit for mistrusting me. The disappearance of my gem was so strange it must have seemed to you like a fraud. Incidentally, sometime I should like to see the gem your friend Mr Ramsey has produced. He must be an exceedingly fine chemist." Mr Tagore went on to say that the jewellery he had given the girls was small reward for all they had done. When they refused anything more, he said, "It would give me pleasure to entertain your whole Emerson safari at a very special dinner Indian style."

"Thank you very much," said Nancy.

A few minutes later Ned arrived with Tizam, who had brought along several wood carvings of the three gazelles standing together. After introductions he presented the first figurine to Mr Tagore, then handed one to each of the young people.

"I have had the pleasure," said the Indian, "of hearing your sister Madame Lilia Bulawaya sing. She has a remarkable voice."

Tizam smiled and said that by the efforts of Mr Nickerson she had been located and had already communicated with him. "I am very happy abou tthis and will see her as soon as her tour is over."

Tizam turned to the young people. "The money she was raising through her concert tour to find me should go to Nancy Drew and her friends."

Again the Americans refused any remuneration for their work and Bess said, "We're just pleased to have had a part in solving the case."

This remark made Nancy realize her work was finished. But not for long. Soon she would be starting to solve another challenging mystery—that of *The Clue in the Crossword Cipher*.

"Mr Tizam," said Nancy, "wouldn't you like to see the spider sapphire?"

"Indeed I would," he replied.

When it was shown to him, he looked at it in astonishment. "It is an amazing gem."

"I should say," George spoke up, "that Nancy Drew has made this spider the most famous one that ever lived on this earth!"